HELL AND BACK

The Protector Guild Book 4

GRAY HOLBORN

✣ I ✣

MAX

Waking up in an incubus's bed was always going to be a disorienting experience. There was just no getting around it.

"You're back," Wade said, swinging around so that he faced me, his angular face sharper than I remembered it. "I wasn't sure if you'd ever be back."

There was hope in his voice, but I could also pick out some lingering disappointment.

"Of course I'm back," I replied, confused by the wall that seemed to build itself up between us, right in front of my eyes.

He glanced down, his dark brows furrowing over his impossibly pretty blue eyes, framed by the world's thickest lashes. Sometimes they didn't even seem real. "After last time, I just didn't think—"

The words died out between us as my thoughts filled with the last time I was here with him, in this room. That particular encounter had gotten quite steamy in all the best ways, and I could still remember the feel of his calloused hands as they desperately searched every inch of my body, could still feel the way his tongue felt as it slid against my skin—warm and wet and intoxicating as hell. It was my first real kiss. The first one that mattered anyway. My first real experience with someone I actually cared about. And man, did Wade ruin me for all future guys.

Staring at him now, his brown skin smooth and blemish-free, like he was a photoshopped model, his lips soft and biteable, I had to stop from closing the distance between us immediately. And those eyes. Wade had the sort of eyes that I could just lose myself in for hours at a time and never get bored with looking at them. So many shades of blue swirled into one. His dark hair and the five-o-clock shadow now dusting the bottom half of his face made them pop even more.

But it was more than just how beautiful his eyes were that drew me to them like a moth to flame. It was the way they looked at me—so filled with hunger and focus, and like our eyes were each designed for the sole purpose of locking on each other's. He looked more rugged here, wherever exactly 'here' was. We still didn't really know. But there was an edge about him now that didn't exist before; he was more dangerous than he was in his other life. Even now, even in his vulnerability.

About two months ago an ambush occurred at Guild Headquarters. Wade left the safety of his home, while he was supposed to be resting up from an earlier injury, to save me. Only, in the process of saving me, his neck was snapped and he was brought to this place. For weeks I dreamt of him in this room, thrashing about in pain, until he eventually woke up. But there was no clear explanation of how he was surviving this, how he was alive again.

Before he died, the protector world thought he was nothing more than a human-protector hybrid, abandoned by a father who was disappointed with producing someone with diluted supernatural blood. Now, he was this powerful, confusing, trapped incubus. If I was smart, I would fear him. Good thing I was perfectly okay with my precarious lack of wisdom, at least in this case anyway.

Back in this room, filled with a damp, dark, isolating sort of vibe, everything about Wade stood out. I sucked in a sharp breath, but the mildewy odor was eclipsed by the warm, masculine scent of him. He didn't belong here. Not in this room that resembled a medieval dungeon. Not alone. Not without me, the rest of the guys, and Declan.

I had to physically dig my fingers into the side of his bed, though it was more concrete slab than a place built for rest, just to keep from latching my lips onto his and kissing him until we forgot about the fact that we weren't together—not really anyway.

And judging by the fact that I was back in this room, in his arms, I had a feeling that back where my body was, I must be asleep.

That was the frustrating thing about having my dreams occupied by an incubus—it was impossible to focus on the things that I needed to focus on. Every single atom in my body wanted desperately to be explored by Wade. My issues in the real world just seemed to melt away, nonexistent on this plane.

And while the desire coursing through my body was all kinds of tingly fun, I needed to focus if we were going to save Wade from whoever it was that was keeping him captive.

"How long has it been since I was last here?" I asked, everything hazy and unclear. My thoughts drifted back to my most recent memory, but everything was so murky, so blurred together, that the scenes flitted through my mind at the speed of light, not one of them sticking long enough for me to grasp. Just as my dream world seemed to slip away when I was awake, it seemed my real world was doing the same while I slept.

"It's been a while," he said, lips turning down slightly as he broke eye contact again. "Time doesn't really make sense here, not anymore. I keep losing track of the hours. But if I had to guess, I'd say it's been a few days—even if it's somehow felt like weeks."

"And still no one's been here?" I asked, sitting up now to look around. No sign of food, no sound surrounding us—nothing. "How can that be? How are you surviving?"

All I could do was hold onto these moments with desperation and hope that, eventually, they'd lead us to him before something—

I shook my head, not willing to finish the thought. We'd get to him. We'd get him out in time. We were protectors. It was our job to protect—and right now, Wade needed us.

"Someone stopped by once or twice. Left some food," his brows pinched in the middle as he studied his hands. They were rough with callouses, the fingers long and lean. "But I couldn't see them properly, couldn't get them to speak. There's not even a door so I have no idea how they were here. Only that one moment I was alone, and then I had food and a bucket. And when I was finished, they disappeared. Even now, thinking back to it, it's like the memory is sand and my mind is nothing but a hole-riddled bucket." He shook his head, before pulling away slightly. Suddenly the small space between us felt impossibly large, like a vast ocean of tumultuous waves. "Max, I think the last time you were—I think that I was feeding off you somehow. I think I might be—"

"An incubus," I finished for him, reaching forward to grip his hand in mine. "I know, Wade, it's okay. Atlas, Dec, Eli—we're all coming for you. We'll get you out of here and we'll figure everything out. The five of us together can find a way to get to the bottom of things. It's not something to worry about right now. Just focus on staying alive."

"I don't think that's something we can just figure out, Max," he said, his nostrils flaring as he inhaled sharply. The smooth tranquility that I usually associated with Wade faded away, replaced by the anger that lingered with the demon under his skin. He pulled his hand away from mine and roughly rubbed it over his face. The sound of his smooth skin rubbing against thick stubble on his jaw created an enticingly delicious scratching noise. Even when he was pissed off, I was drawn to him. Incubus magic was powerful shit. "I've become the very fucking creature I'm supposed to hunt. I don't even know how this could have fucking happened. You shouldn't come for me. None of you should come for me. Just leave me here."

"Your brother is a werewolf," I reminded him as I shook my head in frustration. He could have a moment of self-pity. It was a big deal—falling asleep one day and then waking up only to realize you were suddenly a creature that feeds on sex. But I'd only give him a moment. If he had any chance of surviving, I needed him to focus, to hope. "Tell me Wade, did you give up on him after that happened? Or did you find a way to keep his secret and protect him? The way that family is supposed to do"

His eyes landed on mine again, the blue deepening a touch as they seemed to do so often in this dreamworld of his. "That's not the same."

"Is it not?"

"I didn't literally drag my team—everyone I cared about—to hell, just to try and save him."

"If he'd been in hell, you would have," I said, interrupting his frustration with my own.

"Maybe, but that's because I'm reckless and I don't think things through. And I would have gotten us all killed." He pushed away from me and stood up, pacing up and down the room. It was quite ridiculous looking since the room was hardly any larger than a closet. "And if that's what Atlas is seriously considering, he needs to wake the fuck up. Because honestly, I have to be in hell, there's no other option. Something about this place is just—off. Wrong somehow, filled with a magic I don't understand. Powerful magic. So I know for sure that I can't be in the human realm." He looked down at me, his jaw tight. "I don't want you coming here, Max. You need to promise."

"We're not going to leave you here—"

"And Atlas," he continued, picking up on my other point, "he never hurt anyone. Not once. I've already..." the words melted away until he stood still, head drooping low in shame. "Max, I've hurt you. Don't you see that? How are you not furious right now? How could you still want anything to do with me? If my brother does find me, I hope he does the right thing and removes my head from my spine."

I sat up in the bed, shoving away the blankets and standing on top of them until we were at eye level—almost. "Do I look dead to you, Wade? Because I'm going to be honest, I feel pretty damn great."

As soon as the words left my lips, I realized that they were true. For the first time since Wade was killed and stolen from us, I felt more like me. For months I'd been exhausted, hardly able to catch a night of sleep without waking up more exhausted each day. And then, after my last visit here, I was left weak and drained, my body held together by fragile threads. Something changed, and recently, though I wasn't sure what.

"I do, Wade. It might be unexplainable, and against everything we know, but I feel fine. Better than fine. I feel more—more like me than I've felt in a long time," I said, my voice quiet as if speaking those words any louder would make them untrue. "You did pull from me last time, but I feel better now. And we can find ways to make sure that doesn't happen again." I took a step off the bed and enveloped him in a hug, trying desperately to squeeze some sense into him. Men were stubborn creatures. And I would know, since I'd been surrounded by them my entire life. "We can find a way to help you and get you sustenance without you using your powers to quite that extent again." I pulled back, an enticing idea lingering in my mind as I stared at his plush bottom lip. "Maybe we could experiment with just a...taste this time."

I tilted my face up, angling my lips to meet his, desperate for my skin to be pressed against his again, even if for only a moment, even if only in my dream state. When I was less than a hair's breadth away, he shoved me back, pressing his back into the wall as if he was suddenly desperate to become one with it, desperate to get as far away from me as possible.

"What are y—"

He shook his head, holding a palm up when I made like I was

going to walk towards him again. "I can't stop you from showing up here, Max." He let out a heavy exhale, like the weight of the world was crushing him with each breath. "But I won't put you in the same position as last time. If you visit me in your dreams, that's all that we will do. Visit."

The resolve was clear on his face, his jaw squared and tense, eyes that so often seemed like windows into his feelings were closed and cold.

Not wanting to push him, I nodded, sitting back on the edge of the bed. If we were going to keep our distance physically, this wasn't the optimal meeting space. The room itself had nothing but a bed, the walls themselves so close and confined that there was little way to create space between us. It was like his little jail cell was just as eager for us to resume the events of our previous meeting as I was.

"Okay, we'll just visit." For now, anyway. I exhaled and glanced around the stone walls, the room filled with a hazy, dull gray light, though there was no light source anywhere I could see, natural or artificial.

I looked back at Wade, the strong determination on his face. He was bare-chested, wearing nothing but a pair of black sweatpants that sunk low on his waist, giving me an enticing view of each lean-muscled inch of his torso as it dipped into a V-shape that had my whole body rushing with heat.

He cleared his throat, drawing my attention back to his face, head tilted with a light chastisement. "I mean it, Max. Visitation only. We don't know much about Incubi, they're rare in our world. But one thing we do know is that they take even the barest sexual intrigue and amplify it to dangerous levels. Any attraction you have will be heightened and used against you. I'm no less of a predator than a vampire or a werewolf. You'll do well to remember that."

At the mention of the other creatures that went bump in the night, I thought of Atlas and Darius—two people who filled me with even more confusion and frustration than Wade did. I still wasn't sure how to feel about either of them, about the danger they posed, how much they could be trusted.

How the hell had I gone from no friends outside of Ro and Cyrus to a collection of monsters I was expected to kill? Life as a protector was a wild ride, that much was for sure.

"How have you been spending your time?" I looked around again, like each time I did I expected to find myself face-to-face with something new and exciting. Something that might give me a clue as to where he was being kept. But just like every time I opened the fridge to check for a new snack that wasn't there five minutes ago, the room remained the same, just as disappointing as before. Even if we could find our way into the hell realm, how the hell were we supposed to find him if this empty space was all we had to go on?

I mean, there wasn't even a window for fuck's sake, so I couldn't even try to identify his surroundings.

He shrugged, the tension leaving his body slightly as he realized that I wouldn't push him on his newly outlined rule.

But he didn't need to worry. He'd made a boundary and I'd respect it. Even if the magic in his system was pulling at me like a heavy-duty magnet and making it alarmingly difficult for us both.

"Honestly, time just sort of feels wonky when you're not here. Like I'm here but also not? I don't know, it's hard to explain. I keep losing hours—days even, maybe. Every time I try to remember what I've been doing, it's like I hit a concrete wall in my mind. Like something—or someone—has blocked it off. Every once in a while, I'll spend hours screaming for someone to come by. But then I always just sort of gave up. Hell, I would be happy for a fight, even some torture at this point. The lying in wait has been its own flavor of mind-melting misery."

I frowned, watching his erratic breathing as he studied the walls confining him. He punched into the wall, the room reverberating with the echo of his knuckles cracking. The pain didn't seem to faze him as he pressed his other hand into the smooth stone, like he was searching for some sort of escape hatch.

How long had he done this? How many times had he shattered his bones trying to escape, left with nothing else to do other than wait for them to heal between each outburst.

I couldn't even blame him for the Sisyphean endeavor. I got bored after twenty minutes of not being entertained. Wade had been alone in here for who knew how long. I wasn't exactly sure how time worked in hell.

"Are you okay—" I shook my head at the ridiculous question, "of course you're not okay. I hate when people ask that when the answer is so obviously 'no'. I wish that there was something I could do. Something that could make this better." I stood up and walked forward, ready to give him a hug, but stopped myself at the last moment. I wasn't sure where that stood with respect to our new visitation rule. Touching an incubus was a slippery slope, as I was quickly learning.

A pained expression crossed his face as he took a step back. "Sorry. It's just...until I get a handle on all of this, it's probably better if we didn't." He motioned between us with his broken hand, before letting out a dull, humorless laugh. "Kind of its own version of torture, I guess, so maybe I shouldn't complain too much about the boredom."

I nodded and took a few steps back, feeling guilty suddenly for adding to his misery. The last thing I wanted to do was make this place even more awful for him. "Have you dream-walked with anyone else?"

His eyes widened, like he hadn't even considered that a possibility. "No, just you. When you're not here, I mostly just try and lose myself in some very...tempting daydreams."

I watched as his eyes darkened with an icy heat. I cleared my throat, trying to dispel my own hormones. "Maybe we should try? Might take the temptation out of, you know—" I gestured to him and then back to me, "this."

His face broke out into a small smile, revealing a set of

perfectly straight, perfectly white teeth. Damn, were they straight up giving him some first-class dental treatments in here?

If I was left alone in isolation for months on end, I for sure would have some serious morning breath and mouth slime. But Wade looked the way apocalypse survivors looked in the movies —impossibly perfect given the circumstances. Hell, he even smelled divine.

"Let's do it," he said. He walked towards me and sat next to me on the bed. I could almost feel the anxiety leak away from him now that we had a game plan. He focused his attention on me, gripping my hand in his.

Protectors healed pretty quickly, often repairing broken bones in less than a day. But demons from the hell realm took healing to a whole other level. And now that Wade was a demon —or, now that his demon side was awakened—he was like an evolved version of his prior self. It was strange, knowing him before and after the incubus was triggered—watching him change before my eyes. Still, even with the transformation, he was still indescribably Wade.

We both waited for a long, drawn-out minute, the anticipation so heavy that I didn't so much as breathe. Part of me was terrified that he would zap away and leave me behind, alone in this creepy dream world with nowhere to go. Would I wake up eventually, on my own? Or would I be locked in the trappings of my own mind forever?

Guilt flooded me at the thought—when I wasn't here visiting, that's exactly what happened to him. He was left isolated and alone, with no hope of his circumstances changing any time soon.

"Er, I, uh, don't actually know what I'm doing," he said, scratching the back of his neck with his free hand, like he was ashamed of the fact he wasn't a perfect little incubus just yet. I bit back a smile at the thought. "With you, you just sort of show up. I don't think I'm necessarily the one doing it. And if I am, I have no idea how."

"What are you usually doing before I show up? Are you asleep generally? Do incubi even need to be asleep to pull from people?"

He cleared his throat, embarrassment coloring his cheeks as he broke eye contact. "No, I'm not usually asleep." He glanced up at me again before dropping his gaze to his hands, his fingers weaving around each other like they were fighting a silent, isolated war. "I don't think I really sleep much anymore. Or maybe I'm actually asleep all the time, and just dream of this place, reality blending with my imagination. It's hard to say. Everything's always just so...fuzzy. When you show up, and I mean every single time, I've been thinking about you. But lately, I'm always thinking about you so I don't think that's it either. The thought of you visiting is one of the only things keeping me sane right now. Even though the protector side of me wants you to stay the fuck away, the incubus just bides his time until you're here."

My stomach flipped at that comment, and I had to swallow my grin. Catching feelings for an incubus—especially one locked in hell—wasn't exactly the brightest idea I'd ever had. So as hard as it was, I needed to try and fight them from developing any further. Which was tough because I'd had a thing for Wade long before he was able to ramp up the sex drive. "Okay, well, that's a starting point then. We can work from there. Maybe first we can focus on meeting somewhere else? Like you can try to teleport us to The Guild or something? Maybe your cabin? Some place familiar, cozy even."

"Yeah, that's about as relaxing of a spot as I can think of right now, and I definitely know every last inch of that place so it's easy enough to picture." He held both of my hands in his, like I was an anchor he was desperate to remain attached to, for fear of drifting off into some great unknown all alone.

I closed my eyes, unsure whether or not dream-walking would make me motion sick. One minute passed by. Then two.

For what had to be at least fifteen minutes, we sat in silence, both of us desperate for this to work, desperate for Wade to find a way to keep his mind occupied when I couldn't be here with him, distracting his mind in other, equally dangerous ways.

Finally, with a heavy sigh, he dropped my hands. His eyes popped open, wild and sad, filled with a sort of bone-weary fatigue. "I don't think that's how it works. And if it is, I'm not strong enough to do it." He grinned, but there was no humor in the expression. "Even when it comes to being a monster, I'm not up to par."

I bumped his shoulder with mine, the expression in my eyes stern. I knew that he constantly felt like he wasn't enough, especially with a brother like Atlas. It was the sort of insecurity that came with the territory of growing up with a father who didn't value him and an older brother who was practically a Guild rockstar.

"If it helps, I think you'll be a tip-top incubus in no time. Five out of five stars," I said, desperate to stop him from collapsing into his inferiority complex. I could feel the shit-eating grin spread across my face.

There was only one path I was familiar with when it came to building up an incubus' strength. And Wade had emphatically knocked that option off the table. When I met his eyes, he shook his head softly, as if his new powers included mind reading as well. And damn did I hope not—because my mind was filled with all sorts of things it shouldn't be filled with these days.

Not my fault that being around an incubus made most of my thoughts head in one very specific direction. A girl could only be so powerful. And just like Wade was new to living the life of an incubus, I was still pretty new to life as a protector.

I picked up the scratchy piece of fabric that was doubling as the bed's covering, trying to remember all I knew about incubi and succubi. Honestly, it wasn't much. Werewolves and vampires were by far the most common creatures in the human realm, as far as we were aware anyway, which explained why they dominated human films and books. They were also the only two monsters Cy had bothered to teach me about. Which in a way made sense, since they were the only two beings that had attacked me recently.

But if I had learned anything over the last few months, it was becoming abundantly clear that what we knew, even about vamps and wolves, was alarmingly limited. Either protectors knew very little about the hell realm and the creatures who inhabited it, or else The Guild had some serious hierarchies in place to keep most of us out of the know. And if the latter was the case, I was damned determined to learn the reasons behind it.

Dropping the blanket, I grabbed his forearm excitedly as my mind caught on a realization.

"Wade, every time I've come to you, you've been focusing on me. But I'm already here. You can't get to Guild Headquarters, because it's not a person. Incubi don't feed on places, they feed on people. What if instead, you focused on someone, someone you know just as well as you know your cabin? Focus on your real home."

His lips turned up in a small grin, but I could tell he was trying to disguise his excitement—his hope—from himself just as much as from me. "Like Atlas? Do you think we could try to meet with him?"

Even though I'd been spending more and more time with Atlas, my chest tightened with anxiety at the thought of being alone with him and Wade. Atlas was so hot and cold. I could never tell if he wanted to abandon me on the side of the road or keep me under his eye for constant observation. Or watch as a bunch of demons tore me to pieces. Atlas was a pretty unreadable dude.

"Of course," I said, meaning it, even with my reservations about Atlas. If I were Wade I'd want to see my brother too. I wracked my memory, trying to recall the last thing we'd done, the last place we'd been, in case it would help him get a grasp on his brother.

I remembered breaking Darius out, I remembered my last dream with Wade. And then meeting Darius's twin and getting kicked out of the bar—but that was all. Everything after meeting the succubus—Villette, maybe—felt impossible to grasp, like figments or dreams just out of reach. Little balloons drifting towards the sky.

Not needing more encouragement, Wade picked my hands up, giving them a soft squeeze. I could feel how badly he wanted this to work, his skin was alive and buzzing with anxiety.

Ten minutes of stillness. Nothing.

He tried Declan. Nothing.

I could feel the frustration emanate from him in waves. Failure was the bane of his existence.

"Maybe it's you," he said, swiping some stray beads of sweat off his forehead. His eyes bugged suddenly as he shook his head. "I mean, not like I'm blaming you, but more so the fact that maybe I can only connect to you or through you or I don't know."

I bit back a grin as he stumbled over his words, alarmingly afraid of insulting me, like he'd push me away somehow—the only person capable of keeping him company.

"Or," I said, shaking my head slowly at our oversight, "maybe we're going about this the wrong way."

"What do you mean?" He arched a dark brow as his eyes narrowed in thought.

"Every time I land here, my body is already asleep. Maybe Atlas and the rest of them are all still burning the midnight oil?" Brain spinning with the new roots of an idea, I swung my legs onto the bed and kneeled back down on them. "Just trust me, okay? Try to focus on my thoughts, because you've already got a read on me, obviously. That connection that you and I have, try to extend it to Ro."

I tried my best to ignore how badly I wanted this to work, because my reasons were selfish. I missed my brother something fierce, even if I was only away from him for a few days. And I knew, wherever he was, that he'd be worried sick about me. It didn't matter that I left a note explaining where I'd be, promising that I'd return.

It wasn't everyday your sister ran away from home to descend into literal hell. Not that I was particularly open about where we were going. Just that we were bringing back Wade. I didn't want to give him a heart attack. Ro was a worrier.

But again, after ten long, impossibly-stretched moments, nothing happened.

"I'm out of ideas," Wade said, and I saw the fear in his eyes, the dejection. He'd allowed himself to hope that he'd make it out of this room, and now he was left with nothing but disappointment.

I could see it in the slump of his shoulders, the sweat on his brow as he stared wildly around the small room. It would have been better almost, to not have tried at all.

"I have one more idea, okay? Humor me."

He nodded and I could tell he was only agreeing because I asked him to, not because he expected anything more.

I closed my lids and thought of someone specific, someone who would hopefully be deep in the throes of sleep right now, not that I knew what time it was.

And then, all at once, I opened my eyes and clung to Wade's hands, both of us somewhere else altogether.

No. No, it was more than that.

We were somewhere else. Together.

2

ATLAS

I ran over to Max and Eli, my breaths coming in heavy and inconsistent. Ignoring my shaking hands, I pressed two fingers against her pulse point. The air left my lungs in a relieved rush. She was still alive, for now, just trapped in unconsciousness.

I could feel the wolf close to breaching the surface again, desperate to take over, even though I'd just wrestled back control. The moment my skin came into contact with her pulse, he backed down. For now.

My mind flashed with the image of her bursting into flame as she fried the vamps trying to take out Eli. Did she know that she could do that?

What the hell was she?

As if highlighting her mystery, her hellhound, Ralph, was curled up next to her, resting it's abnormally large head on her thigh, like an overgrown Chihuahua.

I didn't know whether to protect her or protect the rest of us from her. I'd spent my entire life around protectors, but I'd never once heard mention of a creature that could wield fire like that. And she'd done more than light a simple match with her mind—she produced enough energy to cremate some of the most powerful creatures in the world.

My chest felt tight. Jesus, just the thought of what The Guild —hell, what my own father—would do with her if what just happened got out in the open, was enough to make me want to scream. Forget spending a lifetime in the lab. She'd be destroyed.

Satisfied that for now at least, she'd live, I moved over to Eli, reaching him just as Declan did.

I glanced at her, seeing my own concern reflected back in her alarmingly bright green eyes. She glanced over at Max briefly, like she was afraid of what she might find if she looked too closely.

"She's alive," I said, voice as even as I could make it. We'd need to talk about what happened. But not here, not until we were alone and far from prying ears.

Eli looked rough. Ignoring the gaping wound in his neck, he was surrounded in a pool of his own blood, a quick inhale telling me all I needed to know—most of it was his.

Protectors could survive vampire bites. Many of them did. Hell, even Max had survived a bite herself just a few short months ago. My stomach churned at the reminder that the girl had come close to death more often than anyone I'd ever met in my entire life.

But most protectors suffered long term effects from the vampire venom. It was the entire reason that Max's adoptive father walked with a limp. Almost two decades ago, he was bitten. And the injuries from that battle still stalked him daily.

A neck wound was another story. Most protectors died from neck bites within hours. The venom infused the bloodstream quickly, often damaging the heart and brain beyond repair. If they survived, they at the very least wound up in an extended coma, circling the drain of death in a slow, painful, cumbersome battle. Max was the only protector I knew who'd not only survived a neck bite, but healed from one completely. There was no scar, no lingering side effects. She was just...normal.

It was another example of how far from normal she really was.

I glanced down at Eli again, pressing down on the wound to stop some of the bleeding. I wasn't naive though, it was a futile gesture for something like this. This wasn't just one bite. This was many. He was in a bad way. And there was nothing I could do to help him.

If it was anyone else, anyone but one of my own, I'd sink into the realization that this was a lost cause. There was no waking up from this, not really. And even if he did wake up, what would the long term repercussions be? Cyrus was one of the strongest protectors I knew and he still limped from a single bite. What chance did Eli have?

I swallowed back the emotion threatening to escape. Maybe I was overlooking something. Maybe it wasn't as bad as I thought it was. Maybe, maybe, maybe.

"Fuck," Declan shouted, liquid pooling in her eyes as she stared down at him, gripping his hand in hers like she could bring him back to us if only she held on tight enough. His skin was more red than not, his body splattered in blood like a gruesome Jackson Pollock painting. "Fuck, fuck, fuck. You can't die on me you twat. Not now."

I fell back on my ass, readjusting slightly when I landed on a crispy vamp arm. I took a deep breath in, ignoring the sting of my own injuries, holding my head in my hands as I tried to make sense of this. I left The Guild, threw all of our futures into question. I made a series of rash decisions all to save my brother—only to lose another.

Why was this world so fucking cruel? We didn't stand a chance. Not now, not ever. What the hell was even the point?

I'd known Eli since we were kids. He used to follow me around like an obnoxious, lost puppy, copying everything I did like I was some sort of superhero. He was annoying as hell, and his rebellion against so many Guild rules and protocols got us into more trouble than he was often worth, but he'd grown on me over the years. The kid was smart, ridiculously so, and he was one of the best fighters I'd ever encountered. In a year or two, he'd be able to kick even my ass if he trained hard enough. Well, maybe not now that I had a wolf sharing my skin.

I liked to pretend that I was reluctant about him joining our team when he did a few years back, but the truth was that we were better with him than we were without him. He rounded us out, brought in some playful energy in a way that Declan and I couldn't. We needed him. He breathed fresh air into our team. And without Wade, we desperately needed fresh air.

My stomach felt hollow now, my chest tightening like I was being hugged by an iron giant. I couldn't lose another one. We'd lost too much, too many members of this team.

Sarah. Wade. We couldn't add Eli to that list. I refused.

I glanced over at the only two vampires in the room who were still alive: the jackass I helped break out of The Guild and his twin brother.

"We need to save him," I said, fully aware that I was asking two of the creatures I was expected to kill for help. "How can we save him?"

If anyone knew how to survive a vampire bite, it would be a vampire. At least I sure as fuck hoped so anyway.

Darius walked over, passing me up to sit next to Max. I didn't miss the way he studied her pulse, nor the way his expression relaxed once he found it beating in a seemingly acceptable rhythm.

Maybe he knew her from before—from before he was captured. My jaw tightened as I watched him watch her. Maybe the two of them were pulling one over on all of us. Maybe Max was sent in to infiltrate The Guild. Maybe she was one of them.

Part of me knew it was just easier to imagine her as some evil entity. It was infinitely easier than focusing on how drawn I—no, how drawn my wolf—was to her.

"He'll only slow us down at this point," Darius said, not bothering to look up from her throat, like her pulse was hypnotizing him into submission.

I had half a mind to rip his head off right then and there, even in front of his brother who I was certain could kill Declan and I pretty easily if given the chance. We were drained, exhausted from the fight. He'd only come in at the end. And something about him seemed a lot stronger than any vamp I'd come across in my years of field work. I couldn't explain it, but there seemed to be an extra energy about him.

He'd saved us though. My nails bit into the soft flesh of my palm as I thought about what that meant. I understood why he might save his brother, Max too if he knew about her power. But why the hell didn't he finish off the rest of us?

I glanced back at Darius, my lip curling in disgust. I could tell he was trying to come off like didn't give a fuck about Max, but I saw the way he looked at her neck, like the asshole was constantly battling his growing temptation to sink his teeth in. She wasn't his. She would never be his, if it was the last thing I did.

"Our best option is to just leave him here. This one," he nudged Max gently with his foot, "needs rest. We need to get her out of here."

Declan lunged, a low growl emerging from her chest as she moved towards Darius. Her eyes were filled with an emerald fire, and I caught her shirt before she reached him, knowing full well that if she did, she'd be dead. She'd been looking for an excuse—any excuse—to end him, and she was too close to the edge right now to think clearly. I didn't think his brother would sit by and simply watch as she ended his life. And it wouldn't be the first time her hatred of vamps caused a problem for all of us. She was always a short fuse where they were concerned.

We needed to regroup. We needed to figure out what the fuck we were going to do now. Nothing made sense anymore. And if I lost Dec after losing everyone else, I'd shatter into so many pieces that there'd be no going back. Right now, she was the last tether holding me together. There was only so much grief and disappointment a person could be expected to survive.

She fell back against my chest and I closed my arms around her, pinning hers against her body like a temporary straight-jacket. Dec was the only person I knew whose temper ran just as hot as mine.

"We aren't leaving him behind," she ground out as the sound of her teeth smashing together filled the room. "So if you want to stay alive," she said this like she was hoping that deep down, he didn't, "help us save him."

A loud exhale from behind me served as an instant reminder that we weren't alone. It wasn't just me and Declan against a vampire we'd broken out. A very dangerous vampire we'd broken out at that. But it was me and Declan against two very strong, very volatile vampires.

The room shrank as I catalogued the exit. If we needed to get out of here, would we be able to do it? I was fast, especially in my wolf form, but carrying Max and Eli meant that we wouldn't stand a chance. Not really.

And Darius's brother was the reason we were alive right now in the first place. While I didn't understand why the fuck he'd saved us, he had. So I had to hope that he wasn't going to change his mind about wanting us alive ten minutes later.

I turned around slowly, studying Darius's brother. I think he'd said his name was Claude. He looked like Darius, obviously, but much less...feral, maybe? Both had strange, mismatched eyeballs that heightened their already unsettling, mysterious expressions. Claude, though, looked a lot less like he'd spent the last long good while locked up in a lab, having tests run on him day in and day out. Darius on the other hand was un-fucking-predictable. Together they looked like the sort of monsters you'd find terrorizing people in a horror film. Trusting them wasn't exactly an ideal solution.

"We need to leave," he said, his glare like ice. "I don't know how many more will be headed this way, and I won't be responsible for killing any more of my own. So if you want to stick around, I hope you're prepared to save yourselves."

"We're not leaving without Eli," Declan said again, her head held up like she was speaking to a peer and not a dangerous beast from the depths of hell. She could be so thoughtless sometimes.

"She's right, we're not," I said, mirroring her steely posture. Apparently I was thoughtless too.

Claude shook his head before propping it up with his hand, like he was dealing with a pack of children and on his last strand of patience. "Whatever, I don't care. Carry both your dead out of here then, but you need to leave all the same. I'll take you to the gate and we'll be done with this."

Go to hell now? With half of our party unconscious? Was he fucking out of his mind?

"We're not going until she's awake and can defend herself," Darius said, his voice dripping with a lazy boredom as he studied the bloody battlefield with a weirdly calm excitement. Part of him seemed almost amused, like he found the whole experience exciting.

Then again, if I'd spent the last few years locked up in a tiny room as a lab rat, I might feel the same.

The room, scattered with demon entrails, was starting to smell like death. The cloying, metallic stench of blood was fused to the inside of my nostrils to the point where I was wondering if it would be a permanent fixture in my memory. It was impossible to ignore now that the adrenaline was leaving my system a bit. I needed to rest. Badly. I couldn't protect us from much more than another protector, let alone a powerful supernatural beast, in my current state.

I glanced at Declan, seeing my own injuries mirrored in her. Her spine was still straight, her expression still focused. But I knew her well enough to see the slight downward dip of her lips, the way she favored one leg, even if only slightly. She'd drop dead before revealing her weaknesses in front of a pair of vampires.

"So then if you don't want me to take you to hell, what the hell do you want then?" Claude asked, as he searched the faces of the vamps on the floor, lifting up limbs here, decapitated heads there. With each face that came into view, his body sagged into relief. He glanced at his brother, frustration evident in every feature, like he was dealing with an irrational child instead of an equal. Truthfully, that was probably a fair assessment, from what I knew of the guy.

I watched him study the carcasses with a ball of anxiety building in my gut. He'd come in late to the battle. What would happen if it turned out we'd killed one of his friends? Would he still help us or would that be the final straw that would ultimately lead him to snap and kill us all?

"I didn't say we don't want your help. I said we're not going until she's conscious and can defend herself. Plus, you know," Darius waved his hand in the air vaguely in Eli's direction, "they'll all want to wait until he dies or something too."

I dug my fingers into Declan's arm, less to keep her back this time and more to keep from jumping at him myself. There was only so much I could convincingly turn my cheek to.

"Well, you can't stay here," Claude said, pausing when he got to the dead vampires surrounding Max and Eli. "What the hell happened here?"

Darius glanced at the charred bodies and winced slightly before shrugging. "The dying boy is good with pyrotechnics. He's a shit fighter, so that's the only reason he stayed alive as long as he did. Where do you suggest we wait?"

He was protecting Max. Or, at the very least, protecting the truth, though I didn't understand why.

Claude glanced up, for the first time looking uncomfortable. His nostrils flared, jaw drawing down in dread. He swept a hand through his hair chaotically, his eyes searching the place with a sort of frantic desperation. "You'll have to stay somewhere you won't attract attention."

"Any ideas, brother dearest? This is, after all, your city,"

Darius sing-songed, his tone unusually light and carefree for such dire circumstances.

"I know of a place that'll do for a few days." Claude closed his eyes, like he was dreading his own solution already.

"And where's that?" Declan bit out, not at all interested in being cordial.

THAT ENDED UP BEING A LARGE ASS HOUSE BUILT A FEW MILES outside of Seattle. It also ended up being Claude's, if his friendliness with the lock and key was anything to go by. That, and he seemed quite familiar with the pretty, young woman who welcomed us all in, friendly concern and disgust plastered in equal measures across her face.

I didn't blame her. We were collectively a mess. I walked in carrying Eli, trying desperately to keep track of his faint heartbeat, my breath hitching each time it took me a second longer than anticipated to find it. Darius had Max clutched to his chest like a baby, the large hellhound nipping playfully at his feet while Declan monitored the two vampires with an unfriendly focus. I could tell it took every ounce of control she had not to stab them in the heart. Every last one of us was caked in blood and gore like we were extras from a zombie film.

We'd made quick work of the hotel room, piling the bodies into the van Claude ordered as fast as we possibly could. The carpet was beyond saving, as was most of the furniture, but Claude promised to get that taken care of. Or rather, he promised his people would take care of the rest of the mess and the hotel owner, whatever that meant. Hopefully he had plans beyond just draining the poor receptionist, because I didn't have the energy to take him on if that was his approach for making the supernatural gore fest disappear.

I didn't know the guy at all, but he oozed strength and power out of every pore. The way people looked at him when we were in the bar was filled with an unusual mixture of fear and envy—like they wanted what he had but were afraid to have it at the same time.

It made sense, seeing as he had a team to clean up after the mess back there. That meant he was working with some solid infrastructure, an organization of sorts. Obviously The Guild had similar tools available for our missions, but I'd never heard of vampires exercising that same hierarchy of skill and precision.

As far as we'd always been told, they were just blood-hungry beasts with allegiances to no one. Clearly Claude had earned some allegiances of his own. That made him more dangerous in my eyes. And entering into his territory had every instinct in my body screaming in protest.

Part of me wondered if he was one of the masterminds behind the group of werewolves and vampires that had been attacking protectors around the country, which in a lot of ways would make our lives easier. We could live with the enemy for a few days, learn his habits, and plot his destruction. If we could take down Darius in the process, so much the better. We might even learn something about whatever creature kidnapped Wade.

Honestly, if I didn't have Eli's survival to focus on, it would be the perfect mission plan.

"Khalida, these are going to be our guests for a few days," Claude said, his lips turning up in disgust as he stared at our group. "Please ignore them as much as you are able, but tell no one who doesn't need to be made aware of their existence. They won't be trespassing long."

Khalida didn't look much older than Max. She had long, straight black hair, and narrow eyes that were dark as night. There was a wisdom there that raised the hair on my arms, but also a sadness that I didn't want to focus on. I couldn't tell if she was a vampire or not, but I was certain she wasn't human—her body too still, her eyes too filled with a sort of preternatural knowing. She nodded once to Claude in acknowledgment of his instructions, before looking back at us all with a vague disinterest.

And then her face broke out in a wide grin that lit her up from the inside out. She was no longer simply pretty—she was stunningly ethereal.

"Darius? It can't be."

"You forgive too easily," Claude said as he let out an annoyed groan; a groan which Khalida promptly ignored as she back-handed his stomach.

She ran up to Darius and wrapped her arms around him, staining her porcelain skin red as flakes of dried blood landed on her arms and face. She didn't seem to give a flying fuck. Strange girl.

"Hey Khali," he said, awkwardly sinking into her embrace but not moving his arms or hands from supporting Max's small frame. "Long time no see, as they say. Although I've always found it a strange saying, grammatically anyway. Never could fully wrap my head around it."

"You're alive," she said, her voice deep and filled with an echo of disbelief, "I mean, of course you are. I would know if you weren't. But I was half convinced you'd never show your face around these parts again." Her face dropped slightly as she pulled away from him. "Around us."

He winked at her once before walking into a large, surprisingly warm living space, and deposited Max onto a giant gray couch with a surprisingly reverent care.

She looked so small and defenseless as she slept in a house owned by a vampire. How could she have taken down so many of them on her own when she seemed so fragile? She was so small, not to mention ridiculously naive and trusting. Maybe that was all part of it though—a supremely convincing act that made it impossible to fully distrust her. It was like I had to constantly force myself not to fall for my strange desire to protect her.

A hard look from Claude that held a clear order sent Khalida stomping away into another room, but not before she scratched behind the hellhound's ears like he was an adorable Labrador and not a powerful beast from hell. What was it with these women not understanding how fucking terrifying and strong hellhounds were? There was a reason the protectors running the lab wanted him studied and destroyed—they were unpredictable and made vampires and werewolves seem like loveable play things in comparison.

Hell, I'd watched this very creature rip apart a vampire with my own eyes the night that Wade died. Or the night Wade was taken and presumed dead, anyway.

"Before everyone goes for a wash," Claude said, studying his own stained white shirt with annoyance, "I'd like to know a few things."

Ignoring his brother's wince, Darius plopped down on the couch next to Max, settling back against the cushion like he was waiting for a show to begin. Crusty flakes of blood littered the upholstery beneath him.

"As would we," Declan said, crossing her arms and propping her side up against a wall. I didn't think she was doing it to dirty up Claude's walls to spite him, not in the way that Darius was anyway, but because she was in desperate need of some medical treatment and a long, restful sleep. She'd never admit to being badly injured in front of creatures she saw as the enemy though and I highly doubted she'd let herself rest so long as we were in enemy territory, which meant that her recovery would take longer than it should. It went against every one of her instincts to appear weak. "First and foremost, how the hell do we get to...hell?"

She was awake and conscious enough to wince at her own unintended pun, a familiar expression that brought the first grin in hours to my face—the gesture almost felt foreign to my facial muscles.

I laid Eli down on another couch, keeping a close eye on the slow, shallow breaths lifting his ribs. Each rise and fall of his chest felt impossibly erratic and unpredictable in a way that breathing shouldn't be. I was torn between holding onto a naive hope that he'd awaken well and good in a day or so, and calling his father here to give him time with his son in case he didn't.

Jesus. Seamus was going to decapitate me himself if I didn't bring Eli back alive. Didn't even matter if he knew I was a were-wolf or not. He would need no excuse. Eli was all he had and he'd made me discreetly promise over and over again that I'd watch out for him on our missions. Favoritism was deeply frowned upon in our line of work, but no one could begrudge a father for loving his son. And Seamus was like the father I'd always wanted. Disappointing him added an extra heavy layer of misery to the whole situation.

"It's not something I'm going to explain to you. I'll take you to the gate as soon as you are able to go and, judging by the mess you've already created," Claude glanced around at the blood soaking each of us, his nose curled in disgust, "the faster you can do so, the better. For all of us. Now, one of you needs to explain to me how a hellhound came to be glued to this girl? And I don't see any bites on her, none of this blood appears to be hers, so why is she unconscious?"

I hadn't seen him take more than a passing, casual glance at Max, so his confidence that she wasn't bitten threw me.

I glanced over at Declan. Her eyes met mine and widened slightly. I could tell neither of us knew how to explain, even if we trusted Claude in the first place. It was always odd—how drawn supernatural creatures seemed to be to Max—us included. She'd had my entire team tripped up for months, none of us quite sure whether we wanted to do everything we could to protect her or stay as far away as we possibly could without arousing undue suspicion. She was equal parts tempting and terrifying. A terrible mix, as far as I was concerned.

We couldn't pretend she was altogether normal though, that her intrigue stemmed from nothing more than an unusual upbringing, or from being raised by one of the greats. Our instincts where she was concerned were correct—there was something strange, dangerous even, about her. The hellhound's attachment wasn't something we could argue with. He had a knack for showing up whenever she needed him most, like they were bonded in some ancient, powerful way that protectors had no answer for.

At least not as far as I knew, anyway. But I was beginning to realize that The Guild either kept a lot more than they should from the field teams, or else the organization had a seriously alarming deficit of knowledge about the hell realm. If it was the former, I had no idea how to trust an organization that kept us all so entirely in the dark; and if it was the latter, we were right and surely fucked.

And having a beast so often aligned with evil and hell showing up at her side during opportune moments was nothing if not ominous. It was easier to overlook this on occasion, since she'd gone and named the dog Ralph and treated him like he was nothing more than a loveable pet. I was half-convinced myself that he was on our side and didn't mean any harm. Which was absolute madness. I knew better than that. Maybe the girls weren't the only ones who handled the beast with puppy gloves.

No creature associated with hell could be trusted. Not even me.

Not even Wade.

And most definitely not Max.

I'd been concerned about her weird energy since the first second I'd laid eyes on her, before she even moved to Guild Headquarters. Something about my draw to her wasn't right, wasn't explainable in a way that I understood. She was like a beacon, pulling my wolf to that tiny shithole of a town that she called home. She healed too quickly from her vampire attack. And then, more recently, she started dreaming of Wade, a connection none of the rest of us were able to make, despite knowing him longer and sharing half of his DNA. Also weird and unexplainable.

But after the fight? I wasn't sure how to make sense of her at all anymore. Was it better to keep her close so that we could keep an eye on her, make sure she didn't harm anyone? Or was it better to get as far away from her as soon as we used her dream link to find Wade? Part of me knew that if I'd seen anyone else do what she did, we'd be hightailing them back to the lab for research and, eventually, a trip to the morgue. The thought of turning her over though made me feel itchy all over, which was a problem for a different day.

None of us had mentioned the fact that Max had literally created fire with her mind less than an hour ago. For some reason, voicing it out loud heightened the urgency behind the need for action. I half wanted to forget it happened altogether. I could tell from Declan's distance from Max that she was unsettled, maybe even a little bit afraid of the girl now.

And when I glanced in Darius's direction, he shook his head almost imperceptibly. I wasn't sure how I could read him so well in that moment, but I was certain he didn't want us to impart too much information about Max to his brother.

Also interesting. Also confusing. She not only had a hellhound fighting in her corner, but a vampire who was even more unpredictable than all of the creatures I'd ever encountered. Combined.

"The hellhound was also kept in the lab in Guild Headquarters," I said, careful to be as honest as possible so that Claude didn't pick up on any hitch in my breathing or heartbeat. Vampires had powerful senses as they were, but something about Claude felt even stronger than the typical vamp we encountered on our missions. There was a feral lethality in his eyes. He watched every movement we made, not missing a single muscle tense. It was eerie as fuck.

"The girl, Max," Declan continued, voice calm and even, "visited him there often and eventually broke him out. I suppose he feels loyalty to her. As for the lack of bites, it's possible she simply fainted from the heightened emotions of being bombarded by a bunch of creatures bent on killing us all. She's young. New."

I knew that labeling Max a poor, defenseless woman like that grated on Declan's nerves. She'd spent years proving herself as a valuable soldier, and taking away a fellow female protector's agency and strength like that didn't come naturally. Especially since in our world, women were protected, revered even. Their strength matched our own.

Claude arched a single brow, clearly not buying our story or at the very least not ready to believe that was all there was to it. "My bar associates tell me she's being visited by an incubus. You'll want to rouse her soon or you'll be carting around another dying husk. My brother seems fond of this blood bag, so I advise you not to let that happen. He can be," he rolled his neck slowly, as if lost in thought or a distant memory, before grunting, "volatile when provoked."

"Back at the hotel, you mentioned that Ralph—er, the hellhound—brought you to us," I said, ignoring his brother's annoying fascination with Max. I didn't have the energy to dissect that any further tonight. "Why did he go to you and how did he bring you to us?"

A large grin split his face, amusement making him resemble his brother so much more than his usual scowl did. "They really don't teach you lot much in that school of yours, do they? Hellhounds have the power to shift from one place to another. This one isn't fully attached to his powers yet, he's weaker than most." He studied Ralph with narrowed eyes and a look that either read as respect or fear, though I couldn't tell which. "But when it's life or death for the owner of his bond, he's capable of tapping into the power."

"What?" Declan asked, staring at Ralph with an expression of horror. She'd slowly been warming up to him over the weeks, but I could see that progress dissolving in her eyes, making way for a renewed fear. Dec didn't do well with the unknown. She liked things to be predictable, black and white.

"They can teleport," Darius clarified with a shrug, hardly focusing on the conversation at all. "Did I forget to mention that? Oops."

My teeth raged against each other, my jaw tense but unable to move and translate my frustration into words. This explained how he was always able to get to her so easily, especially in the moments she needed him most. I wondered how he was able to sense when she was in danger. More than anything, I couldn't help but think back to that night. How that tall, smug man had scooped Wade up like an unmoving bride and disappeared in a flash, presumably carrying him to a dungeon in hell, if Max's dreams were anything to go by. And now, to find that the hound had the same power—my curiosity, distrust, and anger were competing in equal parts.

"Why did the hound go for you?" Declan asked, making up for my own temporary inability to speak. We were great at balancing each other out sometimes, between my temper and her unwillingness to trust, it could take a while for us to get the information we needed.

Mirroring his brother, Claude shrugged, bored with the conversation now that the answer to his question proved less exciting than he'd likely hoped. "I'm a useful creature to know. The hound is smart. And clearly, it turns out he has good judgment. I was able to get to you while you were all still alive." He arched a single brow, taking a step closer to me, an odd gleam in his eyes. For the first time in years, I felt like I was the mouse and not the cat. "Tell me wolf, what's it like to become the very thing you've spent your entire life learning to despise?"

My stomach squeezed in on itself, a low, warning growl emerging in my chest. My wolf wanted out. It wanted to rip this creature limb from limb and then take on his brother with the same brutal force, until the living room was an entirely new battle scene, much more personal than the last. For once, my wolf and I were on the same page.

"Where can we take them to rest?" I choked out, each word stilted.

I walked over to Max, picking her up again before Darius could beat me to it. I still wasn't convinced that he wouldn't kill her if left to his own devices. And part of me, deep down in a place I didn't want to acknowledge, needed to know that she was okay, needed to feel her breathing against my chest, feel her weight in my own arms.

He narrowed his eyes, gripping Eli in his arms with far less care than he had lifted Max and nodded towards his brother. "Yes, lead the way, brother dearest. One needs rest to wake up, the other needs space to die. And then, in the blink of an eye we'll be on to the next stop in our adventure and out of your precious hair. Don't you worry your pretty little head about that."

"He's your twin, so you do realize you basically just called yourself pretty?" Declan muttered under her breath, face pinched slightly as she moved away from the wall, resigned to follow wherever Claude was taking us.

"I'm known for my brutal honesty." Darius winked and chomped his teeth together in a gesture that was probably meant to be flirty, but really just drove home the fact that he was a fucking man-sized leech.

Declan turned a pale shade of green I hadn't seen since the day she tried eating her aunt's infamous chicken surprise casserole.

His mirror let out a harsh, humorless laugh that turned my blood cold, and walked out of the room with nothing more than a silent invitation to follow.

If hell wasn't the death of us, the fang twins would be.

3

MAX

I stood in a familiar room, the walls decorated in gradient shades of purple and gray. I dug my feet into a familiar black shag rug as I squeezed Wade's hand, grateful for the feeling of his fingers woven through mine.

The grin on his face was contagious, his smiling blue eyes suddenly a swirl of the indigo waves that I was growing more and more fond of. I was beginning to realize that they changed color whenever he used his incubus magic. It was similar to Atlas's eyes and the ways the color morphed as his wolf surfaced. Still, even though the shade was new, it somehow felt like it had been a part of him for as long as I'd known him, like the incubus within was always there, desperate to be let out. And it made sense, truthfully. The incubus was always there, lurking for the chance to express itself.

If I liked Wade, I had to like all parts of him, even though I didn't fully understand how all of this was going to work just yet.

"You did it," he whispered, his face filling with wonder as he took in the room we were standing in, eyes glazed with excitement like a child in a candy shop.

Our dream-walk was exciting for me, of course it was. But how exciting must it have been for Wade? Wade, who'd been locked in isolation, buried in a medieval prison with nothing but fear, loneliness, and a never-ending trove of unanswered questions.

My stomach ached when I thought about him in that room, alone with the realization that everything he knew about his past, about his future—all of it was wrong.

"No, *you* did it. I'm merely mooching off of your ridiculously cool new powers," I clarified, joy rising inside me as I realized what this meant for him. For the first time in a long time, Wade had freedom. He had a way to spend his time, at least until I found a way to rescue him anyway.

Maybe freedom was the wrong word. Maybe what he really had was an escape. A place to go, a way to get out, when he couldn't take being trapped in hell for another moment alone. Hopefully we'd get to him before the situation grew too dire.

Suddenly, a large force rammed me around the middle, squeezing and squeezing until I was certain that I'd explode or die from lack of oxygen.

I craned my neck, expecting to be confronted with an attacker or for the dream world to at the very least evict me. I didn't belong here after all, not in the way that Wade did. I was nothing more than a trespasser, a leech on his mind and power.

My fear morphed into a wildly large grin as my face lined with my attacker's.

I was confronted with smooth, light brown skin and deep gray eyes that were somehow both easy and impossible to read, depending on how guarded she was in the moment.

Izzy.

As soon as she released me just slightly, I wrapped my arms around her, squeezing tightly. We'd only been separated for a few days, but I was still ridiculously happy to see her. If I couldn't have a meeting with my brother, to calm his fears and visit with him, then Izzy was the next best thing.

It was weird, really, to think about how her mere presence instantly relaxed me. I'd only known her for a few months, but it felt like it'd been a lifetime. She just had this remarkable, badass energy that instantly sucked you in and refused to let go. Sometimes when you fit with a person, you just instantly knew. It was like that with Izzy.

"Izzy," I grunted, when her thick grasp became too much to handle. That answered the age-old question then, I supposed. That dreamers really could feel pain. Or maybe dreaming wasn't the best way to describe whatever this was that we were doing. It was simply magic.

How could incubi be evil when they had the power to move time and space and bring me together with my best friend? There was nothing evil about that.

When she pulled back, her eyes were rimmed with red as they glanced at Wade and back at me.

Seeing her that way, suddenly terrified and anxious, like a small lost child, had anxiety gripping at my chest with a fierce, angry tightness.

"Does this mean you're dead?" she murmured, her voice breaking softly at the question in her voice, like she didn't want me to really answer it. "Please tell me I'm not having one of those goodbye dreams my auntie always told me about. I think she meant it as a hopeful experience—to get to say goodbye to your loved ones. But if you're really dead and you're here to say goodbye to me, I'm going to throat punch you until you come back."

"What are you talking about?" I asked, looking back at Wade as if he might know what she was rattling on about. "I'm not dead."

She straightened her posture slightly, her fingers playing with the hem of her silver shirt as she always did when she was trying to make sense of something. "But Wade," she glanced at him again, brows lifting in apology, "I mean, no offense Wade. Maybe you don't realize it yet, I'm not sure how the whole ghost thing works, but you're dead." She turned her focus back on me.

"You're here with him. Does that mean that you're dead too? Since you're visiting me too?

"Maybe I'm just dreaming a normal dream," she shook her head and sat down on her bed, not giving me a moment to respond as she sank into her thoughts. "But I feel more lucid than I normally do in my dreams. More in control of my body and my mind." She waved her hands in the air like she was getting ready to dance a rather ungraceful ballet. "Which is why I thought it might be a death dream. A goodbye."

Finally understanding, I walked over and sat next to her, my body weight sinking into the mattress as it normally would in my corporeal form. I sucked in a breath, grinning as I pulled out the familiar notes of Izzy's favorite perfume—vanilla and spice. "I'm not dead, and this is not a normal dream. And, for what it's worth, Wade's not dead either."

Her dark eyes narrowed as she tried to process her reality with the dream. And honestly, I fucking got it. The only thing that made me realize that my dreams with Wade were more than my typical dreams was the fact that I woke up with indentations of his fingers sunken into my hip.

I wasn't about to mark my best friend's perfect skin, so hopefully my explanation would do well enough. Maybe she'd settle for a sharp pinch if it became necessary.

"Can I tell you something? And when I do, can you promise not to tell anyone?"

"Not even Ro?" she asked, arching her perfectly-sculpted brow in challenge, a devious grin lifting her cheeks, even though her eyes still held some fear and sadness.

My smile responded to hers as I shoved her shoulder gently with mine. "Ro doesn't count, but not anyone else."

My stomach churned at the thought of keeping the truth from Cyrus. While I knew with absolute certainty that Ro wouldn't turn Wade in once he found out the truth about what he was, I couldn't say the same for Cy. I was ninety-percent sure he wouldn't, but that ten percent was too much to risk. And it wasn't my risk to take. I refused any possible future that resulted in Wade escaping from one prison, just to be locked up in another.

"Promise," she said, eyeing Wade with curiosity, "of course I promise."

"Wade's not dead," I said again, figuring that was as good a place as any to start. It wasn't often that the dead came back to life, not even in our world. I looked around the room, holding back a grin. Her clothes were tossed all over the floor and the place looked like even more of a disaster than it usually did. Her dark bedding was bunched up in every direction, like she'd been tossing and turning through some truly horrific dreams. Or, who knows, maybe she had someone over for something more exciting than a shitty dream.

"I thought you said you saw him die that night—that his neck was snapped by a vampire right in front of you?" She leaned back on her elbows, settling in for the story, clearly enjoying it now that she realized I wasn't dead in a ditch somewhere no one would find me.

"I did." I shrugged, mirroring her and leaning back against my elbows as I studied Wade. He was standing awkwardly in front of us, silent, still wearing nothing but black sweatpants. I tried not to focus on his bare chest for too long. I needed to focus if I wanted to get this story out without stumbling on my words. Incubus energy was a heady thing. "Turns out he's not entirely human. Or, well, not entirely a protector I guess. But for some reason that doesn't sound as much like a dramatic reveal. So instead, for entertainment's sake, let's stick with not entirely human."

I turned back in time to see Izzy's jaw drop as she sat back up, spine ramrod-straight. Her eyes narrowed as she studied him, like she was having trouble deciding whether or not to burst out laughing at some tepid joke or go on the defensive.

"Come again? If he's not just protector, what the fuck is he then?" Her eyebrow was arched as she studied him with razor focus.

"Incubus," Wade said, shoulders slumping forward slightly as he dropped eye contact. "Apparently, anyway."

"Well, fuck me sideways. That's wild," she said, standing up to study him more closely. "I guess that explains the whole dream thing then and how you could survive a broken neck. Cool parlor trick. I'm almost jealous. Also explains why I suddenly have an urge to lick you." She crossed her shoulders in front of her chest, staring him down even as she spoke to me. "He hasn't hurt you, has he?"

I shook my head, feeling slightly guilty that I couldn't talk to her like I normally would. I'd tell Izzy about the sex dream eventually, but not until we were alone. I still had to sort out all of those complicated feelings as it was. Was I attracted to him because he was an incubus? Or because he was Wade?

As soon as the thought trespassed through my mind, I knew with absolute certainty that it was the latter. I'd felt a draw to Wade almost as soon as I'd met him. A draw that grew as I started to get to know him—all of his brainy, sweet quirks that were mixed with just the right amount of mischievous edge. That had nothing to do with being a creature who survived on sex.

"No, he hasn't hurt me. I'm perfectly fine. He's locked up and we're going to free him."

"You look good, Wade," she said, voice friendly again now that she was sure he was harmless. That was all it took—my assurance—and Izzy was ready to toss out what The Guild had taught her about incubi and monsters since she was old enough to talk. She lifted a curious finger, poking into his pectoral as if half-convinced her flesh would pass through his. I watched with a grin as her fingertip turned into a whole palm caress. "Death and dreams suit you, I guess. Don't get me wrong, you were always pretty. But now it's just...exaggerated?"

I bit back a grin as Wade took a step back from her. I had to agree with Izzy. Even half-starved, this version of Wade was just so much...more. It was like he was being shadowed in his old life. Now, he radiated power and strength. His chest was perfectly sculpted, not that I'd really had the opportunity to study it in detail before, and his skin was flawless, like he'd been airbrushed to model-like perfection.

But his eyes were the biggest shift. They were just as intelligent as they always were, just as filled with vulnerability and curiosity. But now they had a way of drawing me in and not letting me go. I didn't think I'd ever get tired of staring at them, trying to unravel the thoughts and emotions below the surface.

"Er, thanks," he answered, clearing his throat awkwardly as he glanced between us. "I guess."

"So, where exactly are you freeing him from?" she walked back over towards me, plopping down on the bed again so that she could admire him from afar. She had that lazy focus she always got when she was ready to dive into a good book or movie.

"Hell," I said, hoping we could just glaze past this part of the conversation as quickly as possible.

Her head snapped to me so quickly I was half-afraid she'd broken her spine. Then she broke out in a slow, amused laugh, the lilting sound carrying around the room. Weird how many things the dream world got right. Apparently my imagination was better than I gave it credit for. "I'm serious, where's he being kept?"

When my jaw remained closed, nose scrunching as I cringed, her humor dried up until a look of pure horror and anger eclipsed her face.

"You're shitting me? What the hell are you thinking, Max Bentley?' She stood up and started pacing before adding a quick "no pun intended," and then chuckling like she couldn't help herself.

"I'm thinking that that's where he is now. The night he was

killed—er, killed-ish anyway—a man basically teleported away with him."

"You never told me that before," she said, her brows scrunching together as her gray eyes filled with hurt.

I shrugged. "I didn't remember it happening. Or, if I did, I think the trauma and exhaustion of the moment just blocked it out somehow. If I had seen it happen, I would've thought my eyes were playing games. But Atlas and the rest of Six saw it happen. They confirmed. Straight up teleported away."

"Jesus," she leaned against the wall like she needed to be propped up. "And how exactly are you going to get to hell? Protectors have been trying to find a way for years. Probably centuries. Basically for all of time," she said, shaking her head back and forth like I was ridiculous for thinking we stood even the slightest chance. "And now, not only do you decide to run away and go to hell, but you're doing it without me? What the fuck?"

Ah okay then. Not ridiculous for thinking I could find my way to hell, but for going without her. That was actually pretty on brand for Izzy.

"We made a deal with a vampire, after busting him from the lab," I said, unclear if she'd heard that part of our break out story or not. I wasn't sure how much would be common knowledge for most of the students. Guild members seemed to be pretty tight-lipped—more so than any of us ever realized. "And he's going to lead us there." I paused for a long moment, hesitant to ask what was really on my mind, until the curiosity threatened to swallow me whole. "Um, speaking of which. How're Ro and Cy? They don't want to kill me do they? What's everyone on campus saying about this whole unsanctioned mission?"

Even though I promised Darius I wouldn't go straight back to campus after we rescued Wade, the thought of being banned altogether had my body thrumming with anxiety. I'd just found a home and a best friend, and it was where Ro and Cy were. It would eat me alive if I would never be welcomed back. Where the hell would I go?

Don't get me wrong. It'd be worth it, if it meant we saved Wade from rotting away in a hell dungeon. But it would still suck.

A sly grin crept through her disbelief as she shook her head. "They're not saying much. Mostly because Alleva and the rest of them are pretending it's not happening. At least publicly anyway. As far as everyone on campus knows, Six took you on a sanctioned mission and will be back soon. Reza, meanwhile, has moved back in with her former team. She and her mom are selling it as a final chance to explore her options before her official bonding ceremony, which they're hoping will happen in a few weeks. But you should see her—she's storming around campus, nostrils flared at all times like someone kicked her puppy. I think she's under the impression Six straight up ditched her ass. Er," she glanced at Wade, wincing slightly, "your father is flying into town though. Heard he's expected to be here by the end of tomorrow. So I am guessing Alleva told him what happened—what the guys and Atlas did. And well, you know better than anyone that he's probably not taking the news well."

My eyes widened with surprise. Wade's father hadn't even come to town after his death. It was strange at the time, but to think he cared more about one son ditching The Guild for an off-book mission than the other's death was almost unfathomable.

"Shit," Wade muttered, his hands sweeping through his hair as he turned away from us both, trying to compose his emotions. I didn't know too much about the boys' father, but I knew that he wouldn't handle having an incubus and a werewolf for heirs lightly. He seemed like the sort of guy that clung to Guild beliefs and traditions with an iron-clad grip. "Atlas is going to be in a world of trouble. You can't say anything to him. Not until my brother decides how he wants to handle this whole thing." He looked up at Izzy, his blue eyes wide and striking against his brown skin. "Please. I know he's not an easy person to lie to."

I noticed he didn't include himself in the decision-making process, and I had a feeling it was because he was convinced that despite our efforts, he'd remain a prisoner—or worse. While I couldn't control his confidence in us fixing everything, I could control whether or not we did everything within our power to try.

She rolled her eyes. "I'm not dense, Wade. Even if I didn't have any information, I'd stay far away from Tarren. He's terrifying as fuck. I've only seen him in person a few times, but the rumors surrounding that man are enough to keep me on edge. And I'd never sell my girl out like that."

He nodded, his muscles still tense, but his breathing more relaxed.

"And Ro?" I asked, almost dreading the response. If Izzy was mad I didn't bring her with us, Ro would be irreconcilable. "What's he been told about everything?"

"Well," she started slowly as she swiped a thin hand through her hair, combing through the waves that were mussed with sleep, "Ro is the reason that I even know some of the details in the first place. Cyrus is keeping him in the loop. At least partially anyway. He went a little batty when he came home and you were gone. So thanks to him and his surprisingly terrifying temper, we know that you ran away. And I mean, obviously the note you left for Ro helped explain that some. Although you were annoyingly vague. Now I understand why, I guess. And we also know that you broke the hot vamp out of the lab again. Which, by the way, Ro and Cy are both fuming about." She wiggled her eyebrows at me when she mentioned Darius.

"You're not fuming?" I asked, while Wade watched the exchange in silence, studying Izzy with a bemused expression on his face.

She shrugged and then winked at me. "Figure if he's hot enough, I guess I get it. Plus, while trusting a vampire sounds like a terrible idea, and dangerous as hell, I trust your judgment. He didn't kill you last time you broke him out, so I'm just going to hope that trend continues. And if it doesn't, I'll hunt the fang-hole down myself." She tilted her head, studying Wade again. "Plus, I mean, you're going to go rescue an incubus. And Wade's never seemed particularly evil to me. Moody and difficult to read sometimes, but never evil. Maybe your pretty vamp isn't either. Who knows? Nothing makes sense anymore, everything's changing." Her eyes narrowed as she got lost in her thoughts. "It's strange, isn't it? Can you feel that things are changing too? Like we're on the cusp of something brilliant, or the cliff of something dangerous? Weird how both things feel the same."

As far as The Guild went, Izzy's words were basically blasphemy. Cyrus kept me out of trouble when I let Darius out the first time. It paid to be the adopted ward of one of the most badass protectors in our modern history. But would he protect Izzy if she started questioning Guild philosophy out in the open like that? Izzy never talked about her family—hell, she hardly even mentioned her brother even though he was in our cohort—but I had a feeling that if they held sway over Guild leadership, they might not exercise it for her.

"Just don't go spreading that opinion around. At least for now anyway," I said, suddenly worried about her getting in trouble without me there to back her up. I could handle it if I got myself in trouble, but not if I was responsible for Izzy fucking up her life and prospects. Our world was dangerous enough without garnering enemies from our own people.

"I see how it is," she said, narrowing her eyes at me, "you're the only one who gets to have any of the fun. I'll remember that, Bentley."

I burst into laughter, shaking my head at her, while Wade stared at her, eyebrows raised, like she was a swamp creature from outer space that he had no hope of ever figuring out. I didn't blame him, she was something special, that's for sure. "Anyway, do me a favor and let Ro and Cy know that I'm okay.

The fewer the details everyone knows, the better it'll be. Don't want you to get into too much trouble for harboring a fugitive in your dreams—even if you have no choice in the matter. We'll be back soon." I paused, wondering if it was the truth. The last thing I wanted to do was lie to her—I'd been keeping enough secrets. Adding in another would push me fit to bust. "Hopefully."

Wade walked over and sat next to me on the bed with a heavy clunk, like he couldn't support all of his weight anymore. His face was drawn slightly, and I could tell that he was growing tired. I saw the same exhaustion on his features that I'd been feeling for months. His eyes deepened a shade further, until the light blue color was almost completely eclipsed. The second his hand touched mine, a deep desire to run my tongue through the seam of his lips overpowered me. I leaned into him, my side pressing against his as much as possible, like I couldn't bear for there to be any distance between us. Izzy was suddenly long forgotten.

She shook her head, eyes growing wide. "Oh, I don't think so. You're not getting out of this that quickly. You mentioned that you were traveling to hell. That means you're not currently there at this exact moment."

"So?" I asked, staring at Wade while the rest of the world shimmied and melted away around us. I could feel him losing his grip on the dream, which made it difficult for me to focus on the conversation.

"So you have time to tell me where the hell you all are now so that I can come join you. You think I'd miss out on a chance to go on a rescue mission in he—"

Just as soon as Izzy's room vanished from view, the dark dungeon filled its place.

We both landed hard on Wade's concrete slab of a bed, winded and exhausted.

A glance at Wade's eyes, now practically glowing, told me everything that I needed to know: he was starving.

"Are you okay?" I asked, reaching a hand up his arm, his shoulder, and landing softly on his cheek. "Did that take too much out of you? I'm sorry, we'll find a way to make it easier next time."

He stood up, trying to catch his bearings, only to fall back against the wall, like his legs were made of jelly and he couldn't support himself without assistance.

"Wade?" I reached a hand out to grab his arm, to support him somehow, but as soon as my skin met his, it was like a wave of need devoured me.

His eyes latched onto mine, both of us unable to resist the pull as our faces inched closer and closer together, until I closed the distance completely with one long breath and pushed my lips against his.

Our lips met in an angry war, like they couldn't quite accept that they were already together, desperate instead to get closer somehow. Wade gasped and I slipped my tongue between my lips to meet his.

An intoxicating heat spread throughout my body, my knees buckling as our tongues collided again and again, rolling together in the most delicious way imaginable.

He pulled me against him and spun us around until I was pressed back into the wall, his hands there to cushion my head against the stone.

I bit his lip and draped my hand down his bare, incredibly smooth chest, until I reached the elastic band of his sweatpants. He let out a heavy gasp as I slipped my fingers below the fabric and grabbed him in my palm. Somehow, he felt hard as stone but smooth and silky at the same time.

Just as eager to explore my body, he slid his hands under my top until one grazed the back of my bra, just as the other teased the lace of my underwear. Every touch of his skin against mine, every soft indent his fingers created had me flooding. Part of my brain knew that we should stop, that we should slow down, but as soon as the thought filtered through my brain, I pushed it away—as far away as I could shove it. This couldn't be wrong. Everything about this, about being pressed against him, wanting him as much as he wanted me, felt right. Like this was destined to happen again and again—and we were powerless to fight it.

For a second, he pressed his weight into me with a low, sensuous groan that I felt deep in the pit of my stomach, until I was throbbing with need. But then, instantly, the mood shifted. Suddenly I could feel him changing his mind, could feel the exact moment he decided to stop, even before he acted on it.

With a flash he pushed off the wall and fell back against the bed, creating a few feet of space between us that felt like miles. I felt completely bare even though I was still fully clothed. Chills ran up and down my body as a hollowness filled my belly. I was dizzy with the feel of him, with the taste of him still on my lips —he was somehow sweet and spicy at once.

"I'm so sorry. We shouldn't have—I shouldn't have. A-are you okay?" he asked, his indigo eyes wide and alert as they studied every inch of me. They were glowing and I knew that he'd been pulling from me, but I didn't care. I felt fine. "Holy shit, Max. Your eyes."

"What about my eyes?"

"Ah, I see I'm interrupting. How unfortunate. Interesting that you managed to pull a visitor here, but unfortunate for everyone concerned, all the same."

I spun around and could feel my heart pulse throughout every inch of my body as I came face-to-face with a shrouded figure. He was tall and lean, but his features were all muddled together, like he was perpetually in shadow. I couldn't discern any of his features, no matter how hard I tried.

I felt, rather than saw Wade stand up and push me behind him, like he could protect me from this creature. Even I knew that his efforts were futile. Something told me that if this man wanted either of us dead, there wasn't a damn thing either of us could do about it. Not from here, both of us weaponless and half drained of power.

And the creature standing in front of us was pulsing power—so much so that I felt it down to my marrow. We wouldn't stand a chance.

"Who are you?" Wade asked, his voice still husky and breathy, though now with a different sort of adrenaline and heat. "You need to let her go. Let her leave. It's me you want."

I rolled my eyes, squaring my shoulders. I wasn't part demon like Wade, but I also wasn't a damsel in distress either.

"Where the hell is this place and what do you want with my friend?" I asked, narrowing my eyes where I thought the man's face might be, even if I couldn't quite make them out. "And what the hell are you?"

"Sorry girl, now is not the time for false bravado." He let out a low, haunting chuckle before raising his hands and shoving me with a magic that felt light as air but more powerful than anything I'd ever felt before.

I flew away from Wade, beyond his bed, and into—no, through—his wall. The sound of Wade's screams rang through my ears as he tried desperately to reach me, his body colliding solidly into the wall that a moment before had opened to welcome me.

And then, all I saw was black.

❧ 4 ❧

MAX

My eyes slid open, like the shutter of a camera, heavy and reluctant. Soft sunlight crept through the opening between two thick, dark blue curtains. My hands slid against an impossibly soft set of sheets and blankets. I pressed my head down, letting the cloudlike feeling underneath it wash over me. Beds this comfortable shouldn't be made. Who would ever want to wake up?

I blinked again, trying to remember where I was or how I'd gotten here, but my memories spun in complex patterns and whirls. I couldn't make sense of them in any sort of linear way. It was like I was living my own version of Alice in Wonderland.

The fragments were in such a hurry to get somewhere, I just couldn't quite understand how they were weaving together or where they were going.

I closed my eyes and tried to focus, to think about the last thing I remembered in any concrete detail.

I was alone in a room with Declan, both of us shrouded in a strangely intimate moment, her lips just a breath away from mine.

I was fighting a wave of never-ending vampires as they spilled into the hotel suite, the rest of us trying desperately to survive long enough to reach our next breath.

Flashes, all of them, a moving picture that didn't rest in any one spot long enough to stick.

Villette—sensuous and intelligent, was watching me, toying with me, while Darius tried to pull answers from her that might save my life.

Cyrus—forcing me to stay home while the members of my team went on a mission without me.

Wade—caressing my skin as he tried desperately to keep from giving into temptation.

A shadow figure—hiding in the recesses of a dungeon, tossing me about like it could manipulate the very air around me, like in its presence, I was made of nothing but air myself.

Eli—under an impossibly high pile of vampires, their bodies like quicksand pulling him under, out of my reach—out of everyone's reach.

The thoughts disappeared as soon as I latched onto them, leaving me alone on the winding path of my own mind as I scrambled for purchase.

Was I losing my grip on reality?

I pushed myself into a seated position and I could almost feel the blood rushing through my veins as my body adjusted to the movement. Sounds were so much more intense, my ears suddenly tuned in to each raspy breath I sucked in.

It was too much, too overwhelming. I wanted to go back to sleep—to sink into the cloud bed and forget about all of the creatures that went bump in the night. Waking life was overrated.

"Where am I?" I whispered, my throat dry and charred, though I wasn't sure from what. I pressed my tongue against my teeth, trying to remember the last time I'd eaten. Why did my mouth taste like barbecue?

I ran a frantic finger against my teeth, terrified for a moment that I'd find fangs protruding from my gums.

No.

That wasn't right. Protectors couldn't be turned. Could they? I wasn't sure anymore. Nothing about the supernatural world was as I expected it would be.

"Oh, good. You're awake."

My neck snapped away from the heavy curtains as my eyes tried to chase the quiet, almost musical voice. There was something otherworldly about it.

A girl stood in a doorway, a large pitcher and glass of water balanced effortlessly on a lavish tray. Something about her seemed so timeless, like she'd been standing in that position, holding that vintage silver set for longer than I'd been alive.

She moved towards me in long, languid movements. Her eyes were so black and smooth that they almost looked like they were made of velvet. I found myself strangely wanting to reach out and touch them. Her skin was impossibly clear and blemish free. So much so that I was half convinced she was made of marble, not flesh and bone. Every inch of her long limbs were lithe and graceful as she stood framed in the door.

"Where am I?" I asked again, this time with an audience.

"You're somewhere safe," she said, her head tilted as she studied me, making her look almost like a cat. Only more lethal. A panther maybe. "At least for right now, anyway. I can't promise that you'll be safe here forever. Claude can be quite fickle."

There wasn't a threat in the way that she said it, rather it was like she was simply relaying a fact or an observation to an uninterested third-party.

Her lips curled into a soft grin, both mysterious and beautiful. "There's something very unusual about you, you know? Familiar, almost. Have we met? I can usually place a face, an energy signature." Her eyes narrowed slightly as she studied me. "But I can't quite get a read on you."

She seemed to oscillate between sophisticated and childlike, the transitions so smooth that the strange temperament was almost normal, the seams impossible to identify.

I studied her intently, grabbing the glass as she handed it to me. Part of me was afraid to take a sip of something offered by a stranger. But then if she wanted to attack me, she could've slit my throat while I was asleep.

I touched a few fingertips to my throat, irrationally concerned that someone had slit my throat while I was asleep. Maybe I was dead. Protectors didn't exactly have any sort of religion, despite the fact that we devoted our lives to staving off creatures from hell.

But maybe this was where we went to spend our afterlife. To a house with a strange girl and an impossibly cozy bed set.

"Who are you?" I asked, my own voice not nearly as serene or teasing as hers.

She landed on the edge of my bed with a playful bounce, her eyes dancing with amusement now, like we were old friends prepping for a slumber party. "I'm Khalida. Most of my friends call me Khali though. You're welcome to as well. I'm a friend of Darius's," she said, arching a coy, perfectly-plucked brow as she studied me, "if that makes you feel any more relaxed?"

It didn't.

Darius wasn't the type to have friends. And if he did, it could only mean that they were as detached from reality and as dangerous as he was. I resisted the urge to inch away from her, but I scanned the room slowly, trying to catalogue different objects I could use to defend myself if I needed to.

A heavy lamp on the side table. The glass pitcher on the tray. I slid my hand along my thigh, hoping that I'd fallen asleep with my knife holster as I so often did these days, but all that I felt was my skin. Where were my pants? It seemed strange to enter into the afterlife with a t-shirt and no pants.

Declan and Atlas walked into the room, relief mirrored on each of their expressions as they took me in. Their arrival saved me from responding to the strange girl watching my every move, which was a small reprieve. A moment to catch my bearings anyway.

"Where are we?" I asked them, since I wasn't getting particularly clear responses out of the girl—Khalida, did she say?

"Claude's," Atlas answered, eyes cold and posture stiff. There was something closed off about him, even more so than usual. I had a fleeting suspicion that he was disappointed that I'd bothered waking up at all.

I gripped the blankets roughly in my hands as we stared off.

Claude?

I inhaled sharply, pieces sewing themselves together in my mind.

Darius's brother. The bar. Villette. The attack. The moments wove together into a pattern that started to connect, to make sense. I almost cried from the relief of it.

I stood up sharply, accidentally knocking the pitcher from Khalida's tray, splashing water down my legs and all over the carpet.

At least there wasn't ice.

"The attack." I spun around the room, like I expected vampires to be lying in wait behind me. I took a steady breath in, giving the adrenaline a moment to dissolve a bit. "Is everyone okay? There were so many. How did we survive that? Did we— did we survive that? Or are we dead?"

I ran my hands along my body, expecting to find cuts and bites and broken bones.

Nothing. I seemed completely fine. And, looking at them, they appeared okay too. Declan definitely hid some pain—I could tell in the tightness around her eyes, and the stiffness of her stance, like she was trying to move in very controlled stretches. But aside from a few bumps and bruises, they both looked as good as ever.

They shared a look that I couldn't read before turning back towards me. Silence stretched, like they were both floundering for a way to respond to me.

"You guys *are* okay, right?" I asked again, taking a step toward them.

Declan flinched and took a step back, like she was afraid I would hit her.

It was so starkly different from how she'd acted around me the last time we were in a room together, that I couldn't decide between being hurt or confused. Maybe I was a bit of both. It seemed like every time I took a step forward with one of them, it was only to go two steps back. Their moods were constantly giving me whiplash.

"You really don't remember?" Declan's question came out soft, but with a layer of accusation, like she thought I was pulling something over her.

I shook my head. "Remember what?"

"The fight?" The words left her lips, cold and clipped, with a hint of anger evident in her eyes.

"I remember being overrun—" I wrinkled my brow trying to force the memories back up to the surface, "and then I remember watching Eli get bombarded by vamps on every side—"

"That's it?" she asked, unfolding her arms from in front of her chest. She loosened slightly, relaxed, until I saw a glimmer of the expression she held that night, before the attack.

"That's it." I echoed. "Everything after is just a void. How did we all make it out alive?"

"Claude and Ralph showed up," Atlas said, tone monotonous, as he studied me like I was one of the monsters The Guild kept in their basement—coldly, critically, and with what seemed like a dose of fear or anger. "They got there in time. Helped us take down the rest of the vamps. Brought us back here to heal up and catch our breaths."

"Almost in time, anyway," Declan muttered as she crossed her arms over her chest again, making her transitions between open and guarded easier to recognize. Small mercies, I guess.

My mind flooded with the image of Eli trying to take on as many vampires as he could, the way he desperately fought to keep them away from me—he'd wanted me to run, to leave him there. It was clear as day in his eyes. He was positive he would die there in that battle. I glanced between Atlas and Declan, suddenly acutely aware of the fact that he wasn't there with them.

"Where's Eli?" I held my breath, as my eyes darted from one to the other, desperate for an answer, but terrified of what that answer might be. There was anger written across their features, but not overwhelming grief. Which meant there was hope, even if it wasn't much to go by. "And Darius?"

Atlas's eyes narrowed slightly, nostrils flaring, as if he was annoyed with me all over again for being concerned about a vampire—for uttering his name in the same breath as Eli's.

My chest tightened and my skin felt itchy under his scrutiny. I wasn't sure why I cared whether or not Darius survived, but I'd be lying to myself if I pretended that I didn't. I was trained to kill vampires and I'd watched that particular vampire kill one of our own. But still...

An ethical problem for another day.

"Your friend Eli has been bitten quite a few times, quite severely," Khalida said as she studied the three of us like we were her favorite new pastime, or like she was watching a new episode of her favorite show unfold.

She'd been so quiet since Atlas and Declan's arrival that I'd almost entirely forgotten about her. But now, having her acute focus on me was making my skin feel tight.

I turned away, intent on ignoring her, until I focused on the words that left her lips. My neck pinched, head spinning back in her direction as I processed them properly.

Bitten. Multiple times.

My stomach dipped, and I choked on a breath, everything I knew about vampire bites and protectors pouring through my mind in a heavy rush—how much damage they did, how frequently they resulted in death. None of those numbers and percentages took into account multiple wounds. Had anyone survived multiple bites before? From multiple vampires?

The image of Eli falling under a wave of fanged creatures, the conviction in his eyes that he was about to die. It was the last thing I remembered. Had I passed out? Did I get knocked out just when he needed me most? Had I let the members of Six down again? First with Wade and now...

"Is he—" I choked back my tears, unable to finish the thought, let alone the sentence as my vision blurred slightly.

Declan's face softened momentarily as she nodded out the door, signaling for me to follow her. "He's alive, but it's not looking great. You can come see him if you'd like."

I didn't even focus on the house we were in, on any of the decor, on the path we were taking. Whether we were in a mansion or a dungeon, I couldn't be certain. All that I could think about was Eli under a blanket of vampires.

Would he survive this? Could he survive this?

He had to.

When Atlas opened a large, wooden door, the creak echoing down the hallway, I ran inside. With a quick leap across the room, I dropped down next to Eli on the bed. His neck was a mess, blood soaking through the bandaging and refusing to coagulate. His skin was damp, covered in a thick sweaty sheen. Even without feeling for a pulse, I could tell from the erratic breaths lifting his chest that he was in bad shape.

I'd heard about vampire bites—listened to long, winding explanations in my classes back on campus of how they could destroy the body. Hell, I'd even recovered from one with remarkable speed myself. But I'd never seen someone go through the process. And to see it playing out with someone I knew, someone I cared about—

When I placed my palm on his forehead, I could feel him shiver slightly at my touch. His breathing was rattled and rough, like his lungs couldn't quite fill in the way that he needed them to.

A fierce wave of icy panic swept through my body and I

suddenly wished with a desperation that I didn't fully understand that Greta was here.

She was the one who'd nursed me back to health after I was attacked by a vampire outside of Guild Headquarters. There was a sort of stubborn intelligence about her that had a way of making everything feel okay. If anyone could help him, could save him, it was her.

Another one. I couldn't lose him, not when we were so close to getting Wade back. This felt too much like trading a life for a life. But the thing was, I needed them both.

Eli was confusing and flirtatious and muddled my brain and my hormones more than anyone I'd ever met, but he'd weaseled his way in. I cared about him, even when I hated him.

"Is there anything we can do? Any sort of treatment to help his chances?" I asked as the tears pooling in my eyes muddled the three figures standing outside the door until they were completely indistinguishable from each other.

Until there was a fourth.

The newest figure pushed into the room, like a confident, avenging angel, until he was towering above me.

The panic calmed slightly, though I didn't understand why, didn't see why he of all people would have that effect on me.

"Move aside little protector," his voice whispered, the manic energy I was so accustomed to from Darius flattening into something softer, something almost tender.

I blinked back my tears a few times, drying my eyes against the soft white cotton of my shirt. "I'm not leaving him," I said, gripping Eli's hand in mine—my grip soft enough not to rouse him, but firm enough to make it cumbersome for someone to try and remove me.

Darius rolled his eyes as he pulled his shirt sleeve up to reveal a surprisingly strong, veiny forearm. Something about a creature as powerful as he was rolling its eyes felt so acutely strange in that moment.

His eyes never left mine as he pressed his lips down to the

soft flesh of his wrist, his teeth extending down until they pierced his smooth, porcelain skin.

Even through my fear, I could feel my stomach flip uncomfortably under his scrutiny—a reaction he seemed to pick up on if the soft smile lifting his lips revealed anything.

My lip curled in disgust with myself. The man next to me was a vampire. I'd seen him sink those very fangs into one of my people, right in front of me. Watched him snap a protector's neck and then drain him dry. And before he was captured by The Guild, who knew how many lives he was responsible for ending.

I had no right finding him alluring or intriguing or hot, as Izzy liked to remind me. Darius was not Atlas. He was not Wade. They all hid a monster beneath the surface. But unlike them, he'd killed before. Probably over and over, and probably without an ounce of regret.

He brought his wrist to Eli's lips until the blood soaked between them. Red seeped into the lines of Eli's lips, darkening the chapped skin until his mouth was so bloody that he looked more like a vampire than Darius did in that moment.

"What the hell are you doing?" Declan asked, her voice a mixture of curiosity and disgust. "Get the fuck away from him. Are you fucking mental?" She shook her head, her dark waves bouncing with each frustrated movement. "What the hell am I saying? You're you. Of course you're fucking mental."

"Darius," Khalida warned, her eyes wide with concern, as she took a step into the room. She seemed to almost float over the carpet, her steps were so seamless, until she lifted a thin hand and touched his shoulder softly, "you shouldn't. This is a bad idea." Her dark eyes traced a line from his mouth to Eli's. "Possibly one of your worst. And you've had many terrible ones over the years, so that's not something I'd say lightly."

"She's much less entertaining when she's fawning over the others," he responded, brushing her off, "maybe if I give this one a chance to survive, her fire will reignite."

His brow arched in challenge as he continued to stare at me, refusing to break eye contact. It was like he was expecting something from me, only I wasn't sure what.

"Enough," Declan bit out, just as Atlas growled a low, throaty warning.

It suddenly felt as if we were all acting in a play, only I was the only one trying to follow along without a script.

Brushing past the moment, Darius wiped his wrist against Eli's shirt, like he was nothing more than a living, breathing napkin. "If he doesn't wake within a day or two, he never will. But you can rest now knowing that everything that could possibly be done has been tried."

"You just fed him your blood," I said, disgust and confusion ringing in my voice.

He winked at me. "I did indeed, you're welcome. And I'm even bestowing this favor for free, so hopefully you'll remember it and act accordingly in the future."

And with that, he stood up, stretching his limbs like a cat, his chaotic energy impossible to read.

That didn't sound like a free favor. That sounded like a very loaded favor that I didn't have the tools to fully understand.

"Dar—" Khalida started. There seemed to be real fear in her eyes, even though I didn't know her well enough to read her yet.

"Enough," Darius answered, his voice sharp and revelatory of the demon that lingered beneath his skin. "This stays between us. You'll tell my brother nothing, Khali. I don't need him getting into my business just yet, not when we have bigger fish to tackle, or whatever the hell that absurd phrase is. Now," he rolled his neck from side to side before walking towards the door, "I'm in desperate need of a meal and a very long rest. So unless anyone is volunteering a vein, I should be on my way. We're going to have an intense few days ahead of us, so you'll all do well to follow suit. In the meantime, I recommend everyone steer clear of my brother if you're able. Best to start plotting out how you plan to navigate hell once we get there, since I've held up my side of the bargain. The rest is on you."

I opened my mouth to call him back, to demand that he explain what the hell had just happened, but was spared having my questions dodged by a large, furry train driving into my side and knocking me off my feet.

A warm, slobbery tongue slid up my face as playful chirps filled the room. Sometimes Ralph sounded a lot more like a baby chick than he did a demon from hell. Pushing myself up on my elbows, I grinned as I found him towering over me. He was almost double my size and weight, but his amber eyes were gentle and filled with a warm fondness. The small grayish patch around one of his ears only added to his goofy, dog-like expression.

I wrapped my arms around his neck and used his sturdiness to pull myself into a seated position, his shaggy fur lodging itself in my nostrils and forcing out a sneeze in the process.

"I thought you disappeared," I said, remembering the last time I'd seen him. It was before the wolf attack on campus. He'd torn one of them to pieces but then vanished from all of his usual haunts. I hadn't wanted to admit to it out loud, but even though I knew it was better for him to go back to wherever he was from—hell or somewhere else—I wasn't ready to let him go just yet.

"Huh," Khalida said, an odd grin on her face as she sat on the edge of the bed next to Eli's sleeping form, "I've never seen a hellhound allow anyone to treat it like a pet before, not even their true master. They aren't exactly domesticated, you know?" She shook her head with amusement, her curtain of hair dancing with almost iridescent color in the light. "So strange. I told you there was something very unusual about you, Max. I look forward to figuring it out."

Her words didn't hold the tone of threat, but something about the way she watched me, with intrigued shrewdness, felt like one all the same.

Atlas cleared his throat and studied her, his jaw muscles tense and pulsing as he gnashed his teeth together. I had a feeling that he was deliberately refusing to make eye contact with me though I didn't understand why.

Did he blame me for what happened to Eli? For getting us all into this mess?

I couldn't exactly blame him if he did. Wade wouldn't have been in that field the night he was killed and kidnapped if it weren't for me. Eli and the rest of them would be back home, safe and sound, if I hadn't been convinced that Wade was alive—even if it was only in my dreams.

With a musical laugh, Khalida stood from the bed and walked towards the door. "Don't worry wolfie, I know when my presence isn't wanted in a room. I don't like to wear out my welcome." She turned back to look at me with a wink. "We'll talk again soon. I think you will all be a very amusing addition to my life. I'm very much looking forward to it. Things have been rather dull lately. Claude never invites anyone over."

And then she left. She was just as strange and unreadable as the vampire who'd left before her. No wonder they were friends.

I still wasn't sure whether that was reason enough to avoid her at all costs. Then again, if I was wise, I would have done the same with Darius months ago.

"What Darius did—sharing his blood like that," I started, using Ralph's weight to help pull me back to my feet. "Do you know what he was doing? Have you heard of a person feeding from a vampire before? Outside of the movies, I mean."

Vampire popular culture was rife with legends about a vampire's blood holding the power to transform a human into one of them, but protectors had always been told that it was impossible—that vampirism wasn't something contagious, unlike a werewolf bite.

Unless The Guild had been wrong about that as well.

"I've never seen anything like it," Declan said, patting Ralph on the head awkwardly as he walked towards her demanding attention. As much as she liked to pretend she hated all things hell-related, it was clear that Ralph was slowly creating a chink in her armor.

And if any beast was capable of melting that ice, it would be Ralph. The big dude was quite possibly the most cuddly creature I'd ever encountered.

"I wouldn't expect anything," Atlas said, watching Ralph with a leveled focus. He didn't seem to distrust Ralph specifically, so much as he seemed to just distrust everyone. "That vampire lives in his own world. If vampire blood could be used to cure protectors, I'm certain we would have a record of it somewhere. Hell, if it was that easy to save someone on the brink of death, protectors would die a lot less frequently. Doesn't exactly make sense for vampires to hold the cure to their enemies in their veins."

Even though I knew him well enough now to know that he was trying not to get his hopes up, the chill in his tone sent shivers down my spine.

"Did you dream?" Declan asked, her light Irish accent echoing around the room as she steered the conversation back to me. "I didn't notice any of your usual screams."

I cleared my throat, knowing full well that not all of those 'usual screams' were exactly bad.

Her emerald-green eyes looked past me, like she was doing everything she could to keep from making eye contact.

It was strange and I was probably being overly sensitive, but it felt like I fell asleep and when I woke up, I was back at the beginning in the tentative friendship I'd established with both of them. Maybe it was just the tension of having to rely on vampires to keep us temporarily safe, maybe they both just needed to put their guards up a bit. Protector defense mechanisms and what not.

Declan was leaning slightly against the doorway, her black tank top and leggings highlighting her lean, muscular curves.

Her question caused a nervous flutter to take root in my lower belly. My cheeks burned as I thought back to the last time we'd been talking, before the attack in the hotel. I told her about Villette's warning—that if I wanted to keep from being preyed upon by an incubus, or at least avoid being drained completely, I needed to fall asleep with my sexual energy expended. In other words, I needed to be less horny when dreamland came.

And then, while I couldn't be sure, I momentarily thought that Declan wanted to kiss me after I told her, that she maybe even wanted to help me with that very particular problem. And I, to my own surprise, wanted her to do just that. Did she see it in my eyes? The way that I looked at her while we were both below the blankets, opening up in the heavy intimacy of the dark? For a moment, at the time, I thought there was a chance that she was just as confused about her feelings for me as I was for her. But maybe I'd misread the whole thing. Maybe she was disgusted and just didn't know how to tell me.

It was easier to be open then, when the quiet of a dark room and a few inches of mattress were the only things keeping us apart. Now though, it felt like a giant gulf between us, as if any deepening of our—friendship—was suddenly erased. And we were back to ground zero. Maybe even the prequel to ground zero, if the ice in her eyes was anything to go by.

The way she spoke to me now was even more removed and callous than usual, like I was nothing more than a part of their mission. Like when this was all over, she'd put as much distance between us as possible.

I took a deep breath, forcing myself to focus. Maybe it was the frequent midnight rendezvous with an incubus, but my hormones were all over the place. Catching feelings for or acting on any sexual attraction with anyone in Six wasn't the way to go, not right now anyway. There was too much at stake and getting laid—while fun—wasn't exactly a top priority. It would just turn an already messy situation into an outright disaster.

"I saw Wade," I said, trying to keep the hurt and confusion from my voice as resolve slowly took over. I needed to stick to the mission, Declan was right in making that clear.

Her eyes widened, whether with worry or annoyance, I couldn't tell, but it was Atlas who responded.

"Did he—"

I shook my head, cutting him off. "No. I think he's more aware now. Of what he is and what he can do. He won't let himself cross that boundary again, even if it means starving himself."

I hated the fact that disappointment filled me at that realization, though I desperately hoped it wasn't evident in my voice or expression. The whole goal of speaking to Villette had apparently been for this very reason. But still, a part of me that was growing louder and stronger desperately wanted to ignore all of the reasons that Wade and I couldn't be together in that way— to say fuck the consequences. Maybe the consequences were worth it.

The feel of him ripping his lips away from mine left me feeling empty and hollow.

"Starving himself?" Atlas leaned against the wall, shutting the door so that the three of us and Ralph had more privacy. Vampire hearing was strong enough though that I doubted it would do anything but provide a visual cue to Claude and Khalida.

Was she even a vampire? I wasn't sure. The attacks over the last few months had proven that allegiances across species were much more prevalent than we'd ever realized. And while Khalida had a quiet, lethal power about her, she didn't seem like a creature I'd ever encountered before. There was something so ethereal to her.

"He mentioned that someone has come to see him," I said, trying to remember all of the details. While my dreams of Wade were so vivid that they felt real, they disappeared from my memory as dreams often did, the longer that I was awake. "Someone brought him food but he's otherwise been ignored. He's starving though because he doesn't understand how to use his powers or how to control them. But we did dream-walk."

Ralph hopped up onto the bed and cuddled himself between me and Eli, like he was trying to comfort us both. I scratched behind his ear absentmindedly, his presence soothing my discomfort in a way that surprised me. One day, I needed to focus on the fact that a fucking hellhound had the power to calm my anxiety, but today was not that day.

"Dream-walk?" Declan asked, her eyes glistening with curiosity. "Like, you traveled to someone else's dream? Together?" she glanced at Atlas, her eyes wide with surprise. "I didn't even know that was possible."

"He wanted to meet you," I said, peeling my eyes from her to look at Atlas, "so we tried to travel to you, but you must not have been asleep. So, after trying you both, we figured everyone here was awake and we eventually landed on Izzy instead."

Declan's brows lifted in surprise, her posture stiff with focus though she didn't say anything.

"Why Isadora" Atlas asked. His jaw clenched and I somehow knew that he was blaming himself, as if he was in the wrong for not being asleep at the precise moment his brother wanted to reach him. Men could be ridiculous sometimes.

Most times, actually.

I used every ounce of restraint I had not to roll my eyes. Something told me that Atlas was at the end of his nerves, that the tiniest shove could push him overboard.

"Because I guided him there and the girl sleeps like the dead. She was the best option I could think of, and the only one other than Ro I could be certain wouldn't betray us." A long moment drew out between us in silence, nothing but the sound of Ralph's heavy pants echoing in the room. "She hates being called Isadora, by the way. Though I'm sure you're aware of that."

Apparently I didn't have as much self-restraint as I thought. Something about pushing Atlas was just a little bit too irresistible.

Declan stifled a chuckle and met my eyes for the first time since I'd woken up. Just as they landed on mine, they dropped to the ground again. I swallowed my disappointment. "Didn't that exhaust him even more though? Exerting that kind of energy must take a heavy toll on him."

There wasn't an accusation in her words, but it stung all the same. Because it did exhaust him and I had been the one to encourage the process, to push him until it worked. And then we overstayed our welcome. "He wanted to get out of the prison cell. The cabin fever is really getting to him. And we needed to get the—focus—off of other things."

Declan squared her shoulders towards Atlas, no longer even bothering to pretend I was in the room. "I doubt he'll be able to resist a feed for long. The succubus at the bar told Max the best way to keep him from killing her is to enter sleep sexually satisfied. It might help quell a bit of the attraction she has for your brother so that she'll be less vulnerable and more resistant when it matters. Might also help slow the amount of energy he drains from her if there is a smaller entry point for him to latch onto."

In a single breath, she'd gone from Declan Connolly, a reserved girl standing in a vampire's home, to a bonafide protector in mission mode. I couldn't help but feel a bit annoyed at her tone, at the way she treated me like a problem rather than an equal. It wasn't exactly like I asked to fall into incubus dreams. Then again, I wasn't exactly complaining either.

If my cheeks were burning before, they were damn near on fire now. I cleared my throat and tried to stare at anything in the room that wasn't Declan or Atlas. I knew she was right to tell him, but the way she did it, so callous and matter-of-fact, had my stomach clenching with shame. And discussing my sexual appetites while we were in work mode felt all kinds of uncomfortable.

When I glanced at Atlas, his dark eyes were locked on me, posture stiff. "Then make sure you take care of that from now on," he said, clearing his throat awkwardly. "If my brother accidentally kills you, it will destroy him. So see to it that he doesn't."

I couldn't bring myself to tell them that Wade and I had...worked off some energy before I left him; that I didn't leave him completely drained. I had a feeling that if I told them the truth, they'd do everything in their power to keep me from visiting him again. And those visits were the best chance we had at actually finding him and making sure he was still alive.

With that, he left the room. Silence filled the space between me and Declan until a heavy door slammed in the distance— loud enough that I wouldn't be surprised if it was ripped off the hinges.

"There's food in the kitchen. You should eat." And then, without waiting for a response, she turned from the room and left, leaving me alone with Ralph, Eli, and a pit in the bottom of my stomach filled with nothing but confusion and frustration.

5

MAX

The house—or, rather, mansion—was stunning. Declan didn't exactly leave me with instructions on how to find the kitchen, but I wound my way through the endless halls, hand buried into Ralph's luxurious fur as we explored.

There was something so therapeutic about having him here, like no matter what happened, we'd all be okay so long as he was around. I could almost feel my pulse slow to a normal, relaxed cadence.

"Gotta say, bud," I said, digging my bare feet into the lush, dark gray carpet in one of the empty rooms. The walls were covered in paintings that looked both ugly and expensive, the shelves lined with random knickknacks that were covered in dust from lack of use. The room was dark, with only a single dull bulb ahead to cast it into light. Did Claude and Khalida live here on their own? The place was huge, and only a small portion of it seemed like it was being used. "Totally digging this whole thing where you come swooping in just when I need you. I think I'm officially a dog person."

He yipped playfully in response, head held high with pride. His expression was so goofy that half the time it was easy to forget that he was actually a powerful beast from a different realm. Seriously, if the demons ever wanted to extend an olive branch to protectors, to mend broken ties and demolish bad blood, they need only send a hellhound in their place. Who could say no to a puppy?

I let out a sigh, shaking my head. "Sometimes I wish you could just talk. Tell me why you're here, how you're able to track my movements so easily. Where do you go when you disappear? Why did you show up when you did? Why me?"

I could've sworn that he could understand me, back when I sat with him in the basement of the lab. But Cy looked at me like I was off my rocker when I mentioned it.

I cracked my neck, my limbs all still stiff from getting knocked unconscious—which, gotta say, was completely embarrassing that I just passed right the fuck out in the middle of a raging vamp battle.

Bad habit of mine. And one I'd need to get over if I wanted to have any sort of lasting career as a protector. Especially if I wanted to get sent on field missions. No wonder Cy demanded that I stay home when Ro and the rest of Ten got assigned a new job.

A warm, tingly scent reached my nose and I turned a corner, following the luxurious scent until I found myself standing in a giant, well-used kitchen. Compared to the few rooms I'd explored, this one looked like it belonged in a completely different house.

It wasn't the sort of rich-person kitchen you saw in movies, where you took one look and basically knew that no one spent time there. This kitchen was filled with well-loved appliances, the cupboards lined with mismatched mugs that were selected one-by-one, rather than all at once in a boring, matching set.

It felt so homey. So human.

A large loaf of fresh baked bread was resting on the marble island in the center of the room, knife and butter perched against the charcuterie board next to it. The sight alone sent my stomach into a series of grumbles, never mind the amazing smell. How long had it been since I had something to eat? I forgot to ask everyone how long I was out, lost in my dream world with Wade.

Not waiting another moment, I sliced a piece off for myself and another one for Ralph, my mouth watering as the fresh bread and butter hit my tongue. My tastebuds felt like they were magnified, like I could distinguish between each and every flavor. I let out an embarrassing groan as I shoved another bite in my mouth. Maybe this was magic bread.

"Khali is a great cook," a low, familiar voice echoed behind me. Familiar, but also not somehow. "If I weren't a vampire, I'd double in body weight every time she visits."

I spun around, nearly choking on the bread lodged halfway down my throat. Claude.

He was dressed head-to-toe in black, his platinum hair mussed in that perfect way that looked both effortless and stylish. His eyes, which were so familiar to me in Darius, felt strange and cold as they studied me with a vague curiosity.

There was a darkness to him that I didn't see when I looked at Darius. Or a different sort of darkness, anyway. One layered with a quiet rage, a thirst for revenge.

Maybe it was because so much of Darius's personality seemed married to the fact that he'd been living in isolation for so long, locked up and desperate for anything that seemed even remotely entertaining. He was reckless and wild. Claude, however, was not. A chill crept up my spine as he studied me, until I felt like I was the one suddenly locked up in a research lab.

"Thank you for allowing us to stay," I said, annoyed with my meekness. I was *so* not the sort of girl to cower in a corner, but Darius and Claude were not normal vampires. Normal vampires were scary and strong. This set of twins was on an entirely different level. Their very pores seemed to exude power and strength. Both of them were unpredictable, but in wildly different ways.

I was, for example, fairly certain that Darius wouldn't lose his patience and swipe my head clean off my spine the second irritation crept in. I didn't have the same confidence when it came to Claude.

"I don't have much of a choice," he said, arching a single brow as he cut off a slice of bread for himself.

He broke eye contact and showed me his back in a way that made it remarkably clear that he did not fear me. Even though I was a protector, he didn't think I would attack. Or, maybe it was that he knew he could stop me if I did, without so much as breaking a sweat.

Cocky fuck.

Even though he was probably right.

"Keeping you here for a day or two will require less effort and resources on my part. My brother," he shook his head, nose curling in disgust, "gets into trouble very easily. Best for me in the long run if he's kept out of sight from the community before any of his mistakes land on my doorstep again. If it was up to me, the rest of you would be dead or on your way to other lodgings, but he's promised to make things very...messy for me if I act on those wishes." In a soft, barely-there whisper he added, "insufferable prick."

I gulped, like a goddamn cartoon character, my breath hitching slightly as Ralph stepped between us, growling low and steady. It was a clear warning, and enough confirmation that Claude was as dangerous as my gut was telling me he was.

"And then there's that," he added, intrigue replacing his annoyance in a flash. "If I left you to die, I have a feeling my brother isn't the only one who'd make my life very difficult." He paused and looked at me, his brow arched with an unspoken question. "Curious thing, you know, for a protector to have a hellhound as a familiar. And my brother seems to have decided that you're fascinating enough to keep around as well. I wonder why that is."

His eyes sparkled with mischief and a promise of pain as he took a large bite of the bread, fangs extending just for show. Vampires didn't require food in the same way that protectors and humans did. Just blood. You could starve them for days or months and they'd still survive, though they would grow a bit weaker. It's what they did to the vampires The Guild kept in the lab, and it was why Darius was so much weaker and more unpredictable than his brother. Not only was he starved of food, but he was given very limited doses of blood as well.

"You clearly dislike your brother," I said, straightening my spine in the hope that it would bring me the illusion of courage if not the reality of it, "and yet you saved him. All of us. Why?"

Claude's eyes narrowed, his nostrils flaring imperceptibly. "Everyone who knows him dislikes my brother. It's not a shocking revelation. I suppose in that sense, I'm not the least bit surprised that he's found appreciation amongst a group of protectors—yours has always been the least intelligent species of all. But my relationship with my brother is none of your business, nor are the actions I do or do not take. All that you need to know is that you almost died, but you didn't." He took a step towards me, like a lion closing in on its next meal. "That you're to stay here for another day until your friend upstairs either dies or slips into a more permanent coma. And when he does, I'll be more than happy to end his misery altogether. Then, I'll take you all to hell with a promise in return that you never show your face in my city again."

I pushed back into the kitchen island, as he moved closer towards me, earning a severe warning growl from Ralph. I could feel rather than see Ralph show his teeth as the vampire inched closer and closer. The sound was menacing and, for a moment, even I was temporarily frightened of the hellhound. The very house seemed to vibrate beneath his paws.

I promised to myself right then and there that I'd do whatever it took to never land on his bad side.

Claude's eyes shifted down towards the hellhound and back to me, his brows arching in curiosity but not in fear. Maybe he was just as careless as his brother was. "Tell me protector, how exactly did you come to have a hellhound as a familiar? That is one story I would love to hear. I might even help you survive, if you held my interest long enough."

I cleared my throat, watching as he prowled closer and closer. "I-I don't really know. One day he just showed up." I narrowed my eyes slightly, trying to fill my voice with as much warning as possible. Even to my own ears, the effect was pathetic. "And then when I was attacked by a vampire, Ralph killed him."

It wasn't completely true. He helped assist me with the kill, but the more powerful and menacing I could make Ralph seem, the better. I had a feeling that Ralph could take down most vampires with little to no problem. But something told me that he would have his work cut out for him if he chose to attack Claude.

As if sensing my intention, Claude's lips lifted in a wry grin. His expression was all amusement, no fear. And my not-so-subtle threat didn't stop him from taking another step towards me.

And then another.

"He's actually quite small, you know, as far as hellhounds go. Powerful still, of course. Of that there's no doubt. But when you descend into hell, don't expect him to be the most dangerous creature you encounter. And if he's left the hell realm before, or been kicked out, chances are it was for a reason, and he won't exactly be welcomed back with open arms. That's not how things work there. When you leave, you make damn sure that you don't return without the assistance of some very powerful friends on the other side."

My jaw clenched and I wound my fingers into the scruff on the back of Ralph's neck. Part of me didn't want him to come with us at all. I had enough accountability to worry about—I couldn't risk being responsible for another friend getting injured. Or worse.

Ralph's growls vibrated through me, until they felt like my own. I was so used to him being this loveable furball that I almost didn't recognize him like this. Would he attack Claude? If he did, could he win? *Would* he win?

My chest tightened, like an iron vice was squeezing it. I patted him softly on his back, trying to calm him down a bit. As tempting as it was, we couldn't risk a fight with Claude. He was our best chance of finding and saving Wade. And while I knew that Ralph could easily take on a typical vampire, something about Claude didn't feel the slightest bit typical. And I didn't want to take our chances.

As if sensing my thought process as it filtered through my mind, Ralph sat back on his haunches and stopped his warning growls. He was still menacing, but the threat of him being on the precipice of attack was muddled a bit.

A low, mirthless chuckle escaped from Claude's lips. "Interesting. I've only ever seen a hellhound respond to the wishes and thoughts of one creature before." Appeased now that Ralph wouldn't harm him, Claude closed the distance between us until he was little more than a few inches away from me. "You're an unusual girl, indeed, Max Bentley. Tell me, what is it about you that has my brother tied into such a knot? It's rare—unheard of, really—for him to swear allegiance, however tentative, to anyone. Not even to me, his own flesh and blood. We shared a womb and he's never once shown me any loyalty. But here he is, acting as bodyguard to a pint-size protector, no matter how much he tries to pretend that he's the one controlling the situation."

He raised a hand to the back of my neck, winding his fingers around the strands of hair at the nape until he had enough leverage to pull my focus up, forcing my eyes to meet his above me.

His mismatched eyes were guarded and angry, but I couldn't look away from them.

With a devious grin, he dropped his gaze to my neck, using his grip to tilt my head to the side, baring it to him.

"I wonder," he said, clearly enjoying my discomfort as Ralph resumed the rumbling in his chest, "whether or not you've ever been tasted. Have you opened your veins for my brother? Spilled your blood between his lips? He's a very bad man, you know. You'd do well to keep yourself from falling for his charms, from trusting him. He's betrayed everyone who's ever made that mistake. If I were you, I'd cut your losses and return home immediately. It doesn't have to be back to The Guild for you. I could find a use for you. I'm sure I have friends who would be interested in discovering your secrets. If you had a strand of intelligence, you'd abandon your absurd quest before you get yourself and all of your friends killed." He arched his brow, studying me with the sort of invested patience usually reserved for museum displays. "Of course, if you have a death wish, I'm more than happy to oblige, to see what the fuss is all about myself."

He bent his head down a bit, smiling as his teeth extended into his plush, soft bottom lip. In this moment, he looked nothing like Darius. The playfully amused, occasionally terrifying expression I was used to seeing on this face was cold and filled with a quiet promise of pain instead. His jaw was tight, his eyes filled with ice. I knew with absolute certainty that he wouldn't hesitate to kill me, not really, not if it suited him. That as soon as he decided to, he'd kill us all if we gave him reason, even his brother.

Every inch of my body was vibrating with the need to attack. My fingers danced along my thighs, searching for my dagger but met nothing but the bare space where my long shirt met my skin. Why the hell was I still not wearing pants?

Would he do it? Would he really bring me into his home, give us shelter, only to kill me now? How could that serve his purposes? Why bother bringing us in at all?

"You'd do well to back away," a low, terrifying voice growled. "Immediately."

Claude turned his head, surprised by the new arrival, pulling my head along with him as he moved.

Atlas stood in the middle of the kitchen, eyes almost completely golden as he studied Claude with a deliberate, calculated lethality.

While I wanted to kill Claude in this moment, while I wanted to allow Ralph off his reins to take him out, I wouldn't. We needed him. I wasn't so sure that Atlas was operating on the same long term wavelength. Not with his wolf so close to the surface.

"Not only has the girl got a vampire wrapped around her impossibly brittle finger, but a newbie wolf as well. So very interesting. If I didn't want you all out of my life as quickly as possible, I'd be tempted to keep her around—tear her to pieces until I understood exactly what was so special about her."

"Remove your hands from her," Atlas said, his nostrils flaring as his muscles flexed imperceptibly beneath his shirt, like he was warding off a shift. I hadn't seen Atlas shift before, and while part of me was intrigued by the idea—of watching the creature emerge before my eyes—now was not the time. "I won't give you another chance."

"Reckless boy," Claude said, close to laughing as he shook his head with a mixture of pity and amusement on his face.

I had a feeling that we were all amusing, weak toys to him, that he wasn't the least bit terrified of any of us—neither individually nor as a united front. The realization renewed my fear of him.

"You wouldn't stand a chance against me." With a shrug, he flung me towards Atlas until I went crashing into his chest, his long arms closing tightly around me, only to push me roughly behind him. "Very well then, there you have her. Though I'm not so convinced you actually want her. Half the time you seem split between recoiling and yearning, just as at war with your emotions as you are with your beast. It's pathetic, really. And it will get you killed. Probably sooner rather than later."

Claude grinned wickedly at me, promising we'd meet again and finish this conversation at a later time. "You'll be out of here by morning, whether or not your friend is awake. I don't have time to deal with these distractions and, to be quite frank, the sooner my brother is out of my space, the better it will be for all of you. People tend to become collateral damage when the two of us are together for too long. I don't only think of myself, though it might seem that way."

He ripped off another chunk of bread, not bothering with the knife or butter. He sank his teeth—still extended—into the crust, pulling off a giant bite with an aggressive fervor. With a casual wink in my direction, he left the kitchen as if we'd all just been having a jovial, relaxing conversation, and not threatening each other with an unspoken promise of death.

"Creepy clearly runs in the family," I said, trying to lighten the mood as Ralph slowly followed the vampire out. Hopefully he was only planning on keeping an eye on him and not attacking outright. I didn't think we could get away with killing our host unscathed. Not to mention Wade. We needed Claude if we were going to succeed in our rescue mission.

Atlas was silent, the kind of silent that told me he was trying desperately to swallow the rage flowing through his body. Without acknowledging my comment, he gripped my wrist roughly with his fingers and pulled me from the kitchen. He wound through several rooms and halls, all decorated with an eye towards minimalism and taste, unlike some of the more lavish rooms I'd stumbled upon on my trek to the kitchen. Eventually, he stopped inside of a dark room far enough away from everyone that no sounds chased after us. Was he hoping to have a private conversation with me—away from prying vampire ears—or was this something else?

He shoved me in before him and then shut the door behind us both. Silence swept through the room, the sort of silence that was filled with poorly-contained tension and anger. I could practically feel electricity brewing in the air around us. Gracelessly, I swiped up and down the wall until I found the light switch. After a few clumsy gestures, a final flick up revealed us to be in a medium-sized bedroom with dark bedding and gray walls. There was almost no art on the wall, just a large bookcase filled to the brim with broken spines that spoke of use.

I loved that—books that looked like they'd been read and loved—and I had to physically force myself not to go combing through the stacks to find an exciting tale that could drown my own anxieties out for a little while. This wasn't the time.

Something told me that Atlas wasn't in the mood for lighthearted banter or letting me relax a bit either.

"Are you—"

Before the sentence could leave my mouth, Atlas had me pinned against the heavy door, his forearm pressing across my throat as his body kept me pinned. I was suddenly acutely aware of the fact that I was only dressed in a baggy shirt, as his legs pressed into mine, the fabric of his jeans chafing against the skin of my thighs.

His eyes were that wild yellow they seemed to get when his wolf was lurking close to the surface—the same yellow that seemed to come out an awful lot when I was around, like he was always one smart remark away from snapping and ripping my limbs from my body, piece by excruciating piece. The same yellow that made me feel like the densest girl in the world for not realizing instantly, the exact moment I met him, that he was more than just a typical protector. How had it taken me months to figure out? How had no one else realized it in the meantime?

Then again, maybe he only got this way around me—my presence certainly seemed to correlate with his anger. He made it difficult for me to believe in that whole 'correlation doesn't imply causation' thing.

"I want to know where you come from," he whispered, his voice filled with an unacknowledged hatred as he pressed his forearm into my throat, cutting off the air supply.

I opened and closed my mouth like a fish, hoping he'd get the hint that I couldn't exactly have a conversation when I couldn't even breathe.

Realization smoothed out the tense angles of his features a bit and he released enough pressure for me to speak.

"You know where I came from," I said, my heart slamming hard against my ribs. I was about done with feeling like everyone around me was a hair's breadth away from snapping and killing me. I'd made a lot of mistakes in the past few months, but I didn't deserve this. "I grew up with Cyrus Bentley in a tiny ass mountain cabin somewhere in the middle of Montana. And you know that already," I bit out, anger swallowing my tone, "because you fucking stalked and attacked me there before I even moved to Guild Headquarters."

His nostrils flared, both of our eyes locked on each other in an aggressive battle of wills. We hadn't discussed that moment, the fact that Atlas showed up in my life long before I knew who he was. We hadn't talked about the fact that he was a werewolf much at all. Everything I knew came through Declan and my own deductions, for the most part.

"Before Cyrus," he continued, clearly ignoring my accusation, "where did he find you? Who are your parents?"

Was he joking? We were temporarily seeking asylum in Dracula's castle while on a mission to save his incubus brother from hell. And *this* was what he wanted to talk about? My parents and childhood upbringing? Good old Max Bentley story time?

"How the fuck does this matter right now? And even if it did, I don't know. Cy always said I showed up on his doorstep and he took me in. End of story. He's not exactly the most sharing sort of dude if you didn't realize that already. The conversation about my parents has always been a short one—a simple shrug, an annoyed grunt. Not exactly fodder for a superhero origin tale." I grinned up at him before adding, "at least not for Marvel anyway."

His eyes narrowed, nostrils flaring with each second that passed. Maybe I secretly had a death wish. It wouldn't be the most surprising thing I'd learned about myself this year.

I could feel each breath as he exhaled, his chest pressing into mine. If he didn't look like he wanted to kill me if I so much as breathed the wrong way, my stomach would be flipping for a completely different reason right now. Atlas was equal parts beautiful and lethal, and my brain seemed to get those two radically different things confused far too frequently. If I survived this encounter and, you know, hell, I was totally going to work on that.

"Your parents. Who were they?" His fingers dug into my shoulders like he wanted to shake the answers out of me.

The only problem was, I didn't have those answers.

"Are you not listening to me? Tell your wolf to sit the fuck down and pay attention. I. Don't. Know," I spat out, angry now. I was over this power trip. I narrowed my eyes, glaring right back at him, and then I kneed him in the groin so that he'd back away. He bent over at the waist with a heavy groan. Good. "Cyrus doesn't know either. I'm just a normal fucking orphan; why do you suddenly have a weird vendetta against me? And what the hell does this have to do with any of the handful of things that actually matter right now? Because the top priority is saving your brother, in case that's slipped your mind."

This sudden rage fit didn't make any sense. Atlas had always been suspicious of me, always hated me to a degree, though I didn't understand why. If he wanted to shed all that weight, all those long weeks of repressed anger, fine. I could play that game too.

I took in a heavy breath as frustration washed over me. "How about instead, *you* answer some questions. Why the fuck have you always been such an asshole to me? Why did you show up before I even knew who you were and attack me? If anyone has reason to be suspicious, it's me. But I've never once treated you like you were a speck of dirt beneath my shoe."

He was still bent double, but he grabbed my wrist, only this time the pressure was much more gentle.

"This is a scar," he said, confusion and pain seeping through his expression as he studied me. "Protectors don't scar."

I pulled my arm away from him, looking down at the small star-shaped mark on the inside of my wrist. I shrugged, holding it to my chest before he did something truly ridiculous, like try to chop it off. Not to go all Nicolas-Cage-Moonstruck on him, but this was *my* hand, not his.

"I've had it since I was born. And protectors do scar. You have one too."

I nodded at his arm, where I knew a deep ridge carved along his vein sat etched beneath his shirt sleeve.

"That's different," he said, staring up at me, his brows bent down in the middle. "That's from my attack. We don't heal all the way when we're bit by a demon." He paused, shaking his head slowly as his eyes studied me with less anger now. "Except for you."

He was alluding to the time I was attacked by the vampire outside of the club. When he found me in the back alley, I was bleeding from a super heavy fang laceration. But then, out of nowhere, it healed without a trace. If he and Eli hadn't seen it for themselves, I would've been convinced the fanghole hadn't really bitten me.

I opened my mouth to argue again, to push his buttons the way he'd pushed mine, to launch accusation after accusation at him. But I didn't have words to throw this time. He was right. I healed—completely—from a vamp attack. Not even Cyrus—the strongest protector I knew—had done that.

Why?

If I was being honest with myself, it was a clusterfuck that haunted me many nights when I woke up reliving that attack. The questions would circle in my mind for hours at a time. But then, each morning when the sun rose, I pushed the confusion away. There was too much to worry about, to learn; these questions didn't matter as much. Besides, Cy didn't seem to focus on it. In fact, he told me not to worry about it—so, for the most part, I didn't. It was one of the few times in the past two months that I actually listened to him.

Clearly Atlas did worry about it though. And maybe I was kidding myself by trying to ignore the oddities in my experiences with the hell realm.

Atlas was standing up tall, his height far eclipsing mine, now that the wave of agony had subsided somewhat. Apparently a dick hit only knocked a werewolf off balance for a few seconds. Good to know.

"I don't know," I said, trying to infuse my expression with anger again but the only thing I had to grasp at was a diluted mixture of anger and fear. Anger at my parents for leaving me without answers. Fear of whatever weird blood I had running through my veins. All I ever wanted was to find a community I belonged to. I thought that joining The Guild would be that opportunity. But I was on the outside there as well. "I swear, Atlas. I don't know."

When I looked up at him again, my own torment must've been visible, because his features softened. It was gradual—Atlas never fully relaxed or showed obvious compassion—but it was there. He reached a hand out, like he wanted to comfort me, but he took a step back instead.

"The hellhound," he continued instead, staring at the ceiling instead of at me, "did you know that it can teleport? Do you know why it's glomped onto you like you're its master?"

Shock flooded my system as I shook my head. "He can teleport? Like the dude who took Wade? Can all hellhounds?"

"You really didn't know?" Atlas asked as his head snapped down so that his eyes could study mine again. His brows bent in the middle like he was trying to gauge whether or not to believe me. To trust me. It didn't seem like he landed on a decision yet either way.

"If I knew, I wouldn't have gone through all that trouble breaking him from the damn research lab would I—" I paused, taking a step closer to Atlas as the mystery gripped me. "Wait, if he could teleport, why didn't he just do that when they were about to kill him? Do you think the research team knew? That they prevented him from accessing that power somehow?"

Atlas shrugged, staring at me in silence. "Claude seems to think that his powers aren't fully developed, that he can only teleport now when you're in danger. I don't fully understand it, or know how true that is."

He parted his lips like he wanted to ask me something else or throw another accusation at me, but he didn't. He took a step back and turned away before roughly running both of his hands through his hair and arching his back. Something was clearly tormenting him, crawling beneath his skin, but he also clearly had no intention of letting me in on the mystery of his anguish.

"Why do you suddenly not trust me?" I asked as I took a step forward and set my hand tentatively on his bicep to turn him back around towards me. Touching him was thoughtless, especially when his wolf was so close to the surface. I knew that. I was just clearly reckless. And focusing on the feel of his lean muscle underneath my fingers took me one notch over and made me completely detached from reality. "Why now, why like this? We're in a vampire's house and suddenly *I'm* the one you don't trust?"

I could feel his arm shaking beneath my fingers, so I wasn't surprised when he spun around with a force that pushed me a few feet back until my body collided with the wall again.

The loss of control, the impact of hitting my shoulder blades against the wood woke up my memory, as if jostling the final few missing puzzle pieces back into view.

"Oh my god," I said, the words a cautious whisper.

"I'm sorry," he said, as he shook his hair out of his eyes, "I shouldn't have done that. It's just, when the wolf is this close, it's better if you're not."

"No," I said. I ran forward and grabbed both of his shoulders this time, ignoring his warning altogether. I shook him until he focused on me, terror gripping my stomach. "I've just remembered."

His eyes bobbed down, studying the space between us, as he swallowed slowly. "Remembered what?"

He didn't like it when I touched him, his discomfort was evident enough. If it had been any other scenario, I would've pulled back. But this was too important. "Wade."

His brother's name seemed to refocus his attention—gone was the man who was oscillating between angry intensity and something else I couldn't quite define. Now he was Atlas, the guy I'd seen teach a band of students how to kill monsters with an impressive balance of power and precision. "What about Wade?"

"When I woke up," I said, the words getting garbled in my throat from the tension in my chest. "There was a man—a creature of some sort. I couldn't see any features, and I shouldn't assume gender." I shook my head, trying to grasp onto the memory with all of my attention, to focus. "It *pushed* me out of the dream. It's why I woke up when I did."

"Do you," Atlas's dark eyes were wild with emotion, the gold fading in and out as he tried to regain control, "do you think he's hurt?"

"That's what I'm saying, Atlas. I don't know."

💫 6 💫

WADE

My fingernails scraped against the stone wall as I desperately tried to reach her. I felt my nails break off and bend in angles they weren't accustomed to; saw blood pooling in my nail beds. I didn't care.

She flew through the fucking wall like she was made of nothing more than air. Her eyes were wide and terrified as her arms reached towards me, desperate to latch on.

Letting her down in that moment, watching the wall swallow her up like a ghost or phantom, would stick with me until I died. Again.

"Where the fuck did you send her?" I didn't even try to keep the venom from leaking out of my voice now that Max was gone. I didn't care what this creepy fucker did to me.

He was still shrouded in black, whether cloth or moving shadow, I couldn't really tell. His face was indistinguishable and he showed up in my little cave without so much as opening a door. What the hell was he? And what the hell did he want with me?

I couldn't see his eyes, but I had an eerie confidence that they were pinned directly on mine; couldn't see his mouth, but for some reason knew with absolute certainty that it was positioned in a cocky ass smile.

"Relax, boy," he said, his voice smooth, low, and bored. "She's not dead, if that's what you're so concerned about. Of the two of us, the one with the power to kill that girl in her sleep is you, not me. Hopefully now, she'll be barred from breaking back in."

The truth of his statement stabbed into me like a cold, lethal knife. I'd realized it after that first visit, when I'd felt stronger after she'd left than I had before she'd arrived. Pressing my lips against hers was like breathing air, like becoming new again. It was intoxicating and addictive, and it took every ounce of willpower I had left not to throw myself at her when she showed up again.

My stomach tightened and I found myself reluctantly thankful that this shadow creature showed up when he—it—did. Was I capable of killing her? Resisting Max was already difficult when I was nothing more than a protector. Her presence was like a goddamn beacon, a ray of light that spoke to me on a level nothing ever had before.

But now, now that I was something more complicated than just a protector, she was irresistible. Everything about her seemed sharper to me now. She was like a living contrast—soft and strong, intelligent and naive, adorable and sexy.

"What am I?" I hadn't meant that to be the question I voiced and I cursed myself for uttering it in such a sadboy whimper.

"You know the answer to that question already," the voice responded with a soft chuckle, smug and a bit annoyed, like I was a child in need of supervision.

And honestly, if I could ultimately be responsible for Max's death, that was exactly what I was.

"An incubus," I said, the word a curse on my tongue. "But I wasn't until I was killed, until I was brought here. Why?"

There was a long, impossibly drawn-out moment in which I was half-convinced the shadow figure would leave me here; abandon me in this claustrophobic prison forever. Would Max be able to come back to me now that she'd been banished? Did I want her to? The best way to keep her safe from me was to make sure she stayed away.

That thought struck in the back of my mind and down my spine like a knife sawing through bone, rough and splintered.

"The details don't matter right now, and the story does not interest me enough to get into it at the moment. Suffice to say that your mother was a succubus, not the human your piece of shit father likely thought her to be. She died bringing you into the world; a level of absurd ignorance I didn't think her capable of attaining." He paused a beat, and walked—or, rather, glided—around the cell. It seemed so much larger with him in it, like he had the power to expand the walls beyond physics. I'd been here for weeks or months or however long it was, but it looked unrecognizable with him standing in front of me. "Ignorant or not, she gave her life for an important cause. And she was a loyal confidant while she served me. Least I could do was watch over her spawn while he transitioned."

"How long are you going to keep me in here?" I tracked every single one of his movements, confusion propelling me as much as a reluctant intrigue. If he was watching over me out of some misguided loyalty of the past, perhaps he wouldn't kill me.

"Until you either die from the transition or I can be sure that you won't become a nuisance. Letting a protector loose—even a partial protector—isn't exactly well thought of in this world. If anyone gets wind of what you are, you will be eaten alive. Quite literally, perhaps." I could almost feel him leering at me as goosebumps broke out along my arms and chest. "In the meantime, I'm greatly enjoying watching you come undone. It's the fastest way for you to be reborn into something I can make use of. Maybe one day, you'll become a great tool in this war. It will take a while though, to turn you against the people you think are your own. Until then, you are useless to me."

A plate and glass of water appeared on my bed in a flash. When I turned back to the creature, he was gone.

Suddenly ravenous, I stuffed my mouth with the rock-hard bread as quickly as I could, making use of the glass of water to actually swallow it down. My teeth dug into what I hoped was just a regular steak and not something else. For all I knew, creatures in hell consumed demons...or worse, humans. We had no way of knowing either way, since the creatures we captured had been living amongst humans and protectors for a long while. And they were all surprisingly good at keeping their secrets from us, even through torture.

Still, in this case, the best I could do was close my eyes, chew, and engage in some good old fashioned wishful thinking. I'd need my strength if I had any hope of getting out of here.

Belly full and thirst reasonably quenched, I sat back against my bed and replayed the conversation with the shadow creature over and over.

I couldn't get the image of Max being torn from my hands and flung from sight out of my mind. He said she was safe, that I was the real threat. And while I fully believed the latter, I didn't trust the former. Demons weren't exactly known for their honesty.

An unfamiliar ball of rage grew in my lower belly until, no longer able to control it, I threw the porcelain plate at my side against the farthest wall. The cup soon followed, though the satisfying shatter was drowned out by a loud, anguished scream.

It took me several seconds before I realized that the noise was coming from my own mouth.

My chest lifted in heavy, uneven puffs, as I walked around the small room, the skin of my feet tearing open each time I passed the shattered shards of glass. Suddenly all I could smell was my own stench; the stale air that I'd been living in felt heavy and putrid.

Since the moment my eyes opened, Max was the one thing I had to look forward to. Even when I realized what I was, that I could harm her, I still selfishly lived for the moments when she would show up in my bed, her eyes dancing with that unique mixture of strength and innocence.

And now the shadow figure had taken her from my grasp with a promise that she wouldn't return. If she couldn't visit, how would I keep tabs on her? How would I know she was alive? Safe? Was she still planning on breaking her way into hell or had Atlas and the others finally abandoned that ridiculous plan? He would keep her safe at least, wouldn't he?

Sometimes I was almost convinced that if a demon didn't kill her, my brother would.

Suddenly desperate, I focused all of my energy on trying to reach her. It took several long minutes before my breathing evened out and my mind calmed. I needed a task. Something to fill my days.

I thought back to our time spent trying to trail through our friends' dreams. The way her hand felt in mine. Warm and soft and confident.

The feel of her breaths as they whispered against my skin. The heat in her eyes as she tried not to give in to the incubus now living inside of me. Despite what she'd said, I was convinced that the reason we found ourselves in Izzy's room eventually was because of Max.

I may have been the one with dream-walking powers, but Max was the light, the strength. Grasping desperately to that feeling, to that weird, magical energy that seemed to pull me to her, I focused on her and nothing else. For what felt like hours, I tried to reach her in the way that she helped me reach Izzy.

When it became too painful or too draining, I'd try Atlas instead. Imagine his familiar scowl and stiff posture, his constant battle between wanting to protect everyone and being terrified he was the reason they needed protection.

But always, within minutes, my focus swept back towards Max. My mind was a stubborn beast, never more so than since I awoke down here, alone in my misery and anxiety.

I did this over and over, until I exhausted myself with disap-

pointment, head lolling back on the scraps of fabric I'd fashioned into a pillow. I gave in to the truth—the shadow creature
had taken her from me. I told myself it was for her own good,
that she would be safer where I couldn't reach her. With steady
breaths I begged for sleep to sweep me under. Or, better yet,
death.

HOURS, DAYS, WEEKS. TIME DIDN'T SEEM TO FUNCTION IN THE
way I was familiar with.

A flutter danced along my bare chest, the sensation marrying
together with my dream of Max until it was a deliciously sinful
fantasy. I closed my eyes tighter, desperate to hold onto this
image and feel until wakefulness took hold completely.

The soft flutter grew heavier, until my chest started to shake
from the force. Brushing the strange pressure away, I turned on
my side and buckled back into my dream, desperate to cling
onto it as long as I possibly could. I had no desire to open my
eyes and stare at the gray, empty walls I knew would be
surrounding me.

The shaking resumed and I let out a low, irritated groan.
"Get the fuck off of me."

"Wade," a soft voice echoed into my ear, lodging its way into
my brain.

I blinked harder, filling my mind with the sound of her. This
dream was becoming more and more realistic in the best
possible way.

"Wade, you need to wake up," more soft shaking, "please. Are
you—are you okay? Did that thing hurt you?"

The blast of the question sent my eyelids peeling back into
my skull as I stared at the girl sitting next to me. Her dark hair
was tousled and shiny, her brown eyes filled with a sort of
concern that sent my chest into a flutter.

Unwilling to move just yet, on the off chance that this was

still just an elaborate, wishful fantasy, I stared at her. I took in every curve of her face, eyes following down her neck and then the rest of her body.

My muscles tensed as they always seemed to do here, now that I was transitioning, as that creature called it. My lower stomach flipped at the sight of her plush lips, at her surprisingly full breasts, and the only thing that kept me from lunging at her and claiming her here and now was the sharp voice at the back of my mind. The part of me from before that would die a slow, agonizing death if I somehow hurt her.

My breath hitched as her fingers landed on my chest, the feel of her skin against mine sending chills throughout my entire body. I'd always thought that succubi and incubi simply heightened the arousal of their prey. But since the first moment I saw Max after waking up in this godforsaken torture chamber, I realized that the desire was just as heightened for me, if not more so. She was irresistible.

Pressing my hands into the rough bed and scratchy fabric, I pushed myself up into a seated position, my head almost dizzy with the intoxicating scent of her. I let out a low groan, realizing how much more desirable she was after convincing myself that I would never see her again outside of my dreams.

And the Max in my dreams had absolutely nothing on the Max in front of me right now. The girl here was wild and intelligent and warm and seductive in a way that the version I constructed could never really achieve. All she had to do was sit here with me and I was completely undone.

I shifted, uncomfortably trying to disguise the very real effect she was having on my body right now.

"Wade," she said, her eyes glazing over slightly as she studied me. "Did he hurt you?"

"Who?" My voice was groggy and scratchy from the mental anguish I had put myself through since she was last here. Apparently I was just as good at torturing myself as my captor was. "How are you here?"

"That shadow creature. Did he hurt you? I wanted to—I tried to stay here with you, but he had some sort of power. Ability. He literally threw me from my dream. I have no idea what kind of creature could even do that. Unless he's like a superpowered, boss-level incubus."

I drew in a shallow breath, watching the worry dance in her dark eyes. I hated that expression, hated that she feared for me when she was the one truly in danger. Thinking about the shadow creature would only compound that worry. Especially if I relayed what he'd said to me. About using me as a tool against my people—my real people. My family.

I shook my head and stood up, suddenly desperate to put some space between us as I wove the half lie generating in my mind. "He is the one who occasionally brings food."

"Did he say anything after I left?" she kneeled on my bed, dressed in nothing but a t-shirt that revealed the smooth stretch of her thighs beneath the baggy fabric.

I shook my head, forcing my eyes away. My fingers were desperate to reach for her, to peel that shirt—which looked suspiciously like a guy's baggy shirt—off her body. To press her into the bed and show her exactly how much I thought about her.

Wait. Why the fuck was she wearing another guy's shirt in the first place? Was she wearing it last time she was here too? I shook the suspicion away and refocused on her. "That was the first time he—it—has ever spoken to me. It said nothing once you left. Just left me with some food and disappeared again." I clenched my fingers into a fist, to keep from tracing them along her legs. "H-how are you here, Max?"

Her slim eyebrows bent down in confusion as she stood up on the bed and moved closer to me, her eyes almost leveled with mine from that height. "What do you mean? How am I here? I'm here the same way I'm always here. It took me a while, after waking up, to fully remember what happened. And then, once I did, I tried desperately to fall back asleep. To get back to you."

She let out a soft laugh that sounded musical and light. It sent an electric thrill through my body. "Do you know how hard it is to fall asleep when your body is thrumming with anxiety and you're desperate for nothing but dreams?"

I knew exactly what that was like.

All too well.

I nodded slowly, studying the graceful length of her neck. I couldn't tell her that the shadow creature had attempted to banish her completely from reentering this room in her dreams. What would he do if he found her here with me again? Kill her? Torture her?

Keep her?

It wouldn't be long before he, too, saw in her what I did—that she was the most alluring girl in the world.

"You shouldn't be here," I said, stepping back until my skin was completely pressed against the cool, damp wall. The constant smell of mildew would be forever burned into my nose whether or not I ever made it out of here alive.

She stood up, her eyes narrowing and jaw ticking with frustration. "I thought we were past this already, Wade. I'm here. And I'm going to keep coming here until you are no longer locked up in here. Period. I recommend you avoid this argument in the future, because it's not one you will ever win."

With three small steps, she closed the distance between us and reached her hand out until it wound around mine. Her skin was so warm that I was convinced it could bring me back from the brink of death if I let it.

Her dark eyes studied me as I pushed further back into the wall, trying desperately to escape my own desire—the weird all-encompassing power she seemed to wield over me. How did such a small girl have such a huge effect on me?

Her face softened as she watched me until she let go of my hand and took a step back. Instantly, I wanted to close the distance, at war with whether I wanted to push her away or keep her against me for the rest of time.

"I'm sorry," she said, voice a delicate whisper, "I didn't mean to cross a boundary or to snap like that. I just—I want you to understand that I'm not giving up on you. None of us are. But I'm here for more than a visit this time. A favor."

"Anything," I said, desperate for the distraction, something to keep my mind off of how delectable she looked right now and how badly I wanted to wipe that small frown from her face and turn it into something much more appealing. "But I'm not sure what I'll be able to help with from here. I'm not exactly swimming in resources at the moment."

Her face broke out in a small, guarded smile, and I noticed that her dark eyes were filled with a sort of fear that wasn't there the last time she was here.

"That's just it. I think you're the only one who can help with this." She exhaled and walked back towards the bed so that she could sit down. Suddenly it seemed like the weight of the entire world was on her shoulders. It was a strange feeling, to be mad at the world for doing that to her. "Eli's been attacked. And it's—"

She broke off, her words watery. I looked at her face and saw her eyes were glassy with tears. My stomach squeezed at the sight and I instantly walked over to her and squeezed her hands between mine.

She shook her head and blinked a few times as if she could just clear the emotion away with a bit of willpower. "It's not looking good. The last time I was here, I couldn't quite remember what had happened. But there was a vamp ambush and Eli was bitten. Several times."

It felt like someone had punched me in the gut with a metal fist. Eli had always been like a cheeky, slightly obnoxious older brother to me. A single vampire bite was difficult enough to overcome, but I'd never heard of someone surviving multiple. "How long—"

I couldn't frame my thoughts into anything coherent. How would Atlas handle losing another brother? And Declan? She liked to pretend she hated Eli, but it was a sibling's sort of play-fighting they engaged in.

"I know that when we visited Izzy—" she started, her shoulders slumped slightly with guilt that did not belong to her, "but I thought maybe—"

I nodded instantly, picking up on her plan. "Let's try to reach him."

It took a few minutes, but now that I knew it was possible, so long as she was with me, we reached Eli.

He was in a lush room, lying around in a giant four-poster bed with a grin on his face like he was a goddamned king.

His amber eyes locked on me as soon as I came into view.

"No fucking way," he said, as he shoved himself off the bed and ploughed into me like a freight train. "It's fucking great to see you man."

I patted his back softly for a second until he pulled back; I tried to rein in the fear in my voice. "You too, Eli."

It was strange. In the dream world, he seemed fine. His usual self, if not a bit more energized than usual. Could he really be dying in his corporeal form?

He arched a brow as he took me in. "You look good, man. Like you're more...just more, somehow, if that makes sense?" His face fell and he took a step back. "Ah shit. It's happened to me too, hasn't it?"

"What's happened to you?" Was he aware of the fact that he was in the middle of a struggle for his life?

"I've gone and become an incubus." He shook his head and studied his arms like the limbs didn't belong to him. "I mean it makes sense, I guess. I've always had an alarmingly high sex appeal. So if anyone was going to die and come back as an incubus, it makes sense it's me. Was sort of shocked it happened to you first, if I'm being honest." His brows pinched together as he ran his hands down his sides and then his legs, like he was trying to identify any differences. "But still. Would be nice if we could all stop turning into monsters. Getting a bit predictable and all."

"That's not how you become an incubus, you wank," I said, unable to keep the smile from my words, despite the grim reality. "You know that's not how it happens. My mother was a succubus. It just didn't get triggered properly in me until I was killed and had to rely on those genes to bring me back. The protector side shrouded them, is all. Or something like that. I still don't completely understand it."

"Max," he said, the word a low, reverent whisper. "You're here."

Not waiting for her to respond, he shoved my shoulder and roughly pushed me aside a few feet so that he could look at her properly. I tried to see her from his eyes. She was dressed in nothing but a baggy t-shirt, her luxurious waves of hair rippling down until they reached midway down her back. Her eyes were wide and filled with emotions that I couldn't quite decipher or identify; her lips plump and kissable.

When I looked back at him and saw the lovesick expression on his face, I knew that he saw her in the exact same way that I did. She was delectable.

"I thought you were dead," he said, his voice cracking slightly on the words. "I thought we were both fucking goners."

"I'm a—"

Without letting her finish, he closed the gap between them so quickly that I was almost convinced he was a vampire and swallowed the rest of her words with his lips.

She stood frozen for a moment, but eventually melted into him so that her lips and tongue were moving just as furiously as his were.

He lifted her up so that she could wrap her legs around his waist like a snake, and he carried her a few feet over to the wall, his one hand coiling through her hair while the other swept all over her body like he was desperate to touch every single inch of her.

I'd seen Eli make out with plenty of women. Having shared a house with him for the last few years, he'd made it into sort of a game, trying to screw the girls he brought home in various places around the house. I'd even walked in on him fucking Sharla in my own bed once—payback for accidentally ruining his favorite jeans in the laundry.

But in all of those instances, I'd never seen him kiss a girl like this. Like it mattered.

Watching the fervor with which they met each other, I couldn't help but feel myself getting aroused. Strangely, it wasn't really jealousy going through my mind as I watched them—the way her head rolled back as he drew heated circles down her neck with his tongue. I was jealous that I wasn't a part of it, but not jealous that she was with someone else.

"But Wade," she whispered, her words ending in a moan as Eli pressed his dick, which I knew would be hard as a rock—mine was—into her.

"Forgot he was here," Eli answered, not even bothering to glance in my direction. Or stop what he was doing. "He can watch if he wants. I don't mind."

Strangely, I found myself wanting just that. The thought of her pulling away from him, of this encounter ending left me with an unfamiliar ache.

Her eyes met mine, brown and wild with heat. I nodded, and held her eye contact as I pulled a chair out from the desk, sat down, and gripped my dick. I wanted her to know just how much I didn't mind.

The sight of me slipping my hand beneath the band of my sweatpants made her suck in a deep breath, the desire in her expression amplifying.

Eli turned momentarily to see what she was responding to and cocked a brow as his face broke out into a sly smirk. "Atta boy."

He pulled her from the wall, earning a surprised noise from her, and walked her over to the bed.

"You good?" he asked.

She nodded, her chest heaving with each breath.

"I need you to say the words, Max. If you want me to stop, tell me to stop. And if you want me to keep going, I need to know that too."

And as much as it would have pained him to pull away from her in that moment, with her lips swollen and red, her hair tousled seductively, I knew that he would.

"I'm good," she said, her face lighting up with expectation. "Do your worst."

There was so much heat in those words that I almost came right then and there, like I was a goddamn teenage boy and not a powerful fucking protector. Er, or incubus.

How the fuck did she have this power of me? Over us?

As if that was exactly what he was hoping to hear, a wicked grin appeared on his face. In one swift move, he ripped her shirt off, grabbed her leg, and pulled. She fell back with her head on the pillow, dressed in nothing but a lacy bra and skimpy pair of underwear.

Seeing her in that position was intoxicating and I pulled my dick out and stroked slowly, up and down, as she opened her mouth in surprise.

A short giggle erupted from her until Eli ripped her underwear off and separated her legs. With a devious smirk, he ducked his head down, his tongue slowly licking up and down over her clit. She bucked off the bed with each lap, eyes squeezed tight.

God I wanted her to look at me, wanted her to see the effect her euphoria was having on me.

As if she could hear my thoughts, her eyes sprang open and they lazily traveled from my face to where my hand sat stroking my cock. At the sight of it, she bit her bottom lip, nearly sending me into overdrive. I wanted those lips around my cock desperately.

Without realizing it, I moved the chair closer to the bed so that they were only a few short feet from me. She didn't break eye contact as her hand crept around her back to unsnap the latches of her bra. Slowly, she peeled it off her and tossed it at me playfully, her brow arched in challenge.

I picked it up, hand pumping harder as the scent of her hit me full force. Her chest heaved with each breath as her left hand wound roughly through Eli's hair and her other started to massage into her right breast.

I pumped faster as we stared at each other, her body tensing deliciously as Eli pulled more and more from her.

Eli slipped a finger into her and she melted into him, her body quaking like she was on the edge of a cliff.

"Oh my god," she said, each word coming out on a rough exhale. "Fuck."

Eli chuckled softly—smug ass—as he tilted his head up to watch her. "I've got you," he said, his words both husky and reverent, "you can fall."

It was surprisingly tender for him.

I matched each thrust of his fingers with my hand and I watched as she erupted, her orgasm sending her body into spasms as she screamed.

Unable to sit as the voyeur for a second longer, I walked over to the bed and brought my lips down to hers, swallowing the final whimpers with my mouth as Eli bent down to bring her to round two.

My skin sang as her tongue met mine with a heavy intensity, like she wanted me as much as I wanted her.

I slid my hand lazily down her neck and drew circles around her nipple until I pinched, eliciting a squeal-turned-moan from her.

I grinned into her lips as her hand made its way down to my dick and pulled back for a moment to look at her—to stare at this girl who was fast becoming my undoing.

"I love when your eyes swirl like that," she said, her body already starting to quake with another wave as Eli crawled up her body, nipping playfully along her skin.

I sat back like she'd slapped me, suddenly realizing what I was doing. Incubi heightened sex drives. They took any small inkling of libido and attraction and amplified it until that's all the dreamer could feel.

I wasn't there with them—this wasn't real. Instead, I was joyfully draining my friends of their life force, too focused on my own goddamn horniness to remember what I was, what I'd become.

I was a monster.

"No!" I screamed, dark edges clouding my vision, until the bedroom flew away and I was back in my prison.

Exactly as I should be.

Alone.

7

MAX

I sprang from my pillow, eyes wide and breaths heavy as I looked around. What the hell had happened? It felt like Wade had completely ejected me, not only from the dream, but from sleep altogether.

Panting, I glanced around and reached frantically along the side table, desperately trying to find the lamp.

My fingers latched on the switch and the room was bathed in a soft, luminous glow. Judging from my clear reflection in the window, it was deep into the night which meant I'd slept for a few hours at least.

"You okay?"

I whipped my head around and saw Atlas sitting at the desk a few feet from me—in the exact spot that Wade had been in my dream.

I nodded my head viciously as I tried to catch my breath.

"We should have taken proper precautions before you went under," he said, and even though he was partially cast in shadow, I could see that his face was stern. "Did he drain you too much?"

It dawned on me what he meant by proper precautions. After I'd mentioned that Wade might be in danger, we'd spent hours waiting for me to fall asleep. I even resorted to taking a few nighttime pills to help hurry along the process. Neither of us had given any thought to the idea of what might happen once I was finally with Wade. We were both too desperate to make sure that he was still alive.

Judging by the tightness of Atlas's jaw, he'd heard every sound just as he had when I was in the car on the way to Seattle. I looked down and saw his hands gripping the arms of his chair, his knuckles nearly white.

"I missed most of it," he said in response, like he could feel the anxiety radiating from me. "I went to get a bite to eat. When I came back and you were—I tried to wake you. It didn't work. He didn't drain you too much did he?"

He leaned forward slightly and studied me, like he'd be able to tell either way.

I glanced down at myself, patting down my sides and legs awkwardly, like that might inform me as to whether or not my energy was depleted. I felt fine though.

"Don't worry, you surly shit, it was mostly me anyway. Not Wade," Eli said from behind me, his voice gruff with sleep.

Atlas's jaw clenched for a moment and I could tell he wanted to chew him out for the comment. "That's what happens in an incubus dream apparently, every morsel of desire is amplified out of control," he responded, words clipped.

But then, at the same time, like a bus out of nowhere, we were both hit with the same realization.

I spun around in bed and glanced at Eli, his dark hair mussed and unruly, a shit-eating grin on his face.

"You're awake," I said, as Atlas jumped out of his chair and circled the bed to check on him from the opposite side.

"Look my dude, you're not really my type," he said, brushing Atlas's hands away as he tried to pull his neck into the light. "I'm fine sharing my bed with the lady, but not really with you."

I fell asleep next to Eli out of hope that it would help facilitate a dream-walk to him with Wade. Was he awake now because of that experience? Had Wade pushed him back into consciousness as he had me, or was it something else?

"How do you feel?" Atlas asked, taking the hint and backing up a few feet, though I could see the tension in his body pulling him forward. "You've been out for days."

Eli scratched at the scruff lining his jaw, brows bent in confusion. "I have? What for?"

I cleared my throat and slid out of the covers. It felt too intimate now, being so close to Eli after what had happened. Was Atlas right? Were mine and Eli's actions merely the result of Wade's powers?

I could feel my cheeks heating up and sent a silent prayer that the light wasn't bright enough to reveal my embarrassment.

"You were attacked," Atlas said, his words slow and even like he was worried he'd startle Eli. "By vampires."

"Plural?" he shook his head and grabbed for the glass of water on my side of the bed, downing half of it in one gulp. Atlas or Declan must've brought it for me while I was out. I tried not to stumble on the idea of Atlas doing something thoughtful for me.

"What's the last thing you remember?" Atlas asked.

Eli's dark eyes latched onto mine and danced with mirth. I knew instantly what last memory he was focused on and dropped my eyes.

"In the fight, he means," I added quickly.

"Getting toppled by a bunch of vamps and then," he looked up at me with awe and shock, his face drawn and lips parted. "And then you—"

Atlas cleared his throat and grabbed Eli's arm, pulling his attention from me with a soft tug. They shared a long moment of silence before Atlas glanced at me, his eyes stern and unreadable as always. "You were bitten. Several times. Max, why don't you go hit the other light and we can check his wounds."

"Weird," Eli said, something off about his tone. "I feel totally fine. Better than normal in a lot of ways, if I'm being honest."

Happy for something to do, I jumped from the bed and rummaged along the wall until I found the main source of light.

When I turned around, both of them were looking at me and I suddenly felt hyper self-conscious that I was dressed only in someone's baggy shirt—I hadn't even bothered to ask whose it was.

After we determined that Eli was okay, I was *so* going to take a long, luxurious shower, and then beg Declan to help me locate my backpack. Which, hopefully, one of them had grabbed before we departed from the hotel suite. If not, I was going to be wildly underdressed for hell.

Ignoring their stares and Eli's cocky grin, I walked back to the bed, trying to be as composed as possible while I made sure that the shirt was pulled as far down my thighs as it would go.

With careful fingers, I pulled back the blood-soaked bandages on Eli's neck, terrified of what I'd find when I did.

His wounds had been weeping since he was brought here. I wasn't sure what would happen if the bites didn't coagulate.

"Impossible," Atlas said as he gently moved my hand aside so that he could get a better look. He tore a piece of his shirt off from the bottom and grabbed the glass of water from Eli so that he could wet it. Then, with slow, careful strokes, he wiped away the dried blood on Eli's neck, his eyes focused and assessing.

Eli closed his eyes tight, like he was expecting the worst or, at the very least, for the cleansing to be painful. But after a moment he opened one curious eye and then the other.

"The wound," I said, unable to believe my eyes.

"How bad is it, love?" Eli asked, his voice dramatic and drawn out. "Am I hideous? Tell me. I can handle the truth." He shook his head swiftly before adding, "wait, no don't tell me. I lied. I can't handle the truth."

"How is this possible?" Atlas asked, his voice filled with awe as he rubbed his finger along the spot on Eli's neck that once held a mess of bites and now held...nothing. "You're completely healed. Every bite—"

Eli rolled his eyes. "Well, maybe don't hide that much of the truth from me. I can handle a little bit of reality."

"Eli, you're completely healed," I said, laughter spilling from my lips. "There's not a single mark on you."

Atlas's brows were bent in focus. "I haven't seen anything like this. Well, not since—"

"You," Eli finished for him. He shoved Atlas's hands away so that he could feel his own smooth skin. "Oh thank god. That would've been a hard thing to live with. Still, too bad I didn't get to keep a little bit of a battle wound. Chicks dig scars, you know?"

He turned to me and winked.

"We should go wake up Declan," I said and hopped back off the bed to go do that very thing. Now was not the time to get distracted by Eli...being Eli.

"Have her bring you to the entry hall receiving area. Eli will go rinse up and then we can start planning our next steps," Atlas said as he stood up and stretched his limbs. How long had he been watching us sleep? He probably needed some rest himself —especially considering the fact that we would be venturing into hell soon, if all went well. "Have her show you where you can find your—er," he glanced at me, before immediately averting his eyes and clearing his throat, "clothes."

I ran from the room, too ecstatic with Eli's recovery to be embarrassed by anything else and shook Declan awake. She was just as shocked and excited as I was and her eyes quickly lost that hazy look they had when roused from sleep suddenly. Pointing me in the direction of my clothes and a roomy bathroom, she ran to check on him while I took a few minutes to shower.

Someone had cleaned me up a bit while I was unconscious— unlike Eli, I didn't have any wounds, so no dressings to deal with. But I also hadn't been covered in blood and gore when I'd woken up, despite the fact that I'd been in an intense vamp battle.

I closed my eyes as the water cascaded over me, hoping that

it was Declan who'd seen to the washing up and wardrobe change.

Then again, the thought of her seeing me naked and vulnerable like that brought just as much heat to my body as when I thought about one of the guys doing it.

Instantly, my focus went to that look in her eyes when I'd woken her up, the way all of her attention seemed to beam into me, making it difficult to breathe—to the fullness of her lips as she transitioned from that strange space between being asleep and awake...

Hopefully Khalida then. As strange as she was, I didn't have any confusing thoughts about her seeing me naked.

I wasn't sure what the hell was wrong with me. But I was getting extremely tired of my hormones ruining everything. And how would I face Eli alone again? Did he regret what happened? I should've stopped to think in the moment. It was so good to see him alive and talking, that when he kissed me I didn't even question it.

It just felt...natural. Right.

I thought back to the way it felt to kiss him, to the feel of his hands all over me, to the way it made me feel knowing Wade was watching us. I never thought someone simply watching me in that vulnerable position could amplify my experience of it so much.

My stomach started to flip at the memory of it, so I turned the water to cold, in a desperate attempt to focus on something other than the spot between my legs for a second. I'd need to sort through all of my feelings eventually. It wasn't normal to want two boys at once, was it?

I knew that protectors were a bit more open about polyamory than humans seemed to be, but I never thought I would develop feelings for more than one person—it just seemed so complicated, like adding so much more work to an already difficult thing.

And how would they feel about it? Eli had always been so hot and cold with me, so I couldn't even guess where his head was half the time.

I shook my head, spilling water around me like a chaotic fountain. Now was not the time. We had to focus on saving Wade and getting back to Guild Headquarters in one piece. That was what mattered. It was the only thing that mattered.

A large bark pulled my attention back to the moment, so I rinsed off and threw on a pair of black leggings and a black tshirt, tying it at my hip.

Ralph was sitting outside the door when I opened it, butt popped in the air in the universal dog language for 'play.'

"Don't have time right now, but, how about you take me back to my room and then we can go meet everyone else," I said as I ran my fingers through his shaggy fur.

We walked in silence as we descended the stairs, the halls lit only with a dim glow. I tried to be as quiet as possible, though Ralph stomped around with as much grace as he usually did. Which is to say, not much.

I wasn't sure if Darius and Claude were still asleep, but I was hoping that at the very least, the latter was. After our encounter earlier, I wanted to have as little do with the mysterious twin as I possibly could. Hopefully I'd get away with only seeing him in the morning as he directed us towards the hell gate, wherever that was.

The whole concept of a portal into hell made me feel like I was reliving my Buffy fantasies in the flesh. The problem though, was that now that those fantasies were becoming real, they were also becoming much more terrifying.

When I walked into the room, I saw Eli on the couch, one foot perched on the other leg's knee, his arms spread around the back of the headrests. His eyes lit up when he saw me and Ralph and I ignored the answering flutter in my stomach.

Even now, even while just casually sitting and talking to Declan and Atlas, he had a sly teasing energy about him. It was the sort of look that reminded me that he had no problem getting girls to his bedroom. And I remembered one of our first encounters, when I walked into him pumping into a human girl we'd met earlier that day.

I took a deep breath, drilling it through my head that even if he didn't regret what happened during the dream-walk, it still didn't mean anything. Not to him. Eli was a bedpost notch type of guy. And he never so much as pretended to be otherwise.

"Good of you to join us. I see you used my brother's shampoo," a deep voice echoed around the room, stemming from nowhere and everywhere at once.

I jumped and turned around towards the fireplace where a soft, calm fire was glowing. Darius was leaning against the mantle, his nose scrunched up in distaste.

"I didn't think— will he be upset?" Last thing I wanted to do was get even more on that asshole's bad side. There was only so much stress a girl could take and, honestly, I needed to reserve my capacity for the whole jumping into hell thing.

Darius shrugged, pushed off the mantle, and started to walk towards me at a slow, lazy pace. "There isn't much that doesn't upset him. The word pessimism was basically designed to describe him. But don't worry, little protector. I'll keep you safe."

"Where've you been all day?" I asked, narrowing my eyes at him. After his mysterious visit with Eli earlier, I hadn't seen him around the house.

"Miss me, did you? I had a rest, as I told you I would, and then I went out for a bit. Wanted to familiarize myself with the city again while I got a bite to eat. Who knows when I'll get to see it again. And while it has its annoyances, it was home for a decent while."

I cringed, hoping that by something to eat he didn't mean someone.

"This doesn't matter," Declan said, though there wasn't much animosity in her words. She was staring at Eli like he'd come back from the dead.

Probably because he had.

"I still don't understand how this happened," she said before bending into a crouch and staring into Eli's eyes like she was convinced the answer would be hidden behind his typical shit-eating grin.

"Guess I'm just indestructible," Eli said with a wink in my direction.

"That, or maybe Wade had something to do with it," I offered, remembering the way he'd ejected me into consciousness. I wasn't entirely sure why he'd done it, unless he was ashamed of what we were doing.

"What have you done," a dark voice echoed behind me, sending chills down my arms.

I turned around and saw Claude, dressed head-to-toe in black, his eyes hard as stone as he stared at Darius.

With a gentle hand, Darius pulled me behind him before walking a few steps towards his brother. "I don't know what you're talking about."

Claude's nostrils flared and his muscles were so tense that he looked ready to explode across the room and attack us all. "You know damn well what I'm talking about. That boy was as good as dead."

Darius shrugged, his posture stiffening a bit.

I wasn't used to him taking things seriously and apparently neither were the other three in the room. Eli, Declan, and Atlas all stood to attention and walked slowly towards me like they were afraid of setting the twins off if they moved too quickly.

"Miracles happen, nothing to harp on about," Darius said as he slid a hand towards the knife sheathed at his belt.

And then, without another word, Claude lunged.

8

MAX

The brothers met with a crash that rattled me down to my bones. The room shook and the sounds the two made felt more like a fight between lions, rather than a fight between men. If I thought watching Declan and Atlas spar was like watching masters at work, this was something else entirely.

And suddenly, I realized why protectors worked in teams, why it often required so many of us to take down one of them.

It was like watching a ruthless, brutal ballet. They met each other fist for fist, neither of them even bothering with the use of blades—despite the fact that Darius had one at the ready. And despite being twins and the fact that Claude had recently saved Darius from death, neither of them were holding back now.

Claude threw a punch with so much force and power into Darius's jaw that I could have sworn I heard multiple bones shatter. It was deafening. And Darius, being the absolute absurd creature that he was, just grinned back, using the muscles on the one side of his face that still worked properly.

"What the hell are you doing?" I screamed as the reality of what they were doing swept over me. They were going to kill each other. My words were muffled and lost to the sounds of their destruction.

I ran towards them, unsure how best to get them to pause long enough for us all to figure out what the hell was going on, to talk things through. This wasn't going to solve anything except maybe add an even higher body count to our mission. And right now, we couldn't afford that.

A strong force grabbed me around my middle and pulled me roughly to the ground. My fingers dug into the thick carpet as I tried to reorient myself.

"What the fuck are you doing?" Atlas asked, his breath hot against my face as he shook me furiously by my shoulders. "You don't get into the middle of any fight, let alone one between two vampires. Are you trying to get yourself killed?"

Declan crawled over, her eyes wide as a doe as she reached for me and pulled me back out of the fallout zone.

"And definitely not between these two vampires," she added, grunting as she used all of her strength to drag us both with her at the same time. Eventually, with a deep groan of frustration, she abandoned Atlas, leaving him to his own devices, and devoted all of her energy and focus on pulling me. I could feel the carpet creating a dull burning sensation along my back with each thrust. "There's something off about them," she exhaled with exertion, "they're too strong. Like vampires on fucking steroids."

A loud crash sounded and I craned my neck to see Claude sitting in a pile of broken glass and wood where a side table and ornate lamp had been standing a moment before.

His face contorted with rage as his teeth descended past his lip. "You fucking prick. That lamp was a hundred years old. You just signed your own death warrant."

"What are you going to do about it? Bite me?" Darius taunted, his eyebrow arched and eyes glistening, whether with bloodlust or amusement, I couldn't be sure.

Claude shook off a few stray shards of ceramic and glass, his palms already healing from the superficial cuts, before he stood up, dove forward, and rammed into Darius's chest.

They went down with such ferocity that the ground shook, the two of them nothing but a pile of indiscernible limbs, each trying desperately to claw at or hit the other. They looked so similar to each other that it became almost impossible to decipher which arm belonged to which vampire when they were all tangled up like that.

They lashed out with a fury of fists and kicks that would have killed humans and protectors alike. Watching them, I wasn't sure how even a whole team of protectors could stand a chance, let alone one of us. We were a doomed species if this was the sort of thing we were up against after graduation.

Declan went back for Atlas and I just—watched. Mesmerized.

Their movements brought them closer and closer to us until I could reach my hand out and touch them if I wanted to.

I needed to move. But for some reason, I was frozen. My breath locked up somewhere in my throat and all I could see was the image of the vampire snapping Wade's neck before he fell to the ground in a heap. Lifeless.

My hands tingled and my skin felt itchy as I tried desperately to breathe in and out, my vision blurring between the scene that night and the one in front of me. It was a ridiculous thing for my brain to do in this moment, and a hollow shame filled my belly.

When I located Darius's eyes in the fight, I realized that for the first time, he actually looked concerned. This was no longer a game to him, not anymore anyway. Would his brother really kill him? Would he kill his brother?

How deep did their hatred towards each other go? And if one of them died, what would happen to the rest of us? I knew with a deep, aching certainty that if Claude was the surviving twin, the rest of us would quickly follow Darius's fate. If his allegiance to his brother was gone, we didn't stand a chance at making it out of here alive.

And Wade would remain a prisoner forever, locked up and alone until the cloaked creature decided to do whatever it was he was going to do with him.

And Ro and and Cyrus and Izzy—I'd never see any of them again.

Picking up where Declan left off, Eli slid his hands under my armpits and lifted me up like a rag doll, my limbs lolling loosely like they were boneless. I saw rather than felt him drag me a few feet away until my feet danced above the carpet like I was nothing more than a puppet. After a brief moment of hovering, he let my feet touch the ground, though I couldn't feel them properly. Everything felt unstable and unreal—my body most of all.

When I turned back, I saw that Atlas's eyes were pure gold as Declan held onto his arms, trying to hold him back, to calm him down.

But she didn't stand a chance, not really. The wolf was no longer willing to stay in the small recesses of Atlas's mind that he was allowed to prowl. As if realizing this at the exact moment that I did, she let go and took a few steps back from him. His body contorted in pain. I watched in horror as his muscles snapped and his bones broke. He was starting the transition right in front of us. His smooth, muscular arms lined with the now-familiar dark brown fur. There was pain clear as day on his face as the transition rolled through him and my chest ached at the sight.

Atlas was immoveable; a creature of pure strength and determination. Seeing him struggle through this was like a heavy dousing of cold water on my face.

I could see it in his eyes as they locked onto mine. For once, I could read every emotion there—pain, anger, and most prominent of all, fear. It was like he was using every morsel of energy in his body to keep the wolf back. But as strong as Atlas was, he wasn't strong enough to win this match.

I watched in awe as he lost the battle to his other half, his shadow self; until, eventually, he bared his teeth in a vicious growl—a giant, livid wolf standing where Atlas had been just one moment earlier.

"Calm down Atlas," Declan said, her hands lifted in front of her, palms out as she made eye contact and took a few steps away from him. Slowly, very, very slowly. She didn't quite seem scared of him, but there was enough unease to suggest that she was just on the verge of fear. I wondered how often she'd been around him in this form before. "Remember who you are."

Would he hurt her? Would he attack the rest of us? She told me that generally Atlas had decent control of his wolf, but no werewolf had control near a full moon. Guessing by the anger radiating from the beast in front of us, we were smack dab in the full part of the cycle.

I turned around, desperate to find Ralph in the chaos. He'd kept Atlas's wolf in its place once before, maybe he could do it again, without hurting him. I craned my neck around the room that now looked like it'd seen the depths of a great war, but the giant dog was nowhere in sight.

When had I last seen him?

He'd brought me to the room, walked me through the house, but now he was gone without a trace. He had a habit of disappearing without warning. Better that way, perhaps. Better that he not get wrapped up in this reckless shit show. I'd pulled him into enough dangerous situations already.

My nose itched from the unsettled dust in the room, like the particles were clinging to my skin and trying to fight their way into my body to suffocate me. My palms dug deep into Eli's thighs as we pressed ourselves against the wall, desperate to get out of the way as the brothers thrashed through the room, breaking everything in sight. It felt like a battlefield as the room filled with clouds of dust and the ground rumbled beneath my feet with every toss and fall. How the fuck did this situation devolve so quickly? I didn't understand what went wrong, not even a little bit.

"Stop this, I don't want to hurt you," Darius said, his words tumbling out in breathy puffs as Claude punched him in the gut with so much force that I was shocked his fist didn't go straight through Darius's stomach and out of his back.

Atlas's wolf turned from Declan and studied the brothers, muscles tense like he was waiting until the right moment to pounce. I didn't know whether to feel better or worse about that. It was great that he didn't seem to want to attack his friends, but something told me that if he went after the brothers, he'd end up dead. And almost instantly.

And as much as Atlas ground my gears, I knew with absolute certainty that the last thing I wanted was him hurt. Or worse.

"You selfish, mindless creature," Claude said, his words punctuated with punches until Darius's lip split in a burst of deep red. "You show no loyalty in your whole life, none. Never to me, never to your family. You've saddled me with an impossible debt. And then you go and do this on top of it? You waste your freedom? You're a fucking jackass. I don't know why I bothered helping you in the first place. I should've left you and your friends to rot like the worthless pieces of shit you are."

Darius wasn't even fighting back now, his face nothing more than a punching bag as Claude rocked hit after hit at him.

I wasn't sure what this was about, not really, but I could tell from the darkness in Claude's eyes as he lashed at his brother that it was about way more than recent events. This was the result of a lifetime of anger, built up over time, and now we were all around to watch it spew.

Eli inhaled deeply behind me before letting out a loud, anguished yell. "What the hell?"

I spun around and saw that his lip was broken open, thick blood spilling down his jaw and neck. His left eye was slammed shut and covered with blood like he'd been punched by a hammer. His white shirt was now dyed with splotches of red.

"Eli?" The breath left my lungs. I stared as another line of red carved itself across his cheek out of nowhere. When the hell had he been hit? He'd been standing right next to me the entire time. I reached out to touch his face but hovered an inch away out of fear of hurting him. "What the hell is going on?"

His lips quivered as he looked at his hands, the knuckles now all torn and bloody as he buckled over and held his ribs and stomach. "I-I don't understand."

His words came out in heavy, labored breaths, like he couldn't suck in a full lungful and was trying to disguise the full depth of his pain. When he spoke, I saw that his teeth were blood stained from the gash on his lips, the red coating each crevice along his gums. His tongue pooled with blood, punctured on one side as if he'd impaled it on his tooth somehow just by standing there.

"Declan," I screamed, now no longer paying any attention to Claude and Darius, though I could still hear them meeting in a clamor of bangs and rage-filled yells. "Something's not right. Like, really, *really* not right."

"Holy shit," she said, her jaw dropping as she stared from Eli to the two vampires. In the next moment, she left Atlas's side and tore across the room towards us, her expression revealing her panic. "You guys need to duck!"

Eli and I both hit the ground in time as a vase flew into the wall where we'd both been standing a nanosecond before and shattered into dust after denting the wall. A few stray shards cut into my forearm as I used it to shield my face and eyes. I hovered slightly over Eli, desperate to stop him from incurring any more wounds.

"Leave. Her. The. Fuck. Alone," Darius said. His voice was quiet, stilted, and almost calm. It was terrifying. And something about that sent chills down my spine, like a part of him I'd never seen before was slowly emerging.

I spun and saw him pummeling his brother in the ribs over and over, until I was certain that Claude didn't have a single unbroken bone left in his chest cavity. I had no idea how long it took vamps to repair shattered bones.

Atlas paced back and forth between us and them, like he wanted to pounce into the fight but had no idea which brother to go for. He settled instead for guarding us as he sent out loud, warning growls, his body vibrating with frustrated tension.

Where the fuck had the evening gone wrong? An hour ago I was filled with light and excitement. Eli was alive, awake. And now—I glanced at Eli, doubled over in pain. Atlas, barely able to control his wolf. The vampires, slowly beating each other to death. What the hell had happened?

Claude turned his warped face in our direction. Despite the violence of their fight, it was only mildly bruised and filled with cuts that were already slowly healing. His mismatched eyes glanced down at Eli, now soaked in blood.

"See brother, see what you've done?" He laughed, the sound low and haunting. "Turn around and take a good hard look at the masterpiece you've created. It's only fair you get to see and appreciate your work. You've saved the boy, only for it to result in both of your deaths. A fucking waste. But I can almost admire the poetry of it all."

It took a moment for the words to pull Darius out of his blood-crazed battle rage, and when he finally did turn towards us, I recoiled. Gone were the familiar series of expressions I'd grown accustomed to while visiting the vampire in the research lab.

There was no humor, no amusement, no teasing in his eyes now.

He was nothing but pure, unbridled anger. His eyes seemed to glisten, like he was enjoying the violence as much as he hated it. And I had a feeling that if he couldn't filter that rage against his brother, he would turn it on us. There was no mask of control there anymore. The monster within him was more than a simple vampire. He wrestled demons none of us understood. How many years had he spent in the lab at Guild Headquarters? How much torment and torture could a mind go through before it broke?

I looked closer, noticing that he had a cut above his eye, that his cheek was split, that his lip, now partially healed, was caked in a line of blood.

"Oh my god," I said as Declan glanced between Eli and Darius. Her soft gasp suggested that she was drawing the same conclusion that was slowly solidifying in my mind. "You're connected now. The blood—your blood—did this?"

"Yes, my little brother's gone and tied his life to a fucking protector. The lowliest creature on the planet," Claude said, his tone filled with mirthless laughter and disgust as he leveled a kick into Darius's ribs. "Fucking worthless piece of shit."

Darius was breathing in and out heavily, and I could tell that it was taking every ounce of his self-control not to give into the rage coursing through his bloodstream, not to turn around and finish the battle he'd started with his brother. There was a distance in his eyes now, like he was turning the rage in on himself instead. Much like Atlas had done only a few moments ago, he was waging war with his inner demons. All we could do was hope that where Atlas failed at containing his shadow self, Darius would succeed.

"What does this mean?" Declan asked as she ripped the one semi-clean area of Eli's shirt left and used the grimy, white cotton to apply pressure to the cuts, to stem some of the bleeding.

In the process of her pulling up his shirt, I realized that Eli had several claw marks traversing his chest and abdomen. The gouges were deep and angry. It would take him days to heal from all of this, especially since his energy stores were already so low. But my stomach sank as he fell against the wall and slid down. There was no way that he didn't have internal bleeding to match the external. I'd witnessed the fervor in every single one of Claude's punches.

"This means," Claude said, standing now and smirking down at his brother's glazed expression as he rocked back and forth on the ground, hands sunk into his hair, "that they're blood-bonded now. That if my brother dies, so does your friend." He pounced, lightning fast, and stood less than a few inches away from Eli. "It means that all I have to do is end this measly protector's life and I will take care of my little brother in one fell swoop." He turned back towards Darius and curled his lip in disgust. "By the looks of him, it'd be a mercy. Your kind has already taken his mind, why not his life?"

Judging from Claude's dexterity and speed, Darius had gotten the worst in their fight. I turned back and saw him still locked in his own private battle, his eyes bright and breaths ragged. While both brothers looked like shit, Darius was without a doubt in worse shape. His eyes were locked on Claude, tracking every single muscle he moved with absolute focus and precision as his rocking stilled.

And when I turned back to Claude, I realized that he'd been toying with Darius. Despite the mess in the room and the cuts rapidly disappearing from his skin, Claude looked like he'd done little more than go for a rather strenuous jog. I looked worse after some of my more active sparring sessions.

My blood turned to ice as Declan's words came back to me.

He was no normal vampire.

I was almost certain that even if Declan, Atlas, and I all tried to take him down at once, we would fail. He was powerful in a way that none of us could understand, in a way we hadn't been prepared for.

"What the hell are you?" I asked, forcing myself to look the creature in the eyes as he stalked closer and closer to where we were guarding Eli. We were nothing more than prey to him, and I was convinced with absolute certainty that he would enjoy hunting us down one-by-one. With fervor.

Atlas was in the process of shifting back and I turned my head when I saw that his chest, coated in sweat and pulsing with each heavy breath, was completely bare. I forced my eyes not to sink any lower, knowing that he'd be naked from the waist down as well.

It was a ridiculous thing—that even in the middle of something as dire as the current situation, I could feel my cheeks heating up at the sight of his muscular chest. My stomach clenched as anger at myself gripped me like an iron ring.

Quickly, I turned back to Claude, while Atlas swept the ground for his pants.

"You can't expect me to answer that question," Claude said as he shoved Declan aside into a wall, her head crashing hard with a sickening crack against a shelf, and closed the distance between us, "if you can't even answer the same question for yourself." He leaned towards me, whispering in my ear, "I'll show you mine, if you show me yours."

I stood, stunned, body trembling uselessly as his breath hit my neck.

With a small, humorless chuckle he crouched down next to Eli and dragged a single, porcelain finger up his shirt until he pressed it into one of the claw marks—a perfect match to his own finger.

Eli writhed in agony, his eyes wild and confused as the truth of the situation washed over him. I could tell through his ragged breathing that he was fighting to stay conscious. He was already in such a weakened state, he'd only been awake for an hour or two at most now.

Without thinking, I shook the fear from my mind and latched onto Claude, trying with every ounce of strength I had to pull him away from Eli. My fingers dug grooves into his shoulders and my feet sunk into the ground as I tugged.

Laughing, he brought his blood-soaked finger to his lips and licked, not even budging from my attempts to dislodge him.

Before I could double down on my efforts, Atlas's hands wrapped around me and pulled me away, dragging until I was a few feet back, rendering me once again as nothing more than a puppet.

"Leave him be," Atlas said, his voice so low and dark that I almost didn't recognize it. "Let him go and we'll leave now. We won't bother you again."

Claude cocked an eyebrow before pulling out a small blade from a sheath at his belt. "You think you have any bargaining chips here, wolf? That's almost adorable. But let's see this process in action," he said as his eyes met mine with a wicked glint. In one swift motion, he stabbed Eli's chest.

Eli let out a piercing, heart-shattering scream as he clawed uselessly at Claude's hands.

Atlas left my side and lunged just as Darius shoved me behind him and followed suit.

"Guess I missed the heart," Claude muttered as he wrestled Atlas and his brother to get back to Eli. "No worries, I'll try again."

I ran towards Declan, my legs simultaneously heavy and like jelly, as she watched the process, eyes wide and filled with a disoriented panic. Her forehead was cut and blood carved a jagged line down her cheek and jawline.

"Max," she said, and I realized that some of her panic was directed at me. Her eyes were focused on mine as she raised her hands, like I was the one on the brink of shifting into a wolf. "You need to calm down. Breathe. Take one slow, deep breath in. And then slowly let it out."

I could feel my blood rushing through my body as I turned my focus back towards the tangle of boys. Claude had managed to pull the blade from Eli and was fighting against Atlas and Darius, trying to plunge it into his chest again. My vision blurred and I felt something unfamiliar rising beneath my skin, desperate for escape.

My hands felt hot as I looked wildly around the room and saw Declan creeping closer to me, face a mess of sweat and dirt and blood. Her mouth was moving as she spoke to me, but I couldn't hear anything. I curled my fingers into fists, trying to dissipate the weird tingly heat and closed my eyes, desperate for the room to stop spinning and choking me.

A heavy, unfamiliar rage was brewing in my gut and when my eyes opened, they locked onto Claude. I breathed in, and as my body moved with the heavy inhalation, it felt like it was getting ready for some sort of release. Like the energy corrupting my focus was ready to disperse. Finally.

Almost excited now, ready to jump into the fray and rip Claude from the boys, I started to exhale, breathing the rage into existence—

"Enough," a quiet voice echoed behind me and I felt a sudden calmness wash over the room—over me—in an instant, as a soft breeze blew past my hair.

9

MAX

As if hypnotized, we turned as one towards the new presence.

Ralph was growling beside Khalida in the doorway. She looked so small standing next to him, somehow both fragile and lethal at once. His focus was on Claude as she walked further into the room and I was certain that he had gone to her for help. Though why on earth he seemed to trust her, I had no idea.

She was carrying a large scythe that looked nearly as tall as she was. Within what felt like a moment, she was standing next to Claude, the blade of her weapon less than an inch from his neck.

"Khali," he said, as he swallowed and stared at her wide-eyed, a tenuous smile on his lips, "don't be ridiculous. You're not going to do this and that's too dangerous to toy with. Put it down."

"Don't make me," she responded, her tone was sad but firm. She glanced down at Darius and Atlas, and whatever they saw in her eyes had them backing away immediately, without question or comment. "You will not harm the protector. And you will not kill your brother. Living with you after the sort of torment that will rain down on you is not an option. So don't be an asshole. And drop the blade. Now."

Metal crashed soundlessly on the carpet as Claude dropped his blade and crawled away from Khalida, his eyes glistening with anger and defeat as he stared at her weapon. His jaw was tensed so tightly that I was sure at least one tooth would crack from the pressure. After a moment, his shoulders sank in defeat. "Khali, you don't understand what he's done."

"I do," she said as she bent down next to Eli and rested her palm on his chest, "and it was incredibly ill-advised. But neither of them deserve to die for one mindless mistake. Especially since it was a selfless one. Go clean yourself up and then you can escort them both to hell. The sooner they are gone, the better it will be for you. We'll talk more when you're back."

Claude narrowed his eyes, like he was considering whether or not it was worth the effort he would expend to argue with her. After a long, drawn out breath where the two of them were locked in a silent battle, he stood up and walked out of the room, without a word to any of us left in his wake.

The second he left, the room seemed to erupt into a panic as we all moved like lightning to reach Eli. Each of us stared at him, desperate to help but afraid to touch him—all of us worried about causing him more pain. More damage.

He was in horrible shape and while Claude didn't bite him, he still looked like he was hovering aimlessly on the edge of death, one breath away from falling beyond reach. Protectors could survive a lot, but they couldn't survive the sort of beating that Darius took. Not even one as strong as Eli.

"The blood tie," Declan said, glancing down at Darius, "did Eli incur all of the damage that was inflicted on you?"

It was the first time since before Khalida walked into the room that Declan's eyes left me. And while I knew she could somehow see or feel whatever paralysis had come over me in that moment, my stomach tightened at the fear in her eyes.

For a moment, it had felt like she feared me more than she feared even Claude.

Why? Was it because she blamed me for all of this—for getting her team members killed off one by one.

Or was it something else?

"Blood bonds are unpredictable," Darius said, his voice hollowed out as he leaned against the wall. He wasn't in nearly as bad shape as Eli, but he looked rough all the same. He would need blood soon if he had any hope of healing through all of his wounds in the next day or so. "Sometimes they can be cut-for-cut mirrored, sometimes the bonded person gets hit with more than the one who was hurt in the first place, sometimes the opposite. Hard to say. It's not like a videogame with clearly defined damage points. Magic doesn't seem to ever come with an instruction manual, unfortunately. Especially forbidden magic. Cross-species blood bonds are especially...risky."

Eli's panting slowed down as Khalida pressed down on his chest like she was trying to stem the blood flow. Her fingers pressed gently around the knife wound, almost as if she was trying to push it out of him. I couldn't see her eyes, but Atlas was focused on them with laser-precision, his mouth opened slightly in awe.

"Wh-what are you doing?" I asked as I reached out for Eli's hand, desperate to hold onto him, to feel his skin against mine. We'd just gotten him back. To lose him all over again felt like a cruel, vicious game. One that we'd never win. "Can you heal him again?"

I looked up at Darius as the question left my lips, but he shook his head.

"No, my blood might relieve some of the pain, but it won't heal him again. That's not how it works."

"And if he dies, you'll die too," I said, the statement quiet and wavering with my own confusion. I knew that losing Eli would cut me to the core. But I didn't like the thought of losing Darius either, even if he was technically the enemy.

Darius's mouth tightened into a thin line, but he didn't answer. That non-answer said all I needed to know.

Yes, he would die.

I was surprised by the fact that there was no fear in his eyes, not anymore. Just a hard determination, a level-headed surrendering to whatever the fates would bring him.

Fear clawed angrily at my throat as I watched the mixture of sweat and blood collect on Eli's face, making their way down his cheeks in curved, gruesome trails.

As I watched him, his eyes seemed to regain some of their usual luster and his breathing evened out slightly. It was faint, almost imperceptible, and I held in a long breath for fear of breaking the moment by pointing it out.

I was afraid to hope. Hope was a dangerous thing, especially in our world. That was one of the most difficult lessons I'd learned since leaving the cabin.

Khali turned towards me and I almost fell back on my butt. Her eyes were pure black, no white in sight, and while I couldn't see anything in them besides my own reflection, there was an unfamiliar distance somehow. Like she was there with us but also not. She was beyond reach.

"You being near him, is helping," she said, her voice filled with a ghostly calm. "I have very little connection to him, which isn't ideal for this type of magic. But between the two of us, we should be able to bring him back from the edge. Once you are fully bonded, I imagine your strength will only amplify. Especially since you seem to possess the ability to pull multiple beings into your orbit. You're an interesting creature, Max Bentley."

Her words sent a chill down my spine, like they held the sort of certainty and illegibility that came with prophecy. Not that I believed in such a thing.

I could feel the others' eyes on the two of us, could feel their questions and suspicions lapping against my skin, rough and critical. I saw Declan's distrust and fear from a few moments ago, recalled months of Atlas questioning my heritage and trying to push me away from the people he cared about, and remembered the way that Darius studied me with curiosity, like a toy he didn't quite know how to make function.

Claude was right to taunt me. What the hell was I?

Could Khalida's words be true? Was I really helping Eli?

"What do you mean?" I mumbled, my lips and mouth so dry that I felt like I'd spent months living in the desert, choking on sand.

Khalida turned back towards Eli, waved her hand so that her scythe completely disappeared from sight, and set that hand on his stomach.

I shook my head, convinced that I imagined her weapon's disappearance, but it was gone. There one moment, and then gone the next.

"What are you?" Declan narrowed her eyes, the emerald green glistening through her thick lashes. Even when she was angry and covered in dusty debris and blood, she was absurdly beautiful.

I wasn't sure whether she was talking to me or Khalida, a realization that chilled me to the bone.

"He's healing," Khalida said in response, "and what I am is someone who can help him. And Max, you are helping to heal him too. That is all that is important for now. Expending energy on questions is useless and will only serve to pull energy from him."

That seemed to be all anyone needed to hear. I wasn't exactly sure what I was doing to help heal Eli, but if Khalida thought he stood a chance of coming back from this attack, I was willing to sink into it to the best of my capabilities.

"Is there—is there something specific I should be doing?" I asked as I clung to his fingers with a sort of desperate gentleness.

She tilted her head slightly, studying me with those startlingly black eyes. Carefully, she removed one of her hands from Eli and grabbed one of mine. With a slow precision, she placed it over his eye and cheek. "Stay here, and focus on visualizing the wounds closing. That will be best for now. I will do the rest. And, eventually, hopefully, our combined efforts will succeed."

Her voice was soothing and melodic, and even though the uncertainty and strangeness surrounding her terrified me, I relaxed into her words and did as she said. She had the effect of a gentle balm, like a mother's embrace—or, rather, what I imagined a mother's embrace to be like.

We stayed like that for what felt like hours, though it was probably realistically only a few moments. I closed my eyes, no longer wanting to focus on anyone else in the room. Instead, I pictured Eli. The images came rushing through my mind, from the first moment we met, with his teasing grin, to the moment we shared our first kiss out at his pond, to the intense union in Wade's dreamscape.

The way his eyes always seemed to be filled with clever laughter, the way his lips seemed to be lifted into a permanent smirk, the way his hair was always perfectly messy, the way his lips felt against mine—the rightness of kissing him. I tried desperately to shove the bloodied and pale image of him in front of me away, to delicately but uncompromisingly fold that version of him into the version I knew. The version that was quintessentially Eli.

With my eyes still closed, I moved my hands from his cheek to his lips. They were soft and perfect, even though I knew they were crusted in dried blood. Slowly, I moved my fingers down his chest until they passed Khalida's and rested on his lower ribs and upper stomach.

I wasn't sure why, but something in him seemed to be guiding me there. Or something in Khalida, maybe. I was so desperate for whatever this was to work that I didn't bother questioning it. Questioning would only pull my focus, would only divert my energy, as Khalida had pointed out.

After another few minutes or hours—I couldn't be sure—my breathing felt like it was evening out. Until, eventually, Eli and I were breathing in sync, mirrors of each other that were chaotic at first, and then, slowly, filled with a heady calm.

I felt my body grow more exhausted, which seemed absurd since I'd only been awake for a few hours. Khalida shifted gently next to me, causing a soft ripple of noise that felt so strange in the silence. She'd been so quiet throughout the process that I had almost forgotten she was there.

Was she growing tired too?

Someone behind me inhaled sharply in surprise and I felt Eli start to fidget below me, like he was stirring awake beneath my fingertips.

"Enough now, Max," Khalida whispered as she stood up. She sounded drained and groggy, like she'd been woken from an intense dream she was desperate to claw back onto.

I was familiar enough with those sorts of alarmingly vivid dreams to empathize.

Her hand fell gently on my shoulder but I resisted her pull. Doubling down, I focused on Eli, blocking out the world around us. Pulling each image of him, with all of his personality quirks, even the assholish ones closer to me. Pushing them back into him.

I wasn't sure why, but now that I could feel Eli stirring back to life, healing, I had no desire to stop whatever it was that we were doing. It was almost as if I could feel that there were still more repairs for Khalida to do. I didn't understand why she was pulling back, quitting. He needed her. He needed us.

"Max," she said again, this time with more force behind my name, "you need to stop before you drain yourself. This is dangerous magic to toy with. Especially for one as inexperienced as you. If you go for much longer, you could die."

Her words seemed to drift around me, but they couldn't quite break through. I didn't understand what she was talking about. And, more importantly, I didn't want to stop. We weren't done. She was wrong. She was giving up, stopping too soon.

My shoulders shook, but it was like nothing existed outside of me and Eli. The world around me started to dissolve, my vision blurred, and I could feel that unfamiliar tingling energy beneath my skin again. It was like my blood wasn't liquid but a system of crawling ants bubbling beneath the surface, working to lift pieces of me down a jarring assembly line.

I took a deep breath in, feeling the way my lungs inflated and then deflated, the breaths growing more drawn out with each second that passed.

All at once, my body flew back, my shoulders and head landing against a surface that was somehow both hard and soft. I reached my fingers out towards Eli, an intangible fear licking at my insides when I couldn't feel him anymore. I needed to help him. I couldn't let him die. Why wasn't Khalida helping me anymore? She said we could save him. So why weren't we?

Was she lying?

Disgust filled me the second the thought occurred to me. Of course she was lying. Who'd ever heard of healing someone with nothing but fingers and visualizations before? As if we could fix Eli up by doing nothing but resting our hands against his battered body. He needed doctors. He needed help. We were wasting time with this nonsense.

My stomach clenched with anger as I tried desperately to rip away from whatever or whoever was holding me back. I was part of the reason we hadn't gotten him help sooner. What had we all been thinking? Standing around like that, like we could stitch him up with nothing but our will power and good intentions— with nothing but the desperate hope that he would survive.

I could feel my body shaking, could feel my skin tingling and singing with a foreign, restless energy.

"What's happening to her?" a familiar voice asked. It ricocheted around my head but I couldn't attach it to a face, to a name.

Breath whispered past my ear, and the vice around my stomach tightened even more.

"Fix her," another voice said.

"She's given too much," this one seemed to call to me on a cellular level. It was reaching for me while the others simply reached past me. "You need to calm her down, get her to still. She has to be the one to let go of the power. Only she can stop this right now."

"Max, you need to breathe," the first voice again, filled with a gentle worry.

I turned my head around as my vision clouded and blurred. Until I was staring at a pair of dark brown eyes, streaked through with shades of gold. They were so close and I lost myself in the way one color bled into another. I felt my breathing still momentarily and I settled back, looking up at the eyes that were both familiar and unknown.

My head landed on a firm, muscular chest and I breathed in and out, timing each breath to match the one against my back, until, after a few long moments, I realized that I was in Atlas's arms—that it was his eyes calling to me.

Suddenly all that I could focus on was an acute awareness that his limbs were wrapped around me—his legs around my thighs to keep me still, his arms around my middle, locking mine against my sides. All of his limbs were pulling me back against him.

He was still shirtless, though he thankfully had his pants, and the predator beneath the surface still peered back at me from his eyes.

We stared like that for what felt like forever, our eyes locked on each other, our bodies locked together. It was terrifying and exhilarating and calming.

Everything at once.

"Good, it's working," a soft voice said as I reluctantly pulled my focus from Atlas to stare at its owner. Khalida was kneeling beside us, her eyes were still mysterious and velvety black, but back to their usual form. A warm smile pulled at her lips as her hand reached for mine.

I jumped slightly at the contact, though I wasn't sure what I was afraid of. She squeezed my fingers gently, like we were old friends meeting for the first time in a long while. There was a familiarity to the gesture that raised the hair on my arms.

"You're alright Max. You did well," she said, as her eyes narrowed slightly, making her look more stern, older somehow, "but you must work on your control in the future. You give too freely, too strongly. It will be your demise if you don't learn to harness your energy soon. Power exchange is a complicated process, it can be your undoing if you allow it to be."

She sounded like one of those wise, old creatures from movies and TV shows, not like a girl only a few years older than me. I wasn't entirely sure what she was going on about, but I sank back against Atlas and looked around the room.

Declan stood above us, her expression tense, but not uncaring, as her eyes bounced from me to Atlas to Khalida in quick succession, like she didn't know who was the real threat and where to center her focus or her fear anymore.

Darius leaned against the wall. He still looked worse for wear, but I could tell that his strength was returning to him slowly, even if the normal expression and light behind his eyes was absent. Unlike Declan, it seemed like he couldn't—or wouldn't— look at me. Instead, he was staring off into space, locked in his own battle. His jaw was tensed, his shoulders stiff, his body no longer filled with that lazy carefree posture he always seemed to affect.

And then, as if suddenly remembering, I tore through the room with my gaze until it landed on him.

Eli.

He was awake now, sitting against the wall where he'd fallen, only his posture was straight and the pallor of his face was gone. He was still caked in dried blood and dust from the debris and fallout, but his cuts looked days, maybe even weeks old now. And his eyes weren't filled with that alarming distance and haziness that had been there moments before.

I choked on my breath and unwrapped Atlas's hands from my middle, my fingers shaking with exhilaration as they met his.

For a second, I wasn't sure he would let me go, but after a long moment of resistance, he dropped his legs and his arms and pushed himself back. It was like he went from not wanting to let me go to not getting away from me fast enough, all in one moment.

Ignoring him, I crawled towards Eli and swept my hand over his forehead and cheeks, almost unable to believe my eyes. The cuts were echoes and shadows of what they'd been before. At this rate, he'd be healed back to normal in hours.

But I'd seen what Claude had done to Darius, seen the effects it had on Eli. How was this possible?

"You did this?" I asked as I craned my head back to look at Khalida. What the hell was she? I still couldn't wrap my mind around the idea that a power like hers existed. If we could harness it—if she could teach us how she did it or what she was —we could save countless lives. We didn't need to sacrifice young protectors like we did, didn't need to lose so many, so young, to the demons they battled.

She nodded, bobbing her head up and down once, as her lips tightened into a straight line, like she could sense where my thoughts were going and didn't fully approve. "You did this too, Max."

The realization of her words left my mind filled with a numb emptiness. And suddenly I couldn't bring myself to look Eli, Atlas, Declan, or even Darius in the eyes. Couldn't bear to see the fear or disapproval or disgust that would be written there. Because now I knew with absolute certainty that I wasn't like them. That, in a lot of ways, I recognized parts of myself in Khalida that I hadn't seen, that I wouldn't find, in The Guild.

Shame licked at the back of my throat, down my spine. But there was pride, too. Khalida saved Eli, and by extension she saved Darius too. And I helped. So whatever I was, whatever strange and wrong parts lived inside of me, they couldn't be all bad. Not if they could protect the people I cared about from harm.

"How is it possible that vampire blood can even do this in the first place?" Declan asked, her gaze crossing to Atlas as she stared at him for support. I could see her worldview crashing down around her in the depths of her eyes. "Wouldn't we have known that already? I mean I'm sure that our research teams have fed or injected vamp blood before. They *study* these creatures after all, so I'm sure that includes running countless tests on their blood."

Darius let out a dark chuckle that drew our attention back to him. He glanced past me and narrowed his eyes at Declan like he blamed her for the world burning down around him. "Study is a very loose term for what they do down there."

Khalida's brows turned inward as she glanced at her friend. It looked like she wanted to go to him, to provide comfort, but she didn't know how. Whatever he experienced down in the labs was out of her reach and he was an entirely different person now. I saw the sadness in her eyes, as the gulf between them opened up.

"They've taken our blood and studied it under microscopes, sure. But blood bonds have to be willingly given and taken directly from the vein. It is a magic that does not work without consent or intention. I'm sure there was a period where they had subjects ingest the blood to see what would happen, to see if it had any curative properties." He shrugged nonchalantly, his brow arching, "but they then likely killed the vampire without a thought. And in the process, killed their own, none the wiser. Your kind is not only a cruel species, but an unintelligent one as well. I'm not surprised they've never learned whatever it is that they are searching for in those labs."

My stomach felt impossibly heavy as I realized how accurate that assessment probably was. Even if protectors did somehow learn about the power behind blood bonds, I doubted they would willingly chain their lives to the very creatures they swore to destroy, the very beasts they loathed with every fiber of their being. Many protectors would rather die a thousand deaths than make that kind of concession.

"And these bonds, they last until you both die?" I asked, glad for the temporary distraction from whatever was going on with me. It was much easier to focus my attention on Darius and Eli, even on Khalida.

Darius nodded, meeting my eyes for the first time since I exited my trance. For a moment, I couldn't look away. It was like I was seeing him for the first time, recognizing myself in him. Both of us were misfits, outcast and different from the groups to which we were supposed to belong. Neither of us fit. Perhaps this was why he'd always seemed so intrigued by me—he saw himself.

I cleared my throat, trying to shake away the strange connection. "Why would you do it?"

"Doesn't matter now, does it, little protector?" he grinned, leaning into the bite of that nickname. Had he always known that I wasn't quite what I thought I was? He'd teased sure, but had he been certain? "What's done is done, and now your protector and I will be latched to the grave—however close it may be."

"There will be time in the future, to discuss things," Khalida said, standing now that she had more of her energy back, "hopefully. But for now, the sooner you all can leave, the better things will be for you. I can't protect you forever, and neither can Claude."

"More like he won't," Darius said with a grunt of disgust.

Khalida's eyes hardened on him and my eyes widened with shock when I saw him sink back into the wall, like he was chastised by just one glance. Who was this girl? Why did the Fang Twins cower in her presence?

"Have a meal, clean up and rest if you can, and then meet back in this room within two hours. I will have convinced

Claude to escort you all safely by then." She turned towards me and grabbed my hand in hers again. I followed her pull a few feet away and strained to hear as she whispered into my ear, "I don't know what you are Max Bentley, but there is a dangerous power in you. I can't define it, but I can sense it. And it is imperative that you learn to harness and control it before it destroys you and those you care about. This, above all else, should be your primary mission."

She squeezed my hand with a gentle pressure before turning and leaving through the door.

The second she was gone, I turned and stared at the ground, not quite able to meet anyone's eyes, until my vision was blocked by a sturdy body.

Eli wrapped his arms around me and squeezed. "Thank you, love. For whatever you did, even if we don't quite understand it yet. I won't forget."

My throat choked up, like it was trying to swallow an iron ball, and I felt tears slowly begin to coat my eyes. He wasn't disgusted by me, wasn't afraid of me. He was thankful. Maybe even glad I was different, if only for this one moment. I looked at him, blinking until the image of him went from blurry to clear. Familiar.

I nodded, unable to form words with my own gratitude.

Eli turned away from me and scratched awkwardly at the back of his neck. "And er, thank you too, vamp. You didn't have to do what you did. And I don't understand why you decided to go and tie your life to mine. Only thing that comes to mind is that they scrambled your brains even more than we realized down in that dungeon." He cleared his throat and paused briefly, "I mean, sorry. I'm sure your brains are perfectly fine. Better than average, even."

I stifled my own laugh, caught up in the absurdity of the moment as Eli pulled me to his side and draped a heavy arm over my shoulder.

"Whatever the reason, thank you. And I'll—er—try not to

die anytime soon," he finished with an awkward shrug before mussing up my hair and turning from the room. "Going to go shower some of this gore off of me before we go plunging into the depths of hell, I guess."

The room was silent for a long moment as the four of us who remained eyed each other warily, none of us exactly clear where we stood with each other anymore.

Declan glanced at me, her face warming slightly with a small smile, before she walked towards the door. "Whatever happened there took a lot out of you, Max. I'll go scavenge for something in the kitchen before I pack up our items."

Atlas nodded once before following her out the door, leaving me alone with Darius.

"Are you alright?" I asked, eyeing the dried blood coating his face. I felt uncomfortable suddenly, uncertain how to be alone with the creature in front of me. And equally uncertain how to be alone with myself.

He winked before stumbling in my direction, replacing his arm where Eli's was one minute before, and directing us towards the door. I stumbled as I fell over a pile of splintered wood. As I steadied myself, with Darius's help, I glanced around the room. Glass and furniture parts littered the floor. I gasped in amazement that in the chaos of the last few minutes, I'd almost forgotten about the fact that he and his brother had all but brought the ceiling down upon us all.

"You healed me up some when you healed Eli. Not all the way, mind you, but enough. So I'll live," there was a hollowness in his words as he danced around my real question.

We both knew that he'd live. He was a vampire, difficult to kill. I was mostly asking about how he was doing mentally. I'd watched as he battled through whatever darkness lingered inside of him, watched as the rage and bloodthirst seeped from his eyes.

He squeezed my shoulder gently as he walked us towards the kitchen, weaving casually down the labyrinth of halls, and I relaxed some. It was a small sign, but somehow I knew that's what it was—a sign.

He wasn't completely back to his normal headspace, as chaotic as it was, but he was on his way. And for now, that meant he was alright enough.

10

MAX

Food helped everything. And after filling up on enough steak and potatoes to fill a small family, I was seeing the world with a new, crisp clarity.

Things weren't exactly back to normal by any means, but we all seemed to have entered into a silent agreement that we wouldn't linger too much on what happened between me, Khalida, and Eli. With an impending trip into hell, and a moody twin vampire to deal with, we had enough on our plates without adding to the drama.

Once we were all relatively rested, packed, and full, Khalida dragged Claude into the entryway.

His eyes narrowed as he studied the five of us, and while I could see the depths of hatred that lingered there, he remained silent.

Khalida gently patted his shoulder, like he was a child getting up the nerve to apologize to his enemy. He stood still, glowering instead, which she seemed to take as apology enough.

And honestly, since he hadn't tried killing Eli or his brother again, maybe she was right.

"I have a feeling we'll all be seeing each other quite soon," she said, a genuine grin splitting her face.

I remembered the fear on everyone's face when she brandished her scythe around, and could still almost feel the tingling of her power calling to me. It was strange then, that the gentle and sweet girl in front of me was one and the same.

She walked up to me, her lips turning down slightly as she studied Ralph. He was lying at my feet, gnawing on a bone he'd found somewhere. I was too afraid that it might belong to a human to question where he'd gotten it. Who knew what sorts of things were lying around in this house. As beautiful as it was, I was still under no illusion that the inhabitants were benign.

"I don't recommend that the hellhound join you on your journey." She bent down to scratch behind his ears, earning a slobbery grunt in return. There was a warmth in her eyes when she looked at Ralph, and that, more than anything, confused me entirely. I didn't understand where the good guys stopped and the bad guys started anymore—good and evil just suddenly seemed so blurred and muddled.

"I thought you said that the hell realm was dangerous," Declan said, stepping up next to me so that the length of her arm pressed lightly against mine. My body relaxed at the contact. "Wouldn't it be best if we had all the power on our side that we could muster? " She glanced down at Ralph, her stare firm and confident. "And while he might look and even occasionally act like a puppy, he's pretty damn powerful. Probably just as powerful as the rest of us combined, if I'm being honest."

"The hell realm is dangerous," Darius said, his eyes locked on his brother's as if he was waiting for him to spring, assessing each and every muscle twitch, "probably even more so than I remember. But hellhounds are rare creatures, even there."

Khalida nodded, her face softening slightly with worry as she looked up at him. I wondered, briefly, what her relationship with the two vampires was. There was genuine warmth in the way that she looked at and treated Darius and Claude, and my stomach clenched at the realization that she might be part of the reason they despised each other. Had they both been in love with her? Was she the reason they hated each other with such passion? From the looks of things, it seemed that Claude won that battle, considering she was living with him now.

My stomach tightened at the thought, and I tried to push the unknown emotion clogging up my chest away.

"Exactly," she said, turning back to Declan and shaking me out of my spiraling thoughts. "Hell is a dangerous place for all creatures, but even more so for protectors. Everyone you encounter will be your enemy. Even the creatures who aren't usually filled with malice or bloodthirst."

"You're afraid that walking around with Ralph will draw too much attention," Atlas said, and I could feel him shift position to my other side. His tone was calm, objective, and I could tell that he was in protector mode. Surprisingly, he seemed to trust Khalida's word and suggestion.

Khalida beamed, like he was her star pupil, her eyes dancing with mischief. "You're a smart one, wolf."

There was a flirtatious teasing in her tone that caused my skin to prickle. I dug my fingernails into my palm as they locked eyes, only releasing some of the tension when Atlas glanced down at me, brow arched in curiosity.

I felt my cheeks heating under his scrutiny, so I pulled my focus away from him and back to Khalida. "So you want us to leave him here. With you?"

The words came out sharper than I'd intended, and the brief flash of surprised pain on her face, had me instantly regretting my tone. She was terrifying as fuck, and I had no idea what kind of creature she was, but I couldn't forget the fact that she'd welcomed us here. That she'd saved Eli and tried to make all of us feel at home, even while we were living with Claude.

"Hellhounds do as they please," Claude said, his voice gruff as he broke his silence for the first time. "If he wants to hang around with Khali, he will. Otherwise, he'll go wherever he wants to go. We don't keep intelligent creatures as prisoners. We aren't monsters."

None of us missed the accusation, and I glanced at Darius to see his reaction. He was, after all, a prisoner. And the only reason he was helping us now was because we bribed him with the promise of freedom.

"If he senses you're in need," Khalida said quickly, like she was trying to disseminate a bomb before it exploded, "and if he truly is your familiar, then he will come. But it is safer for you, and for him, if he remains hidden until then. As your powers develop, so will his. That is how these relationships work. And, while Ralph, as you call him, is remarkably powerful in comparison to the creatures you are used to engaging with, he is actually quite young for his species. I will keep him company in the meantime, if he so wishes." Her face lit with a small smile as she ran her fingers over his head. "I've always loved dogs."

As if in response, Ralph licked playfully at her palm, which served to only highlight her warning. He resembled a puppy so much because, in a lot of ways, he still was one.

"If he's relatively weak for his species, I'd hate to run into a full-grown hellhound," Eli said, like he was reading my mind. "Still, we'll miss having you around, little guy." Eli patted him awkwardly before he stood up and rubbed his hands together. "Alright, shall we be off to hell?"

I might have been seeing things, but I was fairly certain that Claude actually rolled his eyes at that before he turned and walked out the door.

Seeing my chance slip away, I wrapped my arms around Ralph's neck and squeezed. "I'll be back for you, I promise. Just lie low and be safe in the meantime."

"You be safe too," Khalida said, her voice a soft whisper near my ears. "It can be a tricky thing—figuring out who you can and cannot trust. Choose wisely, especially once you're through the portal." She shook her head as if changing her mind. "On second thought, I caution against folding your trust completely into any being you encounter there, even the one you're trying to save."

I shivered at her warning, even though agreeing to it was a

pretty simple thing. I hadn't intended on trusting any of the creatures we might come across in hell, except for Wade. And while Khalida seemed wise beyond her years, she didn't know Wade. I could trust him. Of that I was certain.

Not wanting to be rude, I nodded once before glancing towards the door. Atlas was standing just outside, waiting for me. The rest of our team stood awkwardly behind him.

His team. He'd made it clear that I would never belong with them many times.

But did I want to? More and more I was noticing how well we worked together, how our personalities and abilities complemented each other.

No. I was always destined to join a team with Ro—he would always be the person who made me feel like home.

Khalida arched her brow as she watched Atlas, her somber goodbye melting into a smirk. "Something tells me you're in for an amusing adventure, Max. I truly wish that I could join you all as you embark on it. And not many things could make me yearn for a trip into hell."

Her comment was coy and suggestive, as was the way she kept looking at Atlas. I was suddenly filled with gaping relief that she wouldn't be joining us—a sentiment I buried as far down as it could go. I most definitely did *not* have the capacity to argue with my brain about how very bad of an idea it was to think of Atlas in any terms quite so...intimate.

"Thank you," I said, as I gave one final squeeze and kiss to Ralph. "You've been very helpful and warm."

I surprised myself by actually meaning those words. In some ways, she reminded me of Izzy—more guarded and mysterious perhaps, but filled with the same sort of open kindness. If I met her in any other circumstance, if she wasn't whatever it was that she was, we might actually become very good friends.

Her smile brightened, as if she too sensed the sincerity in my farewell. "It was my pleasure. I don't often get the opportunity to meet new people. Claude likes to keep me ferreted away. A bit protective, these vampire brothers."

Hearing her jab, Darius pressed his hands to his chest as if she'd wounded him.

"Keep an eye on him, Max," she whispered, her words so soft that I had to strain to hear them. "He's strong, even for a vampire, but he doesn't have the control that he needs to survive there. And I don't kn—" her voice broke softly, like she was choking back tears, "I count very much on the continued existence of these brothers. I would be quite lost if either of them were killed."

I nodded, once again filled with an almost painful curiosity about her relationship with them. I knew so little about Darius —and as much as I could pretend that I wanted to keep it that way, I knew with absolute certainty that I did not.

Her face brightened once more before she turned her attention to Darius and ran at him until she collapsed against his chest, her arms around his neck.

He squeezed her back and while I could tell that they were sharing some parting words, I couldn't hear what they were.

Their embrace was so familiar, intimate in a way that made me feel like I was trespassing on a scene that wasn't meant for me. I averted my eyes and, rather than waiting for them to separate, I walked out of the old house and into the night.

"YOU MEAN TO TELL ME," ELI SAID, HIS ARMS CROSSED IN front of his chest, annoyance on his face, "that the portal to hell was through your shitty ass bar this whole time? What the actual fuck?"

Claude turned around slowly, his fist closed tight and his jaw muscles so tense I was certain he was going to pop something. The vamp was a walking cliche of anger.

"By which I meant to say, very nice bar. Best bar I've been to in a long time. Top notch, really," Eli added quickly, his voice pitched a few notches higher as he looked everywhere but at Claude's eyes.

Darius slapped his hand down roughly on Eli's back before inching his body between ours. "Now that your life is tied to mine, how about you at least pretend to try preserving it, yeah? At least for a day or two?"

We were standing in front of the now-familiar bar. Claude simply nodded to the doorman before ushering the rest of us through. Marge was working behind the counter again and when she saw all of us spill around the bartop, her mouth dropped open.

"You sure this is the best idea, boss? After what happened the last time this lot was in here, might not be a good look. Don't exactly want our patrons thinking this is a protector joint now do we?" Her voice was low and hushed, and while she'd seemed so jovial and welcoming the first time I'd met her, there was a dark cast to the way she looked us all up and down now. The lines around her mouth and eyes that spoke of a jovial spirit when we met, now seemed to reflect fear and anxiety. "I don't want anyone coming after you like they did Darius, is all."

Claude exhaled on a soft chuckle. "Don't think anyone who comes into this bar is under the illusion that they stand a chance against me, Marge. My brother and his new band of friends will be here for only a moment. We're just heading out back."

If she was surprised by our arrival, then she was downright shocked by the thought of us going out back. Her ruddy green eyes dulled as she looked at him. "You can't really mean—"

"Not something for you to concern yourself with," Claude said, cutting her off. He nodded towards the room in the back and we all followed.

I didn't miss the regret that carved lines in her expression as she watched Darius follow.

A second before he was out of reach, she shot her hand out to grab his, her short red hair bouncing from her rushed movement. "I can't make you reconsider?" She paused a beat and waited for Darius to shake his head in response. Her face fell when he did, her eyes wide with a profoundly sad concern. She shook her head, eyes glazing over with unshed tears. "You're a reckless, reckless boy."

She didn't say it unkindly, more like the way a mother might chastise her son for doing something that brought him harm; it was the sort of statement filled with regret, with abject, terrifying powerlessness.

He brought his palm up to her face in a move that appeared so tender and heartfelt I almost forgot that he was a bloodsucking vampire whom I'd watched snap a protector's neck with little thought or concern. "I'll be okay." He winked before adding, "I'm pretty tough to kill. Keep an eye on this place." He turned, like he was finished talking before he thought better of it and spun around again. "And keep an eye on him, will you? He's too tense. Needs to live a little."

She tsked softly before tapping him playfully on the cheek. Without another word, she turned back to tend to her customers. The bar wasn't exactly full, but I spotted several guys waving her down for a refill.

I scanned the room, looking at the few dozen tables and stools, most of which were filled with people huddled over pint glasses and shots. How many of them were vampires and were-wolves? Villette didn't seem to be present tonight.

It was strange how much the scene resembled ones I'd seen countless times at the restaurants and bars from back home on the mountain and back at Guild Headquarters. I had to remind myself that these weren't just humans or protectors out enjoying a night with family and friends. That a whole group of them had attacked us only a few nights ago.

That they had almost killed me and my friends.

That no matter how innocent or human they looked to me now, they were anything but.

I spun that reminder on repeat as I followed the group,

desperate for it to grab hold in my mind, for it to feel unflinchingly true. More and more, I could feel myself pulling away from The Guild—questioning everything I'd ever been taught about the supernatural world. And I wasn't entirely certain that I was ready to have my entire universe turned upside down. Not when there was so much at stake.

We disappeared through the door behind the bar, winding through a dark hall that was lined with a series of closed doors until we made our way to the very end. It seemed like such a typical bar. Maybe a bit larger on the back end, with all of the mysterious rooms, but typical in all other ways. The walls were lined with a deep wood paneling, the carpet a plush red.

Maybe they'd chosen that color to disguise all of the blood shed? I shook the gruesome thought away and tried to refocus on what we were doing—on where we were going.

Claude inhaled deep and slow, like he was preparing himself for what lay behind the heavy metal door. For the first time since I'd known him, some of his calm slipped away to an emotion other than anger. If I didn't know better, I'd say that there was a sort of sadness in the hunch of his shoulders, in the guardedness of his eyes.

"Why exactly is the portal to hell located at the back of a Seattle bar? Seems kind of like a strange place, no?" I asked, drawing my attention away from Claude and whatever sympathy was stirring in my gut. I turned to Darius, my skin buzzing with the tension of the moment. We were going to walk through some mystical portal and land our asses in a world filled with our enemies. And we were doing it on purpose. While I knew that was the goal from the moment we left The Guild, I hadn't let the fear and realization settle in until now. Not exactly great timing. "I thought you said that you weren't certain where the portal was?"

I didn't mean for my tone to sound like it was filled with accusation, but if my brother worked so close to a hellgate, I'd make damn sure I was aware of it.

Darius shrugged, not at all phased by my rambling. "I wasn't. It moves. This time it's apparently gone and attached itself to the bar."

"The portal is unstable," Claude said, though I could tell he was holding something back, telling us only half truths. "It goes where it can latch onto power, where it can both control and be controlled. Right now, that location is here."

"Seems like a dire business plan," Eli said with a dry laugh, "your kind doesn't exactly speak fondly of hell, so I imagine it can't be great for business—your customers having the potential to get sucked into another realm while guzzling down a pint."

Darius cleared his throat like he was uncomfortable with where the conversation was going. It was strange, as he generally seemed to embrace the awkward and uncomfortable with a weird, sadistic relish. But where Claude and his old life were concerned, he seemed to take on a wholly different persona.

"Let's stop the chatter and speculation and get on with it," he said, sweeping his arm in a gesture for his brother to open the door.

When he did, the heavy breath I inhaled spilled out in an anticlimactic sputter. It just appeared to be a vaguely rundown back patio, with grass growing between cracks in the concrete. There were a few forgotten beer bottles littering the ground and when Claude flipped a switch, a buzzing, flickering light cast the small area in a soft glow.

"Not exactly what I was expecting," I said, as I craned my neck around, half-expecting to see some whirl of light or fire that led to the depths of hell. Why did everyone seem so frightened of...this? "Kind of looks like any old back patio."

Claude turned towards me, his eyes narrow, but stiff. "It's meant to appear non-threatening. Can't exactly have a mystical force field drawing attention to every creature who walks by it. Would make gatekeeping it a big problem, wouldn't it?"

His spine straightened as he glanced around, and while I didn't know the vampire well, he seemed more tense than usual, like he desperately wanted to turn around and close the door, to abandon this lackluster alleyway as quickly as possible.

His fangs descended in a quick, fluid movement. My breath stopped and I was momentarily convinced that this whole thing was one elaborate ruse; that he'd turn on us all, now that we were outside of a building filled with his friends.

The logical part of my brain knew this wasn't the case, knew that if he'd wanted to, he could have killed us all back in his home. But fear was a fickle fuck that loved playing mind games and distorting reason.

He arched a brow, like he knew exactly where my mind had gone, before he pressed his fangs into the fleshy part of his palm.

I watched, fascinated as deep red blood pooled in his hand. I stood, entranced, as he took a few steps towards the back of the alley, and swept his hand delicately around, like he was caressing an invisible wall.

His blood-streak stuck, like a smear in midair and then was quickly absorbed, like the air was nothing more than a hungry sponge. He breathed in deeply, like the cut actually drained some of his energy—a false notion if ever I'd had one. I'd just watched him demolish his entire living room in a blood-filled pissing contest with his brother after all.

I blinked, confused, as the air seemed to shimmer, like it was contained by plastic wrap that was blowing softly in the wind. And then, just as I convinced myself that what I was seeing wasn't simply my brain playing funny tricks, the air stilled, and a quiet, hushed whisper filled the atmosphere around us, calling us forward, before quieting altogether.

Claude took a few hurried steps back, studying the area he'd just been standing on with a deep focus. Then, with a swift kick, he lodged one of the empty beer bottles towards the brick wall at the farthest spot from the door and my mouth fell open as I watched it disappear completely from sight, swallowed by air or an invisible force, at the exact spot he'd offered his blood.

Satisfied that this was the spot, Atlas took a few steps

forward. I could feel the adrenaline coiling off his skin as he studied the area where the bottle no longer sat. "We just walk through? Is that all there is to it?"

When Claude nodded, Atlas turned back towards the rest of us and exhaled softly, running a hand through his messy black hair.

"Anyone can turn back now if they want," he glanced quickly at Darius, his lips tightening slightly, like he was debating the next part of his speech. "That includes you vamp. We got you out, you got us here. We can call it even if you want to cut your losses and go do whatever it is that you do with your time."

Eli stepped forward next to Atlas and gripped his shoulder in that bro way guys always pulled off. "Can't get rid of me that easily, my friend. Like I'd give up on the opportunity of chasing baddies in hell."

Declan nodded, no mirth in her expression as she locked eyes with Atlas. "You and Wade are my brothers in every way but blood. I'm going."

Atlas's jaw tightened as he looked at his two teammates, and I could see the strange bond that connected them all.

I was filled with an unrecognizable longing—to be connected with them in that way. I'd experienced something similar with Ro, of course. And Izzy and I had grown close in a really short amount of time. But to be a part of a team, to have someone's back and them have mine, no matter what reckless or ridiculous things we got into.

To belong.

I cleared my throat, shoving the rising emotion back down. I'd get back to my family after this if it was the last thing I did, but I wasn't backing down now. "I'm in too."

Beyond finding Wade, beyond using my dreams as a way to uncover our path to him, I was enthralled by the idea of exploring hell. For some reason that I couldn't quite understand, I'd felt a pull towards that bottle as it disappeared from sight. A strange desire to chase after it was building and building, like I needed to explore whatever it was that lurked on the other side.

I'd learned so much in my short time with The Guild, but if the last few days taught me anything, it was that I didn't know nearly as much as I needed to—not about this world of supernaturals and, more importantly, not about myself.

Something in my gut told me that the answers I needed would be through this invisible portal, hidden in the backyard of an old dive bar. Maybe I was just being naive, but I couldn't back away from that intuition.

Darius stepped up next to me, his lean build towering over mine. His eyes fell on mine as he answered Atlas. "I'll be seeing this through. Not least of all because I want to make sure all aspects of our bargain are held up."

Atlas glanced at me, his expression filled with steel as he took in Darius's statement.

My stomach dipped as I stared up at him. In all of the strangeness of our journey, I'd almost forgotten about my particular role in our bargain. That if we survived our descent into hell, if we rescued Wade from the shadow creature or the man who'd kidnapped him in the first place, that everyone would return to The Guild.

Everyone except for me. I'd made a promise to Darius that if we were successful, if we survived, that I would stay with him. At least for a while. An agreement I made, having no idea what exactly it was that he even wanted with me in the first place.

I nodded, a silent acknowledgement that I hadn't forgotten our bargain.

Darius's face split in a peculiarly chipper grin as he walked towards the brick wall. "In that case," he said, glancing quickly at his brother, "we'd best be off."

With a teasing salute, he winked at me and took a large step back.

Declan and I let out a mirrored breath of surprise as he disappeared from sight.

It was strange. I was a protector. I grew up knowing that vampires and werewolves were real. I was training to hunt all of the monsters that went bump in the night. I knew that the hell realm existed, that it's where the beasts come from.

But to see the magic take shape before my eyes felt like a peculiar dream. Everything suddenly felt real, more tangible somehow.

Claude cleared his throat and I saw the muscles in his jaw pumping as he stared at the spot where his brother disappeared. Something told me that he didn't expect to ever see his twin again. And while he'd spent part of the afternoon attempting to kill him, I knew that their relationship wasn't as clear as we'd thought. It was a mixture of love and hate and everything else in between.

With nothing more than a quick glance at each other, Eli and Declan followed Darius, leaving me alone with Atlas and Claude —the two most intimidating men I'd ever encountered.

My skin felt tight as the air around us all grew heavy with tension. Desperate for Eli's or hell, even Darius's dark humor to lighten the mood, I took a quick step in the direction of the portal, ready to chase after them and swallow my fate whole.

A harsh grip tightened around my wrist, stopping me mid stride. I turned around and found Claude hovering over me, his lean fingers digging into my forearm but not enough to bruise.

"My brother is fixated on you. That much is clear. But you'll do well to remember exactly what he is." His tone was hard, monotonous, and he wasn't looking me in the eyes.

I swallowed, unsure how to respond, but unable to look away from the sharp angles of his face all the same.

"Those people broke something in his mind—a mind that was already a complicated place to spend time in before them. He's a predator and he's dangerous. Forgetting that will not serve you or whatever strange destiny you have before you."

"Why are you telling me this?" I squinted up at him,

watching as his breath hitched slightly at the question. "Why do you care?"

Claude quirked one side of his lips in the shadow of a smirk that made him look more like Darius than any of his mirrored features did. He glanced down at me, his mismatched eyes boring into my own. "I don't care. But I don't understand you—what you are. And I've spent enough time tied to hell to know that the energy containing it is stretched too thin. And the tether tying everything together grows more tenuous by the day. Our world is on the precipice of a big change, and I have a sneaking suspicion that you will be at the center of it. I don't know what your role is, or why Khali and my brother are so intrigued by you, but I do know that you should watch your back. It's not too late for you to turn away, to leave all of this and this ridiculous mission behind."

I glanced over at Atlas; his eyes were lined in gold, all of his focus drawn to the spot where Claude's skin touched mine.

I tore my gaze from him and shook my head. "I'm going."

Claude loosened his grip until his fingers fell away one-by-one. "As you wish. Just don't be surprised if what you find there isn't what you expected. And be aware of the fact that you may very well be walking into your own doom." He let out a sigh and, for a moment, seemed softer than he had before. I wouldn't say that it was compassion radiating from his expression exactly, but something close to it. "It is your fate. Navigate it how you will. I've done my due diligence in warning you."

I ripped my focus from him as Atlas walked towards us. The gold in his eyes was lighter now and he threaded his fingers through mine, pulling me away from Claude. My skin felt electric in the places that it grazed his. And I hated the way that proximity to him seemed to make my heart rage against my ribcage, like it was desperate to get out, or worse, get closer to him.

With a last look at Claude I nodded. "Thanks for, er," I looked around momentarily, like the small patch of land might give me something concrete to say. It didn't. "Not killing any of us, I guess. Even though you tried. Hopefully if we meet again, you'll continue with that approach." I paused a beat, clearing my throat. "To be clear, I meant that I hope you continue with the not killing us approach, not the trying to one."

Claude didn't move, but something told me from the way his eyes were glistening, that he was swallowing back a grin.

I shrugged before turning back towards the brick wall, gripping Atlas's hand tightly in mine. I hated that I was afraid of walking into the portal alone. Part of me was filled with fear that this wasn't actually a portal into hell—that we'd land somewhere worse somehow, or separated from each other altogether.

As if sensing my anxiety Atlas pulled my body closer to his and stepped through the invisible barrier into the unknown abyss. I wasn't sure why, but having him next to me felt safe somehow, like we could—and would—accomplish what we were after.

I heard Claude chuckling behind us, his voice trailing off as I followed Atlas. "You are intriguing, Max Bentley. For that reason alone, I hope that you aren't stepping towards your death."

At first, there was nothing, I heard nothing and saw nothing. The portal was simply absence. There was no sound, not even my own heartbeat or breath. Just empty. It was the most terrifying thing I'd ever heard.

I found myself clinging with a childish desperation to Atlas, drawing closer so that our hands weren't the only place of contact. Instead, I circled my arms around his waist, grounding myself by pressing against him. For a long, whirlwind of a moment, I almost deluded myself into feeling safe in his arms.

11

DECLAN

My heart beat so quickly that I was certain it was on the edge of exploding. The heavy drum of it rang in my head like a countdown to my final moments. What a ridiculous way to die—bounding into a portal opened by a damn vampire and his creepy magical blood. What the hell were we thinking?

A heady flash of light blinked so brightly that I could see it even through my closed eyelids. A swirl of movement that I felt rather than saw had me feeling so dizzy that it took everything I had not to throw up. A sharp, piercing whistle penetrated my ear drums, so loud I wasn't sure I would even call it a sound at all—it seemed like a trivial word for the thing cascading through my skull like an ice pick.

Just when I thought I would pass out, that my brain would burst from the pressure, everything quieted. With a heavy thud, my knees hit a hard, jagged surface, my hands following seconds after.

Rocks dug into the flesh of my palms and I could feel my blood being absorbed into them, like a sacrifice to the land or, more accurately, an unwilling offering.

After watching the vamp open up the portal, it probably shouldn't have surprised me that hell was a blood-hungry place.

If that's where we even were. I still wasn't totally sure, if I was being honest.

But if we were in hell, what made us think that the realm would allow protectors inside in the first place? None of our kind had ever gained entry before, as far I could tell. It was part of the reason the lab was so desperate to find answers, to get to the bottom of where and how the monsters breached the barriers in the first place. At least Atlas stood a chance—the one benefit of being a werewolf was probably that he wouldn't be outright ejected from hell.

Then again, I didn't know that I would actually consider that a benefit.

And Max—well, I wasn't sure what the hell she was but I knew for damn certain that she wasn't just a protector. I wondered if the rest of The Guild had any idea. Did Cyrus and Seamus know? Had they willingly encouraged us to watch after some sort of demon? Put all of us in danger? Gotten us attached to a creature we might be forced to eventually kill?

I exhaled sharply, remembering the way she lit the room on fire with nothing but her mind. She'd saved Eli, sure, but it was clear she had no idea what she was doing with her powers, if she even realized she had powers in the first place.

I hadn't decided yet if the whole naive innocence thing was for real or if she was playing a part in some grand master plan to take us all down.

I'd been so close to—

I shook my head, tossing my hair around my shoulders. I did not want to explore that line of thought any longer. I'd rather brave whatever beasts hell was going to throw at me than try and validate any winding paths my mind wanted to carve out for me where Max was concerned.

New plan.

Find Wade. Save Wade. Get us all the hell out of...hell. And then figure out the rest when we weren't fighting off creatures that were aching to watch us die.

Surviving long enough to do all of that was the first thing I needed to focus on. The creepy demon at the bar, Marge, seemed to be able to sniff out species. I just had to hope that we didn't run into any of her kind while we were here. If we did, we'd be screwed. Especially me and Eli. Since we were, all of a sudden, the only two protectors in the group left.

I was going to kill him if it turned out that Eli was a secret banshee or something.

Carefully, I opened my eyes. I had to wait a moment for things to adjust, the way your eyes have to readjust to your surroundings after you've been staring into the sun for too long. It took a moment for the contrast to balance out a bit, but I didn't catch any movement other than the blurry light dots around me, so I assumed we were safe. For now anyway.

While it was dark when we entered the vamp's bar, the land surrounding me seemed to be glowing slightly from a distant atmospheric light source, though I couldn't exactly see anything in the sky like a sun. And since no protector had ever made it to hell and demons remained notoriously tight-lipped about the place, we knew next to nothing about what we'd find here.

I pushed off the ground, which appeared to be made out of a burnt orangish-brown rock, and wiped the gravel and blood off on my pants. There was already an angry hole in my knees from the landing and I was far from naive enough to think my favorite pair of pants would be the only casualty of this journey.

It looked like we landed in a ruddy desert of rocky hills. The whole place seemed dried up and dead, like it'd been baking in the sun for too long.

I couldn't catch much in the horizon ahead of me, and while I wouldn't say it looked like we were still in the human realm, this place also didn't scream fire and brimstone either. More like somewhere in between the two. Which, seeing as I wasn't immediately swallowed up by lava or a river of dead souls, I guess this was as good as I could reasonably hope for.

Maybe this was purgatory? Such a place didn't actually exist in our history, but maybe there was something to the human theory. This place certainly looked like what I imagined nature's waiting room would look like.

I craned my neck around, hoping to spot Atlas so that we could start forming a plan, when my lips parted on a gasp.

I was so not a gasping sort of girl. But when I turned around, I expected to at the very least get sight of Eli trying to recalibrate his equilibrium on impact or, hell, even the obnoxious vamp we'd been carting around standing over us with that smug look of his plastered across his face.

I did not, however, expect to find myself alone.

Utterly and completely alone.

I spun slowly in a circle, like maybe I'd see somebody if I took a steady breath and just, I don't know, looked.

But after a few minutes of spinning like a goddamn ballerina, I realized the truth: that while I'd clearly made it through the portal, it was entirely possible that they hadn't.

My breath was coming out in quick bursts and, even though I could feel my lungs expanding and contracting, it felt like all the air had been sucked out of me. I crouched low and dropped my head into my hands as I tried to remember with a desperate focus exactly what the fuck had happened.

I wasn't the only one to go through the portal. We'd all watched the vamp stumble through first, aloof and infuriating, even then.

And then what?

Did Max go through next? Atlas?

I shook my head, like I was having a conversation with myself—probably because I was.

Eli and I went next. I was almost positive that we took the leap together, him maybe even half a step ahead of me as we walked through the creepy invisible wall.

So where the hell was he?

I stood up again, too fast this time and I nearly fell back down as the blood rushed through my body. I tried to force slow, steady breaths in. I'd had enough of them to know that if I didn't calm down a bit, I was a hair's breadth away from a panic attack. And a panic attack while unguarded in the heart of enemy territory was just all sorts of bad.

Okay, so it was just entirely possible that I'd gone and gotten myself stranded in hell. Solo. With no way out.

I would deal. Or at least I'd try. Because one thing was certain, I wasn't going down without a fight.

I willed my heartbeat to regulate and I took in my surroundings. This place was unnaturally quiet. I didn't know if it's because all of the human media subconsciously made me buy into the whole screams-of-agony-and-never-ending-torture thing, but it almost felt like hell was the absence of sound. There weren't any creatures around yelling in pain, or buildings collapsing under a wave of fire. It was just...empty.

And I wasn't expecting it to look like a slightly distorted and exaggerated version of the sort of rocky terrain you could find in the Dakotas.

Nothing seemed to be moving as far as I could tell either. I inhaled deeply, expecting to smell sulfur or some other unpleasant scent, but it just smelled like the outdoors. Maybe with a touch of smoke, but nothing that I wasn't used to.

I didn't know whether to be freaked out or mollified by the fact that this place didn't seem to align with my expectations.

Satisfied that I wasn't in any immediate danger at least, I started to walk. Part of me was torn between searching and staying, on the off chance that Eli or Atlas or even Max would eventually show up to join me on this spot. But the isolation getting to me and I half convinced myself that something happened to them all while I was crossing over.

Maybe they got here first and something captured them?

And when it came to choosing between doing something to

protect my friends and standing around waiting for the other shoe to drop, I was definitely a proud supporter of opting for the former.

Maybe the portal wasn't entirely linear. Maybe they got tossed to another location close by. My landing didn't exactly scream friendly and planned. And the fang twins did mention that the portal was unstable and had a tendency to move around. Maybe spitting us all out in different spots was part of it?

Satisfied with the hope that that was a very real possibility, I made quick work of covering the plain. I cringed every time my feet landed too harshly and disrupted some rocks, creating a loud, cascading echo around me. It wasn't exactly stealth mode to sound like a small stampede, and on the off chance that some demon was lurking nearby, it was best to keep quiet.

I walked for what felt like half an hour, maybe even longer. The dryness in the air, mixed with a faint scent of smoke, had my body begging for some water. I dug through my bag and my stomach sank when I saw that my water bottle was almost empty. Why hadn't I filled it properly before leaving? I tapped the last few dregs onto my tongue and kept walking. It wasn't enough. It wasn't nearly enough.

Did hell have water? Or food that we could consume?

I shook my head as I tied my hair up into a ponytail. We didn't exactly think this whole thing through very well. Seamus would have our heads—not only for going on an unsanctioned mission—to hell of all places—but for being thoroughly unprepared for the endeavor as well. The constant surprises since leaving Headquarters had shaken us—more than we'd prepared for.

We were better than this. Hell, we were one of the best field teams The Guild had to offer. And I worked my ass off to make sure that I was worthy of my team—that I could protect my friends and operate at full capacity. But apparently, when you went and threw emotional attachments into it, we forgot all of our training, all of our foresight.

Still, even if we starved to death, it'd be worth it if it meant we could save Wade.

I stilled for a moment as distrust crept over my skin like a wave of tiny insects. What if Max had been lying? What if she hadn't really been seeing Wade in dreams? Even if she had, what if her whole goal was to lure us here? And, without question, we'd followed. Now we were separated and way out of our depths.

I focused on my breathing, trying to dispel the anxiety taking hold around my chest. And when I did, I saw an image of her, head lying gracefully on her hotel pillow while she spilled her heart out to me. I saw the look of raging compassion in her eyes when I told her about my parents, when I talked about Sarah. My stomach tightened when I thought about how badly I'd wanted to kiss her in that moment, how badly I wanted to say fuck The Guild and bondmates and all the trash they fed us about procreating. That was never going to be for me, not in the way my people wanted anyway.

When I thought about it, when I really focused, I knew with alarming certainty that she wasn't pulling something over on us. That she truly believed Wade was here and that he was in danger. That I was just falling into old habits and refusing to trust anyone outside of the members of my team.

And while it had taken years and years to build up the vulnerability to trust my team, Max made my head spin in new and thrilling ways. It was like my skin buzzed when she was in the room; my entire body called to her, reaching. I just didn't know what it was reaching for.

Maybe that was the problem. I always treated her with suspicion, not because she deserved it, but because I was so fucking conflicted and confused about how drawn to her I was. Maybe the right way to proceed was to treat her like a member of our team. We were kidding ourselves if we didn't think she was eventually going to be a bonafide member of Six. She fit with us like she was always meant to be ours. And while she confused the hell out of me, the thought of having her around in a more permanent capacity didn't fill my mouth with bile.

If we couldn't convince her to join, if we couldn't convince Atlas to stop being such a ballsack, well, the alternative was Reza. I blew out a loud puff of air. Hell by myself I could handle. Permanently living and fighting alongside Reza, having to trust her in any capacity—that I wasn't so sure about. I'd rather take my chances on an alarmingly pretty protector who just happened to light shit on fire when she panicked.

I just had to keep my interest in her firmly in the teammate category, and not go confusing things with my emotions and hormones. Easy.

Probably.

"You look miserable," a deep, taunting voice said behind me, "but I guess it makes sense. I would be too if I was stuck all by my lonesome in that grumpy head of yours."

I spun around, fingers clenching around the dagger at my side, ready to strike whatever hellbeast I was about to encounter. And then, to my own chagrin, my muscles relaxed and I rolled my eyes.

"It's you," I said, half-relieved despite my annoyance. I looked at the vamp as he towered over me, his silvery-blond hair slightly disheveled from his trip into hell, willing myself to summon the sort of fear or anger that I was supposed to feel around a vampire. My jaw clenched when I realized that all I felt was just a bland annoyance. And, even worse, a lukewarm excitement that I was with someone I knew. It was like my brain and my body were getting used to his presence, which was dangerous. Once our guards were down where he was concerned, we were well and truly fucked.

I couldn't let that happen.

We were alone. He'd gotten us into hell and we didn't really need him anymore. Now was my chance to end him without having to deal with Max's wide, shell-shocked eyes watching the whole thing and trying to intervene.

So why didn't I?

My mind filled with the image of having to relay the asshole's death to Max once I found her. The way those dark brown orbs would glass over with tears while she tried desperately to process whatever emotions she was feeling. Truth be told, she was just as emotionally stunted as the rest of us, just as clogged up and confused as I was. But I knew that she'd be upset if the vamp were killed, even if she didn't understand why.

Fucking empathy and compassion. The girl had it in droves. It was going to get her—and everyone close to her—killed one of these days.

And then I thought of Eli, which made me metaphorically let go of the blade altogether. The vamp was now tied to one of the few people in this world I actually gave a shit about. I'd never get to act on my desire to decapitate him.

My lip curled in frustration as I watched the obnoxious fuck smirk at me, as if he could read my thoughts as they circled around my mind.

"Don't pretend you're not excited to see me. Hell isn't a fun place to wander alone. Especially for a so-called protector. Trust me," he said. His creepy yellow eye darkened until it was just a few shades lighter than his dark one, his face growing uncharacteristically serious as he glanced around the perimeter. "Hate me all you want, Grumpy, but if we're to survive the night, you'll want to keep me near. We're stronger together than we are apart."

"Have you seen the others?" I narrowed my eyes at him, frustrated with the realization that he was right. As much as I didn't want him to be the person I ran into, I also had no idea where I was going. My chances at finding the rest of my team went up exponentially if I had backup. Especially if that backup was actually an exile from this realm. "And where did you come from? I've been walking for a while and didn't see or hear you until you were right behind me like an annoying, desperate-for-attention shadow."

His brow arched as he started walking in the direction I was heading, arrogant enough to assume I would follow him.

And in all fairness, I did.

"You didn't see or hear me until I was in a position close enough to kill you because you were lost in your own thoughts. That's a dangerous thing to do in a place like this, especially if you're alone. They don't train you lot very well in that big old fancy academy do they?"

I opened my mouth, ready to argue, but then I snapped it closed again, my mouth tasting sour with the acknowledgment that he was right. I was being reckless. This was why I fucking hated emotions and relationships. They stole your focus. They got you killed.

Look at Wade—he went charging recklessly after Max when he was still half-dead from his last mission and that decision got his neck snapped. Then again, if he didn't do that, Max would probably be dead too. Any option we chose, any path we traveled, we were screwed. That's what being a protector was. The key was finding ways to hold our deaths back just a little bit longer, and then a little bit longer than that, again and again until eventually we got swallowed up by the monsters anyway. It was always a losing battle, the goal was to just make it a long one.

"And I haven't seen the others yet," the vamp said, his tone quieting a bit with what sounded almost like concern, "but I'm sure that they're okay. Portals are just fickle things, even more so now."

"Yeah, what makes you so fucking sure?" My tone was hostile, but I'd be lying if I didn't acknowledge the hope that was starting to stir in my stomach at his proclamation. I wasn't exactly the type to trust anything a vampire said, but I was starting to get desperate. The sheer emptiness of this hellscape was starting to make my skin tingle with fear. I should've come across them by now. And why was hell so...empty? It felt like I was standing on the edge of a cliff, waiting for the storm to sweep me away.

Darius shrugged. Even that small gesture made him look like a smug asshole. "I'm still alive." He turned back to look at me, a shit-eating grin on his face that only served to heighten his particular brand of chaos. Without even slowing his stride as he hopped over a pile of rocks, he added, "pristine in fact."

I narrowed my eyes as I climbed up the small hill he was dragging us towards, my feet sliding a few times on some of the loose pebbles. Why didn't hell come with clearly marked hiking trails? At this rate, I was going to sprain my ankle seven times over by the time we hit three miles. And I was actually pretty graceful on my worst days, so that didn't bode well in the long run.

"You're a vampire. You're, unfortunately, very hard to kill. Doesn't mean the others are," I mumbled while I glared daggers at his back. I couldn't kill him, but I could certainly paint elaborate images of how I would in my fantasies. Those wouldn't hurt El—

"Oh," I said, catching on. I could feel some of the tension dissolving from my shoulders as my lips quirked up a bit. Maybe having this vamp around wasn't totally useless. "You're okay. So that means that Eli is too. Alive at least, anyway."

He winked back at me and fury boiled in my stomach. I wanted to punch that smug face next time it turned in my direction. Eli could survive a broken nose. He healed quickly. And he'd understand. Hell, if he was here, he'd probably beat me to the punch, ready and willing to take one for the team. And since the link was so random and hard to predict, it was possible that the injury wouldn't even mirror itself at all.

"Catching on, are you?" the vamp said as he reached the top of the rocky hill and paused, waiting for me. "And while I don't like the wolf, he seems a lot more capable than Eli. So I'm sure he's fine too."

"And Max?" I asked, though there was no venom in my tone. I wanted a clear, logical explanation for how she was safe too. I'd swallow and internalize my grumbling so long as he was talking sense, easing some of my latent anxieties. Because, as much as I hated to admit it, having the douche-canoe around was actually making me feel a little better. There was nothing worse than being alone with your thoughts when you were navigating through the rocky terrains of fear.

He shrugged and scratched the back of his neck as he surveyed whatever scene lay in front of him. "You saw her flambé a pile of vamps, didn't you? Something tells me she can hold her own if she's alone. At least for a little while." He turned back again as I closed the distance between us, a line forming between his eyes. "Hurry up. While I'm fairly certain she's okay, I can't guarantee it. The slower you are, the longer it will take for me to track her."

"Track her?" I echoed as I reached him and looked out across the distance. More rocky plains, peppered with weird hilly mounds like we were walking in the hell version of the Badlands. If it wasn't hell, it would almost be beautiful. I squinted until I realized that there looked to be some sparse buildings a mile or two ahead of us. I felt my face scrunch up as I tried to decipher what I was seeing. "Is that a town? Does hell have towns?"

He exhaled, impatient with me already, as he started making quick work with his descent. "Come on, Grumpy, we've got some ground to cover. The portals aren't always consistent with where they drop their passengers off. And from what I've heard, they've been less predictable as of late. It's possible everyone got plopped down a few miles apart. It's rare for people to enter through the portals, most are trying to leave this place. And we, well, we entered through the exit."

"Insufferable prick," I mumbled, but I picked up my pace all the same. "Would've been a good thing for you to warn us about before we all drank the koolaid. How exactly are you going to track her then? Is vamp smelling really that strong?"

I knew it wasn't. That if she was that far off, there wasn't a chance a vampire could scent her out. But it had become alarmingly clear over the last few days that the vamp twins weren't your average set of fangholes. And while generally being in the presence of one of them would make my skin crawl, right now he was my best chance at finding my friends. So for once, I was almost happy that he was stronger than most, even if his brother blew his strength out of the water if their little battle royale was anything to go by.

"What was that?" he snarled, not bothering to turn his head now. Instead, he picked up his pace.

"Oops, guess I spoke that last part out loud. Sorry," I said. But I wasn't. Prick could use a little ego hit as far as I was concerned. It seemed to be the only weapon against him I had since I couldn't physically hurt him.

"Are you familiar with this ar—" my words cut off as something bowled into me and knocked the wind out of my lungs. As I stumbled and fell like a damn cartoon character, I watched the vamp get attacked by what looked like a werewolf, but I was spinning downhill so fast that I couldn't be sure what the hell I was seeing. Fur, definitely what looked like fur, but that was all I could concretely identify.

When I finally stopped tumbling like a fucking nursery rhyme, I was face down on a flat surface. I could feel small cuts all over my body and I was certain that my clothes were torn to shreds. Thank god I still had my small bag on my back so I could change after I sawed off the head of whatever the hell attacked me.

As soon as I was still enough to do so, I grabbed the dagger out of my thigh strap and raised it up just as a giant white wolf sprang towards me like a rabid torpedo. The beast was obviously faster than me and leapt directly onto my chest. I was pinned beneath the creature's heavy weight, my vision filled with nothing but a pair of yellow eyes and the dust that my fall had stirred up.

I coughed as the cloud settled into my mouth and lungs, tears streaming from the irritation. Just as the creature moved to sink its teeth into my shoulder, I freed my hand and sunk my blade into its side. I wasn't positioned to reach its heart for a kill shot, but it was enough to hurt and fast enough to catch the wolf by surprise.

The wolf let out a pained howl and instinctively backed far enough off of me for me to escape. I crawled away quickly, like a crab, and ripped my blade from its body, watching as its snow-white fur turned a deep red.

Not waiting long enough for the creature to regroup and spring on me again, I flung my body into it, shoulder first, to try and unsteady it before it went on the offensive again.

Large tufts of white hair crept into the seam of my lips and went up my nose as I tried to tackle the creature to the ground.

With a cringe, I felt it dig a set of claws into my side, but the adrenaline coursing through my body was too strong for me to be aware of the pain. I needed to end this quickly, before I lost too much blood. I used all of my strength to wrestle the beast underneath me and forced myself to clear my mind as much as possible.

Ever since Atlas was turned, I'd been having trouble killing werewolves with the same amount of vigor as I used to. I knew that the creature below me was trying to kill me; that this sort of situation was kill or be killed. But when I caught sight of those yellow eyes, chills ran up my spine and all I could see was my best friend.

Before I could think about it any longer, I shoved my dagger through the wolf's diaphragm and angled up until I was certain the blade sank into the heart. I watched as the life drained from the beast's eyes and a sort of hollowness carved into me. I used to be filled with so much pride, so much excitement when I took down one of these beasts. Now, each one that died made me worry about how long Atlas had before a protector did the same to him.

With a heave, I pulled my dagger from the carcass, my lip curling at the squelching sound the movement made.

I spun around, ready to help the vamp in case he needed it

when I noticed a giant gray wolf diving for me. It was less than a few inches away, it's long teeth bared around an aggressive growl.

I braced myself for impact, knowing I didn't have time to dodge.

But it was too heavy and when it landed on my chest, we both went down with the momentum in a pile of limbs. My blade was knocked from my fingers as we hit the ground and my heartbeat picked up as I fished around for it. I didn't stand a chance against one of these without a weapon and this one was significantly larger than its predecessor.

After a long moment, my body stilled. The wolf hadn't moved—no attempt to close my neck within its jaw, no set of claws raking against or through my abdomen.

With a heavy shove, I crawled out from under the creature. A giant blade was sticking out of the body, aimed perfectly at the beast's heart. It was dead.

I swiped some stray strands of hair from my face and glanced around. The vamp stood over me, his hand extended to lift me up.

"You killed it?" I asked, the words little more than a whisper.

He arched his brow and grabbed my hand, clearly bored with waiting for me to accept the offering. "Yeah, that's sort of what you do in an ambush, no? Kill the enemy? I would think your kind is particularly used to that."

With a heavy yank he pulled me up, his eyes narrowed slightly as he scanned me for injuries. My head swam from the movement and I held onto his forearm for support.

He swiped his fingers carefully against my side, lifting my shirt to get a better look.

I shoved him away and in the process fell back down. I'd lost more blood than I thought.

"Stubborn woman," he mumbled as he turned around and went through his bag. He must've stolen some things from his brother's house. He didn't exactly come with any luggage when we broke him out. "I wasn't trying to come onto you, Grumpy.

You've got a wound there that needs dressing if you want it to heal quickly."

"You could have let me die," I said as I watched him pull out a water bottle. It's what I would have done if the circumstances were reversed and he wasn't connected to Eli.

"Is that what you would have preferred?"

I narrowed my eyes in answer, but there was no malice behind it. For a brief moment, it had felt like I was taking on a pack of wolves with a member of my team—a notion which sent a series of repulsed shivers down my spine. A vampire was not a part of my team, nor would one ever be.

"Yeah well, I know this might come as a surprise to you, but while I am a vampire, I'm not a monster." He tore my shirt open so that my stomach was exposed. I held in my wince as he gave the wounds a water bath and cleared out any of the sooty debris that lined the gouges. "Besides, if you died, I'd have to deal with your friends. And she—"

He shook his head, which I took to mean he wasn't going to finish the thought.

"Thank you," I said, the words tasting unfamiliar in my mouth—not because I'd never said them before, but because I'd never said them to a vampire. It felt foreign and strange, thanking him for saving my life, when I'd spent so many years hating his species for taking the lives of my parents. "Whatever your reasons, I'm glad you didn't just sit back and let me die."

I glanced down at the wounds. The claw marks looked nasty but they weren't too deep and I'd be mostly healed in a few hours if I was lucky. Considering I'd taken on and slaughtered one of the werewolves solo, I'd consider this particular battle a very solid win.

I started swiping up and down my legs before trying to glance at the back of my shoulder.

"What on earth are you doing?" The vamp looked at me like I was the one whose mind was broken.

"Trying to make sure I wasn't bitten," I mumbled as I craned my neck trying to make sure the scrapes on my back were from tumbling down the hill and not from the scrape of a tooth.

He rolled his eyes before gripping under my arms and lifting me back to my feet. I froze as he spun me around and lifted up the back of my shirt. "You're fine. Devil forbid you get any beastie cooties. No bites here."

I shoved away from him and pulled my shirt back down; well, as much as was possible anyway with all the bottom of it shredded to scraps. Ignoring his bemused expression I grabbed my pack and pulled out a fresh tank top. "It's not a cooties problem, you asshat," I said as I swiped my shirt off in one quick motion, trying and failing to ignore the sharp stab of pain as the cloth swept over my wounds. I glanced at the vamp and he was doing a very good job of staring at my face and not my boobs. Points for that at least. I pulled the fresh top over my head as I added on a cloth-muted mumble, "we can actually die from those bites. And on rare occasions, be turned altogether."

"Ah right," he said, as he grabbed up his supplies and surveyed the dead wolves. Looks like he'd managed to kill two before taking down the one that charged me. "That's what happened to Alpha Asshole."

I arched a brow at his nickname for Atlas. Did he have one for all of us? Still, I loved Atlas and all, but that nickname wasn't exactly far off or unreasonable. His personality wasn't for everyone.

I nodded and picked up my bag as my throat clogged up at the memory of that night. It was one of the worst moments of my life. Watching Atlas and Wade come back without Sarah was like being stabbed in the chest and losing my ability to suck in a full breath all in one go. We were all so consumed with grief that Atlas was able to hide the bite from us at first. Our focus was on other things—my aunt, debriefing Seamus on the turn of events. It was a lot. And everyone just thought he was ignoring us because of the particularly acute pain of losing a bondmate, but really his body was being ravaged as the disease coursed through him.

And then when Wade finally noticed the telltale wound on his arm that wasn't disappearing as the days went by, we decided to keep it from everyone at The Guild on the off chance that he was one of the few to turn into a wolf. Protectors who were bitten and survived with no ill effects were pushed back into their normal lives, lauded as heroes who'd fought against death and won.

But those who died or transformed were quietly swept away into the recesses of the lab—or worse. We weren't really certain what happened to our fallen soldiers. It was a topic no one discussed in The Guild.

None of us were ready to lose another member of our family so soon, not if we could help it and keep a close eye on him. Atlas was a stubborn ass—if anyone could keep the monster locked down, it was him. And when we learned that he was able to keep his affliction under control, that he had enough power over his own mind to keep from hurting anyone, our stance on the matter solidified. It bound us together with even deeper ties. Secrets had a way of doing that. We became a team so tightly connected that our bond stood against the rules of The Guild.

The vamp had already started walking again, so I hobbled after him, downing a few gulps of water from his water bottle he'd left next to me in the process. If he wasn't going to make use of the hydration, I was.

After what felt like an hour of unbearable silence, in which the heat of the sun, or whatever was in the hell-sky, beat down against my back, baking my neck, I started to get bored.

"Why did you leave hell anyway? And why do the creatures here hate it so much? Why risk dealing with protectors just to mingle around some humans?" I asked, staring at the vamp's back. He hadn't made any more attempts at conversation since the ambush, both of us too preoccupied with looking out for new attackers and keeping our eyes peeled for the rest of our team.

My team.

His back stiffened, almost as if he'd forgotten I was behind him. With a quick look back, he shrugged and then started moving again, this time his pace faster.

I exhaled sharply, my breath puffing the few stray strands of hair away from my face. I was caked in sweat, dried blood, and desperate for a bath. "Is there food and water in this realm that won't kill the rest of us?" I tried again.

"Yes," he said, his answer drawn out like he was only half paying attention to me.

"Do you know how we can find where Wade's being kept? Do you have like a map of hell memorized in that warped brain of yours?" I narrowed my eyes at him, getting frustrated with the fact that he suddenly seemed uninterested in bickering with me. From what I knew of the dick, he desperately loved to hear himself talk.

He stopped walking before slowly spinning around on his heel. The movement was so smooth and sudden, and I was so focused on not upsetting any rocks as I walked, that I bumped into his chest and dropped his water bottle on his foot.

"Sorry," I said as I bent down to pick it up. When I stood, his brow was arched and he was staring at me like he'd never seen one of my kind before. "What?"

"Nothing," he said, shaking his head, "I'm just not used to you talking to me, let alone apologizing. Trying to figure out if your brains got liquified in the portal or if the werewolf slapped some friendly into your personality."

I narrowed my eyes at him and shoved his shoulder as I continued walking. It wasn't what he said that had my mouth tasting like metal, it was the fact that he was right. I was warming up to him and I wasn't sure how I felt about that. Which made me even angrier because I should have felt damn devastated at the realization and corrected course immediately. It was hard hating someone who literally saved your life.

But honestly, the bottom line was that this asswipe was going to be connected to one of my best friends until he died. So maybe it was better to just find a way to stomach his presence.

But then again, maybe not. "You know—"

He cut off my snarky retort as he rushed past me. At first I thought he was just being a douche about me changing up our follow-the-leader game and the fact that I was taking my own stab at directing us, but after a second I realized that it was something else altogether.

I took off at a run, trying to keep us as best as I could, but I wasn't nearly as fast as a vampire on my best day, let alone after taking on some werewolves.

"Slow down," I whisper-yelled at his back, too worried about who might hear us to turn up the volume. He was a vamp though, so I had no doubt that he heard me just fine if he was listening.

But he sped up, so clearly he wasn't. Or he just didn't give a fuck, which was much more likely.

After a few minutes, I lost him entirely and pumped my legs so fast that they started to feel like jelly. I paused, catching a quick breath and pressed lightly against the claw marks on my side. The exertion opened them back up again, which was frustrating. They'd been healing just fine until I pushed too hard.

Bending at the knee, I took a steady breath in and out. My chest felt tight all of a sudden and while I wanted to think that it was because I was in pain or dying or something, I realized with a sinking frustration that it was because I was alone. I was anxious because a vampire went and ditched me.

What the fuck was wrong with me? I shook my head, ready to chase after him in the direction I'd seen him moving so that I could give him a good dick punch once I found him—sorry, Eli— when I stopped breathing altogether.

My eyes caught sight of the now-familiar white-blond hair,

but it was what I saw standing next to him that had me falling to my knees with a relief so sharp it almost hurt.

Max and Atlas.

They were alive.

And I hated that I was going to have to thank the fanghole for finding them just like he said he would.

⚜ 12 ⚜

MAX

The moment I saw Declan and Darius, I physically felt the weight lift off my shoulders. Atlas and I had been wandering for what felt like an hour, with no one sight, and I was starting to fear the worst.

He didn't help alleviate any of my anxiety either, as we moved at what felt like a snail's pace so that he could check around every corner to make sure no one was lying in wait, ready to feast or capture us or whatever.

Not to mention that he'd been on the edge of a shift since the moment we dropped down in the middle of a small valley. His wolf was so present that I half expected he couldn't speak to me even if he wanted to. Seeing him so on edge just amplified my own anxiety and it wasn't until I caught sight of Darius that I realized my hand was still gripped in Atlas's.

A realization that was made only more shocking by the fact that he was holding onto my hand just as tightly as I was holding onto his. As if he noticed it at the exact moment I did, he relaxed his fingers and mine fell away.

"Are you both okay? Where's E—umph." My face burrowed into Declan's chest as she barreled into me and wrapped her arms first around me, and then around Atlas. Her squeeze was so tight that it was difficult to breathe, but I didn't even care.

She was alive. They were both alive.

Slowly, she peeled away from me and she and Atlas stared at each other with that peculiar focus that only genuine companionship could bring. He was slowly coming back to himself, so he listened with rapt attention to every detail she gave about her experience in hell so far.

My heart raced against my chest as she recounted the attack in vivid detail—it was so at odds with our own experience here. I hadn't so much as seen a single thing move or breathe. It was like we'd been dropped into a wasteland.

Just as I opened my mouth to ask her more about the wolf attack, my blood coursing furiously underneath my skin, Darius gripped my face in both of his hands and studied me with more focus than I'd ever seen him show.

His eyebrows were bent, creating a small line between them, and I could tell from his rigid stillness that he wasn't so much as breathing as he tilted my face first from one side, then to the other.

"You're okay?" he asked, as his eyes and hands swept from my head, to my torso.

His perusal was objective, calculating, but I couldn't hide the shiver that rolled through my body as his hands caressed with a gentle familiarity. Each time his fingers lightly brushed along my skin, I could feel my blush deepening, my breath quickening.

I took a step back, so that I was a full arm's length away, and glanced up at him, trying desperately to ignore the fact that while my brain wanted distance between us, my body most certainly did not. In fact, it was downright screaming in protest. The traitor didn't seem to care that the creature standing before me was a fucking vampire, the very thing I was built to destroy.

Either not sensing my need for space, or simply not caring, he closed the distance between us again, so that he could continue his assessment.

"I—" the word came out as a squeak so I nodded instead, using the extra few seconds to force my body to behave itself. "You are? I mean, you're okay? Are you okay?"

He was crouched down now examining a few cuts and scrapes along my legs, his head near my lady bits. He looked up at me and arched an eyebrow, his lips lifting in a cocky grin. Something about that sight did wild things to my stomach. "I'm perfectly fine, little protector." He glanced over at Declan, as she and Atlas glared back at him. "We both are."

I took a quick step back again, like we were doing little more than a dance now, my skin burning as Declan and Atlas studied the space between Darius and me. "What about Eli?"

I craned my neck, like he was merely hiding between a boulder, ready to pounce at us in surprise. Letting me worry for an elongated second was exactly the sort of thing he would find hilarious, all while leaving him an excellent opening for a dramatic appearance. It was quintessential Eli, and right now, I desperately wanted that to be the reason he wasn't standing here with us.

Declan's face fell and she shook her head as she shared a knowing look with Atlas. My chest tightened with worry, but I glanced back at Darius.

"But you're okay?" I asked again, my eyes sweeping over Darius now just as thoroughly and thoughtfully as his had swept over me.

"Pretty sure he's made it clear he's fine," Atlas bit out, his voice filled with venom. It was the longest sentence he'd uttered since we'd gotten here. I wasn't sure why his rage was directed at me, but I was getting used to it. Enough at least, that I didn't even bother acknowledging it.

"Yes," I said slowly, trying to swallow my frustration, "which means that Eli is too."

"You've got to hand it to her, wolfie," Darius stood up and stretched, his long limbs reaching high as the tension evaporated away, "she's a lot quicker than you are."

Atlas took a step forward and squared off with Darius, his eyes a flash of pure yellow.

I thought Darius might back away, give him some space, but the laziness that had suddenly crept over his body, disappeared just as quickly. His spine straightened and he narrowed his eyes before he used both of his hands to shove Atlas back.

A low growl built up in Atlas's chest and Declan and I stood still, both of us afraid of doing something that might escalate things even further. If the showdown between Darius and Claude taught us anything—it was that the two of us didn't stand a chance at coming between a disagreement between beasts.

Darius let out a sharp, humorless laugh before shoving Atlas again, like he'd found a new toy and was pleased as pie.

"You need to get that wolf of yours under control before you get yourself or someone else killed," his gaze swept briefly in my direction and I was taken aback by the steel in his eyes. The usual shit-eating grin was absent from his face, and I could tell that the demons that lingered beneath his skin were surfacing once more. "Embrace your monster while you have the chance. Pretty soon it'll be too late and you'll be nothing more than one of the countless late bloomers driven wild as the wolf takes over. When that happens, your wolf won't be so discerning about who it deems an enemy."

Fur sprouted along Atlas's skin, lining his forearms like magic, and I could tell that he was losing his hold on the monster, no matter how hard he tried to hold it back. As much as we all liked to pretend that he was different, that he was in control, we all knew deep down that it wasn't true. The wolf was no less a part of him than it was of any other werewolf.

"Atlas," I said as I took a step towards him. Declan tried to pull me back but I stepped around her before she could grab hold of me and reached for Atlas's hand. "Just breathe. In and out."

I mimicked the breath for him, my lungs expanding and deflating with exaggerated movements. Darius grabbed my shoulders and tried to pull me away but I leveled a glare at him, stopping him cold. We all knew that sudden movements right now would not be received well by the wolf, no matter how well-intended they were.

Atlas helped me through the portal, let me cling to him like Saran Wrap until I calmed down. It was only fair that I do the same for him. If we were going to work together, it was time we all stopped pretending like he wasn't a werewolf. We needed to learn how to work with the beast, just as we needed to learn to work with the man.

His head turned towards mine, yellow eyes studying me with an intelligent, but unfamiliar focus. For the first time, it felt like I was actually seeing his wolf, separate from him in some ways, but not in all.

He tilted his head in an almost cat-like gesture and the hand I clasped jerked back, pulling me until I was pressed against Atlas's chest, our bodies glued together as I stared up at him. With a gentle precision, I felt fingers caress the side of my face before sliding back behind my neck and gripping the hair at the base of my skull. His hold was firm, but gentle all the same—just enough to let me know that I wasn't in control of this situation.

My stomach lurched as he tilted my face towards his and I didn't dare so much as breathe. His face inched slowly towards mine as the yellow started to swirl and bleed back to brown. With lips so close that they ghosted on mine, I closed my eyes.

The glance of his lips against mine sent a ripple of tingles down my body and I felt a low, buried need stir to life in my belly. It was like something in me was waking up, responding to the wolf.

Instead of meeting the expected pressure, I felt Atlas push away from me until I stumbled back, knees still weak from what-ever was coursing through my body. Darius gripped my arms and steadied me before I fell down on my ass, embarrassing myself even further.

My heart beat furiously against my ribs as I turned towards

Atlas. He was back to himself again, the wolf hidden once more beneath the surface, his dark eyes just as guarded and unreadable as ever. Shame and regret filled my chest as he refused to look in my direction, his jaw tensed and pulsing. I could almost taste the rage radiating from him, it was so strong.

What the hell was happening between us and why did I try to get close to him when the monster was in control? And why did I get the feeling that the monster tolerated my presence far more than Atlas did?

"I—" I started, unsure what to say or do, when a harsh inhale distracted me and Darius let me go.

I slammed my lips closed and spun around, only to find a deep gash running down Darius's cheek.

Where the hell had that come from?

He buckled over and held his stomach. When he lifted the edge of his shirt up I saw another deep, angry line carving down his side. Blood flowed down his lined abdomen.

The world spun for a long moment, as my brain caught up to the situation.

"Eli," I said as I watched the similar realization fall on Declan's face. I looked up at Darius, every muscle in his body seemed tense, like he was perpetually waiting for the next strike to come. It had to be a strangely disarming feeling, but I didn't have time to linger on it now. "Can you run?"

Without a word, he nodded before wrapping my hand in his. He took off with a speed I struggled to keep up with at first but, to my surprise, I fell into step with him as we blew past rocks and, eventually, entered into a dark, sparse forest.

We ran for what felt like miles, both of us weaving effort-lessly around the brambles and tree roots. I'd grown up running through the woods back home, scaling the mountain on morning runs with Ro. Darius was just as adept at handling the terrain as I was, even though he was battling the added difficulty of getting attacked by some phantom creature.

He let me lead. I wasn't sure how I knew where to run, but I didn't question it. Hell was a place literally filled with magic. If my instincts were pointing me in the direction of Eli, I would follow them.

My breath came out in harsh clouds as the trees opened up into what looked like an abandoned street. The terrain in this realm was all over the place, from what felt like a bumpy Burning Man land, to an enchanted forest, and now this. There were a few scattered buildings around, with concrete sidewalks and buildings that were being reclaimed by plant life.

It was like hell was a lifeless Earth, with all of its landscapes condensed down and shoved together in close proximity. A terrifying sort of Disneyland.

Darius stopped as soon as we reached the edge of the tree line and I went colliding back into him as he pulled my hand.

I opened my mouth to ask him why he'd paused when he lifted a thin finger to his lips.

My eyes traced over him and I noticed that his shirt was now coated wet with blood, whether because Eli had obtained new injuries or because the first ones were deeper than we'd realized, I wasn't sure. Either way, my stomach clenched with fear.

I sucked in a slow, steady breath, reminding myself that Darius was still standing—still alive. And that meant that Eli was too. I closed my eyes for a moment, desperately trying to get my pulse to calm down so that I could focus and listen to whatever was around us. It was quiet, strangely so. And while I had no logical or rational reason to give, I was certain that Eli was close by.

I glanced back at Darius, ready to tell him just that. That we needed to push forward and keep going. But I swallowed my words when I saw him. His body was tensed, his eyes narrowed as he studied the perimeter. He looked every bit the lethal predator that he was. And something told me that while I didn't see any monsters near us, they were there. As Declan's story had proven, hell was anything but the lifeless, empty terrain it seemed. The beings here were just far better at lingering in the shadows, out of sight.

Atlas and Declan weren't behind us, so either they hadn't caught up to us in our pursuit or something happened to them. My hands clenched, fingernails digging into the flesh of my palms as I sent a silent prayer that it was the former. We could only handle one catastrophe at a time.

"Come out, come out," a playful, devious voice rang out, the echo haunting as it bounced around the abandoned buildings. "I promise I won't hurt you too badly just yet. I like my games to last. But if you make me chase you around for much longer, I'll make your death draw out in the most exquisite sort of agony. That can be a fun game too."

The voice broke into a childish giggle that had the hair on the back of my neck standing to attention. The flesh along my arms pebbled as the echoes ran through me.

Darius positioned me so that I was behind him and grabbed the blade fastened at his hip. I had a feeling he'd stolen it, along with all of the supplies he brought into hell, from his brother. Claude's wrath was neither here nor there right now.

Mirroring him, I pulled out my dagger and nodded, signaling that I was ready to move. I wasn't sure what sort of monster this creature was, but there was something in the way that it spoke that hinted at a deep appreciation for evoking pain. The voice was the stuff of nightmares and horror films, and as much as I wanted to run and help Eli, to protect him from whatever was happening to him, I was equally terrified of encountering the creature too soon, unprepared. I didn't want to get him killed— we had one chance at this.

"I want you to stay here," Darius said, his voice low and filled with an authority I hadn't heard before. He almost sounded like Atlas, like the leader of a team, not like the aloof vampire who seemed to thrive on chaos. "I'm not sure what we're dealing with here, or if she's alone."

But whether he'd realized it or not, I wasn't very fond of

following Atlas's directions, and the same was true for his.

I arched an eyebrow at him and took a step forward so that I was no longer hidden behind his lean bulk. "I don't think so. We either go at it together or we go at it separately. Your choice, but I won't stand here and wait for that thing to kill Eli—or you— one slice at a time. I'm not some delicate flower, despite what everyone seems to think."

He squared his shoulders and I could tell that he was preparing to argue, when the clash of bodies rang out around us in a series of grunts and bangs.

My teeth clenched as I heard a loud groan, followed by the girl's taunting laughter. When I looked up at Darius, there was a new deep, red line that looked like it was carved by a sharp blade, running from his brow to his jaw.

His eyes flashed with anger as he nodded at me. "Together then. Let's go draw some blood, little protector. I need a meal anyway."

My stomach lurched at the comment, not because I was disgusted by the idea of him feasting on the creature's blood, but because I wasn't. My blood rushed with the thought of killing the beast responsible for injuring the boys. And I not only wanted Darius to kill her, I wanted to watch as he tore her limb from limb.

No. I wanted to help him do it.

He arched a single brow, like he was expecting me to challenge him, but all he got was my hardened resolve. He'd get no fight from me on this, my bloodlust was growing with each second we waited.

A greedy grin lifted his lips as he studied me. I felt like an onion, being peeled back layer by layer, terrified of him seeing whatever darkness was lingering at my core. He tightened his fingers around my wrist, just above my pulse point. For a second, I thought he was going to draw me towards him, do something we'd both regret.

Then, in a flash, he was on the move, my hand in his, both of us stalking our way out from the trees. We crept silently from building to building as he listened and tracked the beast's movements.

I held my breath, straining my ears to try and pick up whatever it was that Darius was hearing. As I watched him, another thin slice appeared on his right forearm. Whatever the hell this creature was, she was toying with Eli right now. This was nothing but a dark and twisted game. My stomach turned as I noticed that the slice stretched and morphed until an entire swath of skin was missing.

"What the hell is this thing?" I mouthed to Darius out of fear that whatever it was had good enough hearing to catch my words as they traveled through the wind.

His lips turned down as he stared at his arm, his eyes hard as ice. Something changed in his demeanor, though I couldn't quite put my finger on it. He took a steadying breath in and gripped his blade. This wasn't the Darius that I was used to seeing. He was no longer the creepy, taunting vampire kept behind glass in The Guild's research basement. Instead, he was the fierce monster who'd torn his brother's living room apart in a battle no protector would have stood a chance at surviving.

One moment he was there next to me and the next he was disappearing in a flash behind the corner of the building we'd been ducking behind.

"Shit," I mumbled, wincing as the word formed off my tongue. Shit, shit, shit. I chased after Darius, though I knew I didn't stand a chance at catching up with him. Vampire speed far outweighed that of protectors. And my tracking skills were mediocre at best. The most I could hope for was to provide backup by the time I got to him—that, or find the creature first myself.

About twenty feet away, I saw a door to a decrepit building close. It looked like an abandoned warehouse, large and square, with far more attention to utility than aesthetics. Still, the way that vines crept along the sides, and the fact that half of the windows seemed to be busted, suggested that whatever purpose this place was built for, it was no longer being used. What happened to this place? Why did hell feel like a damn dystopian novel, with most of the population long gone?

Hoping that Darius or Eli entered the building instead of whatever creepy creature we were hunting, I inhaled a calming breath and followed, cursing the fanghole for ditching me less than two minutes after we'd agreed on going after this thing together.

I don't know why I was so surprised that a fucking vampire went back on his word. They weren't used to working in teams, not like we were. And I had a feeling it had been years and years since Darius worked with anyone or trusted someone else to have his back.

Hell, even his own brother wanted him dead.

The place was dark and cluttered with debris along the grounds, papers and broken glass lining the path. I could only see a few feet in front of me, so I kept one hand along the wall as I walked further inside at a painfully slow pace. I slowed my breathing down and tried desperately not to rustle any of the shit littering the floor. If the monster was in here, I didn't want to send an announcement of my presence. Far better for me to catch it off guard rather than be the one caught.

A high pitched peal of laughter echoed around the walls.

I jumped, shivers traveling down my skin, like every atom in my body was telling me to run away, that I was not prepared for whatever creature I might find here. It was like every instinct I had knew that this was dangerous, that something about the childish laughter was unnatural.

"Tasty, tasty," the girlish voice trilled. "Time for another bite."

There was a brief pause that felt cloying and claustrophobic, like a vice was squeezing around my chest, waiting with a heavy anticipation.

"Best not to fight it, dinner is served," the voice said, its echo ringing around the empty building like a strangely macabre chorus.

"Darius," I whispered, my voice hushed and strained. "Where are you?"

A loud thump, and then a heavy crash.

"Back off, you creepy shit," a deep, familiar voice shouted, followed by a strained yell.

Eli.

No longer willing to take things slowly, I took off at a quick pace, running in the direction of his voice, desperate to get to him as soon as possible. With one hand along a wall, I ran down winding halls, losing track of how many different turns I took, how many different doorways I entered.

And then I saw him.

His face and arms were bloody as he leaned against the window, face bathed partially in whatever light was left outside. Each of his breaths seemed to come out in ragged gasps as his wild eyes searched around the room, like he wasn't quite sure where the creature would crop up next in their twisted game of Whac-A-Mole.

When he saw me, he jumped, like he thought I was the owner of the girlish laugh, but then his eyes grew wide and filled with worry. He shook his head as he started to walk towards me, but his movements were stilted and rough, like he was fighting against his own muscles.

"Max," he said, the word low and constrained, "run."

As I reached a hand out to him and moved to close the distance, his face distorted with fear.

"My, my, tasty one. Earning your keep already. You've brought a friend."

Before I had a chance to turn around and confront the beast, something sharp scraped against my neck before a heavy object smacked into my skull. A low, piercing sound filled my ears and bright dots of light obscured my vision until, eventually, my body fell against a wall and slid to the ground.

❧ 13 ❧

MAX

My vision blurred but I blinked past it, desperately trying to ignore the pain in the back of my head. Did the monster walk around with a damn baseball bat like some sort of Harley Quinn knockoff? Because while that was generally quite a vibe, I was *so* not feeling it right now.

"It's a party," the girl yelled, her voice filled with a childish glee as she crouched down and stared at me, her head tilted at an odd angle like she was trying to study me from upside down.

She looked human in form, with long black hair and smooth pale skin, though both were covered in dirt and what looked suspiciously like paint. Black lines were drawn across her cheeks like she was auditioning as an extra in a football film.

Her eyes were wide, but cast in shadow so I couldn't get a read on their color. They didn't appear to be yellow from where I was, so not a werewolf, but my vision was doing weird things at the moment. For a second, she reminded me of the young vampire I'd come across in The Guild labs, a strange mixture of terrifying innocence. The very thing nightmares were made of.

Except where my reaction to the young vampire had been one of confusion, my body seemed intuitively certain that the girl standing before me was a threat—the sort I hadn't come across before.

I wasn't sure how I knew, but I did—she was neither vampire nor werewolf, but something else altogether. I just wasn't sure what. The only other creature I'd encountered was a succubus and I was overtly aware that whatever this girl was, she wasn't that.

There was no sex appeal, no unexplainable draw luring me in. If anything, every atom in my body seemed repulsed by her, like she was death embodied. Or maybe it was just because she reminded me of those creepy kids in a horror movie—the ones who instantly cued you into the fact that they were about to murder someone while humming along to a terrifying lullaby. This girl had that whole mood on lock.

"I wonder, friend," she said, studying me with rapt attention and excitement. "If you've had your dinner yet. Do you taste as good? I hope so, I hope so, I hope so!"

She punctuated each phrase with a playful little hop that sent her hair bouncing wildly around her petite form, her voice growing louder and more daring with each repetition.

Her face pulled into a grotesque smile that made her seem like a macabre caricature of a teenage girl. I could see from where I sat, my back pressed against the wall as Eli inched closer to me, that the lines between her teeth were filled with blood, and what looked like a flap of skin was hanging awkwardly over her lip.

Bile rose up my esophagus as I noticed Eli's jerky movements to my left. It was like he was fighting a weird paralysis or some invisible force that was holding him back. Every muscle seemed like it was working on overdrive but getting absolutely nowhere.

What had she done to him? And how had she overpowered him when he was easily twice her size.

She began dancing in strange circles, laughing that bone-chilling laugh of hers. Her movements were both graceful and clumsy, like she was performing a strange balancing act on a tightrope. As erratic as her limbs were, she never once stumbled or tripped over any of the broken pieces of wood or piles of trash lining the floor.

I reached my fingers out along the cement ground until I found Eli's hand and squeezed it. The skin on my fingers felt strangely stiff, like the feeling I got from trying to hold too many shopping bags at once. Brushing it off, I tried to focus. I would get us out of here, I just needed to know what the hell I was dealing with. I glanced around the room, trying to find anything that might be useful. I had my blade clutched behind my back, but my bag was no longer hanging off my shoulders.

As if she could read my thoughts, the girl shook the black bag in front of her, pulling out my clothes and weapons and scattering them around the room with a wide grin on her face.

"New, new, new," she whispered, her voice giddy and strange as she eyed all of my things, almost as if she'd never seen clothes or weapons before. She held each item before her eyes, studying them with the sort of attention you might expect from someone visiting a museum exhibition. "I can't wait to play later. But for now, I think it's time for a taste."

I was still dizzy and disoriented, but I gripped my dagger all the same, steeling myself to stand up and attack.

Only I didn't.

Or, rather, I couldn't.

It was like my brain and my body were suddenly disconnected and despite how much my mind tried to tell my limbs to move, to fight, I couldn't. My fingers were gripped around Eli's, but each muscle suddenly felt like it was weighed down by bricks. I could barely untangle my hand from his let alone lead an ambush against this girl.

"Wh-what—" the single word was a struggle to push past my lips.

The girl turned back to me, dumped the rest of my things haphazardly on the floor before throwing the bag down on top of it all, and started to laugh like the entire thing was a hugely elaborate joke. And one that she'd orchestrated all on her own.

There was pride, excitement. It was terrifying.

She waved a small knife at me and I instantly realized that it wasn't one of mine. The blade was rusted and coated with grime, which meant that it wasn't one of Eli's either. Protectors were notorious for treating weapons with the sort of care one would treat a child.

My thoughts flashed back to the small prick at the back of my neck before I was knocked to the ground. I tried to lift my hand to feel for a small cut, but it felt like my limb was weighed down by a boulder—completely useless.

The creep walked forward, slowly, while hopping from one foot to the other, like she was deliberately trying to play into the horror-film vibes her appearance already strung together. She grabbed the arm that was holding my blade, my fingers frozen around the handle in a useless deathgrip.

"Tsk, tsk, tsk," she clicked as she peeled each finger back with ease until the metal dropped to the floor with an echoing clatter. She picked up my dagger and dangled it blade-down in front of her face, swinging it back and forth like it was some sort of morbid pendulum, her eyes wide and filled with a strange mirth.

This close, I could see that her eyes were dark, almost black, but there wasn't anything to distinguish them from one super-natural creature or another.

With a harsh belly laugh, she whipped my dagger across the room until it crashed and slid along the floor into a pile of garbage. I cringed. That blade was a birthday gift from Cyrus.

I could feel my fingers slowly starting to regain movement, and I was able to unclench my jaw, but only slightly. At this rate, I might stand a chance at taking her down in a few moments.

She didn't look particularly strong, but that was the thing. Demons didn't exactly scream professional wrestlers in terms of their appearances. She was lanky and looked underfed, but for all

I knew, she possessed the strength to fling me across the floor just as easily as she did my blade.

With a quick movement, she pulled my forearm towards her and drew her knife down in a jagged line until my blood spilled all over my legs and the ground.

She brought her nose down until it was barely an inch above my skin and inhaled deeply, the sound strange and guttural. With a renewed fervor, she carved another slice down my skin and pulled a patch away with it.

A scream I didn't recognize as my own left my mouth as pain flared up my arm like I was being prodded over and over with a fire poker.

Her blade must have been dipped in some sort of weird poison. At least it seemed to be temporary. Not that it would matter if she kept using it repeatedly until we were nothing but skinned corpses. And being skinned alive was about as awful a way to go as I could imagine.

My vision went dizzy again and any strength I was gaining over my muscles seemed to be moving in reverse, though slowly. Eli and I gripped each other's fingers and I dug my nails into his palm when I saw him start to move towards her out of the corner of my eye.

He seemed to be coming out of his paralysis moment-by-moment but he was still too stuck to take her on like this.

My stomach twisted at the sight of her holding my flesh above her mouth like she was dropping something as normal as a strand of spaghetti onto her tongue.

The second it hit, her head whipped down until her eyes were locked on mine, her expression filled with an intoxicated reverence.

"Good, good, good," she sang, as she clapped her hands together. She brought her blood-coated fingers up to my face, manually shifting my expression into a smile.

My muscles were stiff and held where she placed them.

"Such a tasty treat." She patted me on the cheek like I was a well-behaved child before digging her blade into my arm again. "I won't play with my food anymore, time to feast. If you're good, maybe I'll shar—"

The word fell on a breathless gurgle, her face frozen in shock. Her mouth spilled over with blood and I watched in morbid fascination as a stretch of red materialized across her neck. Strong, pale hands, gripped her head on either side and twisted, tearing and dragging until she was out of sight.

I tried to follow the movements from the corner of my eyes, since I couldn't shift my head to get a proper view of what was going on. My heart raced against my ribcage as I sent up prayer after silent prayer that whoever the newcomer was, they were friend not foe. I didn't want to be passed from one cannibal-like creature to another.

A loud shuffle ensued and my body jolted with fear as I waited for the heavy crashes to silence.

Please please please let her not be the victor of this battle.

After a long, drawn out moment, a pair of familiar eyes met mine from just a few inches away. One gold, one dark brown.

"D-dar—" I started, frustrated with my body for failing me in this moment. I never thought I would be so desperately happy to see a vampire, not least of all when I wasn't even able to protect myself from an attack.

"She's dead," he said as his eyes moved to Eli briefly before coming back to me. He grabbed my arm in his and ran a careful finger above the spot she'd carved. "There were two others in another building, but I took them out as well. I think she was the last of them." He shook his head and let out a frustrated breath before falling back on his ass in front of us. "I shouldn't have left you like that. I thought it was only one, maybe two. They don't usually work in groups like this, but it seemed to be a sort of family unit." He exhaled, his shoulders sagging under an invisible weight. "It seems even more than I've realized has changed here in my absence."

I tried to reach out my arm toward him, to ease the expression of pain creating harsh angles on his face, but settled with trying to relax what was a probably very disturbing grin on my own.

He winced and gently relaxed my facial muscles himself, his long fingers gentle. "This should wear off completely in an hour or two, and you'll likely have most of your muscle control back in a few minutes. The venom they use isn't very strong, and I don't think it will hold you down for too long. You're a formidable opponent, so I have a feeling your body will dispel it quicker than most."

"Wh-what the h-hell was that thing?" Eli asked, his voice sounding strange and strained as he spoke through his teeth.

Darius stiffened, his jaw muscles pumping furiously. He stared at Eli in a harsh silence for several long moments, like he was gathering his emotions and thoughts together until they were something more legible to share. "They are a sad abomination. The closest thing from your world I can think to describe them would be the Ojibwe wendigo. Although I suppose they also share some similarities with human portrayals of zombies." He let out an exacerbated breath and turned his head, likely looking at where the girl's body was discarded from their skirmish. "They survive by eating the flesh of other demons, but they are doomed to exist in a permanently starved state. No matter how much they consume, their hunger never dies. And since they aren't really any stronger than most supernatural creatures, they've developed a sort of poison that causes paralysis while they feed. Dead flesh isn't nearly as tasty as that from the living, apparently, so their victims often exist trapped in their bodies until they eventually die or are discarded and abandoned."

"Are they born?" Eli asked, tone in full protector mode. I felt him shift slightly next to me. "Or made?"

Darius rolled his teeth over his bottom lip, his fingers now playing unconsciously with my own, clenching them into a fist and then relaxing, like he was trying to force movement back into my body. "They are made. The magic here, the lack of resources—it can sometimes be enough to turn them. But we don't always know how or why it happens. They exist as a perversion of the magic that contains the creatures of hell. It's why vampires are sure to never consume their blood. They are considered bad luck, but unfortunate byproducts of an unstable and cruel land all the same. They are pitiable beasts, victims of circumstance."

I arched my brow, or at least I tried to. The girl was anything but pitiable as far as I was concerned. She literally *ate* a chunk of my flesh. And when it came to zombie movies, I was never one to be on Team Dead Guy Who Likes To Eat Brains For Breakfast. No thank you.

That said, I could understand that it wasn't entirely her fault. But if it was us or her, I was supremely glad that it was us.

"The o-others," I said, squeezing my fingers gently around his. "Where?"

Darius's mouth turned down, like he'd all but forgotten about Declan and Atlas. "Oh, right, them. I guess I could go track them down if you want me to. I don't think the grumpy one could keep up with us, so she's probably still making her way with the wolf, trying to track us here." Darius shrugged, lip curled slightly in disgust. "And since he's not exactly in tune with his wolf, I imagine it will take them a while if they carry on solo."

I thought back to the way that Darius had guided me as we ran after Eli. How I'd somehow felt intuitively that I could find Eli.

And I was fucking terrible at tracking.

Had our pace really been that fast? Maybe vampires were somehow able to transfer some of their speed if they held your hand. Weirder things had happened. Today, even.

WITHIN AN HOUR OR TWO, DARIUS WAS BACK WITH A VERY angry Declan and Atlas in tow. The two were glaring daggers at him as they checked Eli and I over for any permanent damage, like they didn't trust his assurances. We filled them in on what happened with the wendigo creature, the expressions on their faces mirroring the disgust likely visible on my own.

Atlas was currently bent down, studying the dead girl with that objective fascination he seemed to have about anything pertaining to the hunt. The tension in his body suggested that he was partially upset he missed out on all the fun. That was two attacks on us now, since we arrived in the hell realm, and he'd been absent for both of them.

I could tell the control freak in him was itching for a battle of his own. I held back my scoff though, knowing that if I were him, I'd be feeling left out of the action too. Protectors were a ridiculous species. No wonder we died so young.

For now though, I was just happy that we were all together. And that the creepy girl didn't devour more of Eli and I than a few scraps of skin—as disgusting as that was.

For the most part, Eli and I had control over our bodies again and our wounds were on their way to healing. I'd used the rest of my water cleaning them out, on the off chance any of that grimy nastiness was lingering. Protectors didn't develop infections very often, but something told me that if anything was going to fight its way into our system and do some damage, it was hell slime.

Temporarily satisfied, I searched around the room and collected my dagger and all of the contents from my bag the little creep had dumped throughout the room. I tried not to grimace at the fact that my stuff was lying around in a pile of garbage and what looked peculiarly like some discarded bones. She'd clearly lured us back to her nest of sorts.

When in hell, I guess.

"We should get moving," Atlas said, shoving the girl's body with his shoe. Darius had not only stabbed her in the heart, but decapitated her for good measure. "This must've been their hunting ground."

Darius collected his things from the ground and shook his head. "We can't just move through the night. We aren't in the human realm. It's dangerous enough moving about during the light hours." He nodded towards me and Eli. "They need to rest up, make sure that they are back to full strength before we take on anything else. The venom they use can linger for hours and wandering through hell without full control of your body is a dangerous and reckless thing to do."

"So you want us to just stay here for the night, with the dead body?" I tried to keep the disgust from my voice, but it was definitely there. The wendigo creeped me out more than any creature I'd ever encountered before. Maybe because I'd never heard of one. And while a bloodsucker wasn't entirely different from a flesheater, it would take some time for the heebies to disappear. I didn't even want to think about what kind of pain I'd be in now if Darius hadn't rescued us—who knows how much of me would even be left.

Darius's expression was stern as he turned towards me, but I caught the way his lips pulled slightly in that devilish grin he wore so often. "There are other rooms here. You don't need to stay in this one. No one is asking you to play naptime with a corpse."

I narrowed my eyes at him because it sounded suspiciously like he was planning on leaving us here. After we'd spent our first however many hours in hell trying to collect everyone in one place. "And what do you plan on doing while we rest up, exactly?"

"I need to see if I can track down some of my old contacts. It's been years since I've been in this realm and if we try to traverse it carelessly, we will fail. Hell is not the sort of place you try to conquer without a plan. And things—they're different here than they were before. The magic and environment are devolving at a speed I hadn't anticipated."

I opened my mouth to argue but he raised a hand stopping me.

"If we fail, that means your beloved incubus will not be rescued, little protector. Which, last I understood, you were willing to sacrifice everything to achieve. Has that changed? Because tell me now, and I'm happy to brainstorm a plan that involves everyone telling ghost stories around a campfire while I fill up on food."

My lips snapped closed, answer enough. But I glared at him all the same for his taunting. If Darius could use his contacts to speed up the trip to hell, all the better. But—

I hated to admit it, but I was actually worried about him getting himself killed. He clearly wasn't exactly popular amongst his kind, so who knew what sort of reception he'd meet with once he found whoever it was he was going to look for. And would the rest of us just be left here in the meantime? Waiting around on the off chance he actually returned to us?

As if he could read my thoughts, he nodded towards Declan and Atlas. "You two should scout for some food, water. She needs resources, as do you all. We're almost out. Most vegetation is an offshoot of what you'd find in your realm, so it should be edible. But to be safe, bring everything you find back here and let me check it out before you ingest anything. Last thing we need is to worry about you lot either dying or hallucinating from eating the wrong kind of mushroom. Protectors don't exactly live in this realm, so it might be a bit of a guessing game as we figure out what works for you and what doesn't. Resources are, unfortunately, quite limited. More so even than they were last time I was here. Luckily, water is relatively plentiful, so that should be easy enough at least.

"All the same, it's dangerous here so move about mindfully. The wolf should help you blend in if necessary, but I'd rather not have to come hunt you both down and save you if it comes to it." He paused and turned towards me, his expression an innocent pout. "And just to be clear, I'd have to save them, right? We couldn't just cut our losses and keep going if it came down to it?"

I shot him a glare in answer.

He shrugged before moving towards the door, his posture lazy but confident. "Doesn't hurt to ask. It's not like my life is tethered to either of theirs."

❧ 14 ❧

MAX

Twenty minutes later, Eli and I were clearing out a room, layering the floor with our extra change of clothes. Alone.

"I can't believe they just left us here." I couldn't keep the dejection from my voice, even though I knew it made me sound like a child. "I feel perfectly fine now. I should be helping. What if they get ambushed and need us? Sitting around just feels so useless, like we're wasting valuable time."

Eli chuckled and threw down his jacket before pressing down gently on my shoulder until I sat down on top of it.

"You were almost eaten up just a couple of hours ago, love. You do realize that, right? If they think we'd do more harm than good, it's best that we stay hunkered down here and take sleep in shifts. When they get back with provisions, we'll keep watch while they get rest." I glared at him but he shrugged me off and ran his hand playfully through my hair, knotting it all up. Thank god there weren't any mirrors around, I was better off not knowing how terrible I looked. "Sometimes working in a team isn't as glamorous as it appears. You have to share the glory and make sure everyone is at the top of their game, whatever it takes. Right now, it takes us staying here and out of the way until we can be certain that all of that nasty shit is out of our blood-stream. Glory and stubbornness aren't so great if the result is someone getting hurt or killed."

I exhaled and gave him a reluctant nod, thinking about the last time I'd forced my way into a battle I shouldn't have been in. If I'd stayed back then, it's possible we wouldn't even be in this mess in the first place; hell, it's possible Wade's incubus side would never have been triggered at all if I hadn't gone barging out that night, determined to rescue Ralph.

So on some level, yes, I knew that he was right, but it didn't stop the lingering frustration and helplessness. I wanted so desperately to actually *do* something, to help. I hated feeling powerless, and like I was the weak link in the group, constantly being rescued instead of doing the rescuing. It was infuriating.

I wanted to be strong. Powerful. More.

We sat in silence for a few long moments, until I became acutely aware of the fact that this was the first time I'd been alone with Eli since I'd woken up from that dream with him and Wade. The memory of it sent a rush of heat flooding through my body and I suddenly found myself embarrassed about being in his presence. Alone. In a quiet room with our clothes ripped to shreds.

My dreams with Wade tended to fade after a while, but the details of that one still lingered along my skin. I could almost still feel every stroke of Eli's finger, of his tongue. Did he remember what happened? Did he regret it if he did?

"I wonder how things back at The Guild are going," he mused, completely oblivious to the maelstrom of emotions fluttering through my stomach. His lips turned down and he started to fiddle with the fabric underneath us. "I hope my dad isn't too upset about us leaving," he chuckled and stared down at me, his brown eyes filled with a soft vulnerability that I rarely saw in them. The rare occasions it had made an appearance, we'd been sitting out at his peaceful lake. This room...had a completely different vibe. "I mean, of course he's pissed. But I hope he isn't too worried. Maybe having Cy there will help take some of the edge off." He paused and shook his head, his lips turning up slightly in a shadow of a grin, though there was no humor behind it. "Doubt it though. Neither of them are particularly warm and comforting, least of all Cyrus."

I could tell in the short time that I'd known them that while Eli and Seamus were both incredibly guarded and stubborn, that they cared deeply for each other. And I knew that leaving without telling his father was ripping Eli up inside. It was a sharp betrayal. Not only was he acting without his father's knowledge, but he was directly working against everything The Guild stood for—all for the chance to save Wade.

It was something I acutely understood—I'd been forcing Ro and Cyrus from my thoughts as much as possible, otherwise the guilt at leaving them behind without a thorough explanation would unravel me completely.

"Did your father talk much about Cy?" I asked, realizing that Eli and I had never really discussed this before, despite the fact that Cy was his uncle. Part of me was filled with a petty jealousy that he had a tie to Cy that I never would—blood. It was an undeniable family connection and one, I was learning, that protectors seemed to value above all else. My own lack of a family gene pool was something I was only becoming more and more aware of, the more entrenched in Guild society I became.

He shook his head and leaned back on his arms, his brows pinched together slightly in thought. I tried to ignore the way his shirt pulled up slightly from the stretch, revealing the toned lines of his lower abs. He was an infuriatingly beautiful creature and sometimes it felt almost impossible to ignore my obvious attraction to him.

"Not really. I met him maybe once or twice while I was growing up. My father would go to see him on occasion in this small town a few hours out and he'd occasionally bring me with him. But Cyrus was always standoffish and gruff when we met, barely sparing me more than a nod and sentence or two, before sending me off to go run some useless grocery errand while he and my father caught up." He bit his bottom lip, lost in the memory. "I always got the feeling that Cyrus didn't want to be there, that he was just doing it as a formality to keep his brother happy, you know? Like it was a strange family obligation more than anything else—the only way to keep my father off his back about returning to The Guild." He ran a lazy hand through his hair, pulling out a few leaves and debris from the fight. "They were close, you know? Not like you and Ro close, maybe, but close all the same."

"I didn't know that," I let out a humorless chuckle. "Cy never even mentioned he had a brother until Seamus greeted us at Headquarters that night." He was always standoffish and private, even when it came to me and Ro. So while I could tell that Eli took it more or less personally that Cy brushed him off all those years, that was just the way that he was. I learned to love that about him, as frustrating as it could be. "What about us?"

Cy wasn't exactly the sort of proud father who'd carry pictures around in his wallet, but I wondered if he'd ever mentioned us before preparing to move back into the society he'd so mysteriously left behind.

"My father mentioned on occasion that Cy had adopted kids, but it wasn't something we discussed very often. And I was forbidden from mentioning our meetings with him to anyone else. Their rendezvous were always shrouded in absolute secrecy." He grinned, a wistful expression creeping over his face. "Back then I thought that was the coolest thing ever—like I was being allowed on a secret mission, despite being a student. And there was something sort of intoxicating about walking around Headquarters, having met the infamous Cyrus Bentley. Especially since so many people were convinced he was dead."

I studied Eli, wondering what it would have been like to grow up at The Guild, surrounded by family and friends. And, perhaps more than those things, knowledge about our world, about my heritage.

"That's good that Seamus didn't keep everything a secret with you, that he shared those meetings even if they weren't frequent," I said, my words hushed as a familiar bitterness settled in my stomach. As much as I tried to ignore it, I was hurt by how much Cy had kept from me. I was strong and I could fight, but Ro and I would have been so much better prepared to take on this world if Cy hadn't tried to hide us from it for so long.

Eli's lips tightened and he nudged my foot with his. "I wouldn't take it personally, Max. Uncle Cyrus had a difficult past. I think he wanted to keep himself as far away from The Guild as he could, to be honest. Not telling you about his brother, about his career—I think that was his way of protecting you from the pain that comes with being a protector. You and Ro were the life he chose, sounds like he just wanted to erase everything that came before that and focus on the life he actually wanted, rather than the one he was born into."

Much to my surprise, his words felt like a soothing balm, like it was something I always knew more or less but needed to hear all the same. Because as frustrated as I was with Cy, Eli was right. He chose to raise me and Ro. He chose to devote his time and energy to training us and keeping us safe when he didn't need to.

"He's never seemed particularly paternal," I said, considering my words carefully. "I was always shocked—as were most of the people in town—that he even adopted us in the first place. He seemed to crave isolation something fierce. Raising a couple of kids in the middle of nowhere when he had no obligation—it just always seemed so out of character." I swallowed, my throat clogging a bit with emotion. As much as I loved Cy like a father, sometimes I worried that he didn't feel the same. Abandonment issues were a bitch. "But I think you're right. He did choose me and Ro, even if I don't always understand why."

A guardedness came over Eli and he slouched slightly, considering, his eyes suddenly averted from mine. I got the feeling that he knew something I didn't. Which was pretty on par for me. Most people seemed to know more about Cy than I did.

"Do you know much about your parents—where you came from?" he asked, the words falling out in a rush like he had to get them out before he could think twice about saying them at all.

I shook my head, my limbs suddenly antsy with the familiar frustration that sense of lack built up. "He's only ever told me that I showed up on his doorstep with nothing at all, not even a name. Any time I've tried to press for more, he's shut down. Like he was just as guarded about my past as he was about his own. It always infuriated me. Eventually, I just stopped asking."

And part of me had hoped that I'd find the answers to my questions once I joined The Guild. Learning that no one seemed to know where I'd come from had pierced more than I thought it would. It was like my entire history was simply erased, like it didn't matter to anyone since no one had any answers.

After a long, drawn-out moment, he turned back to me, a sad smile pulling his lips up at the corners. Pity. I much preferred his usual cocky, devilish grin on him. "He might just be a guarded dude, Max. Heartbreak has a way of doing that to a guy. I'm sure he'll open up one day. If he opens up to anyone, it will be you and your brother. Of that I'm certain."

I broke out laughing, puncturing the quiet moment like an overextended balloon. The idea of Cy ever experiencing something remotely like heartbreak was absolutely ridiculous, but after Eli didn't join in with me, my reaction died down.

"Wait. You're serious?" I waited for him to join in on the joke with me, figuring he was just trying to lighten the mood. "You can't really mean that Cyrus left because of a relationship? Like, with another person?"

Cyrus Bentley, the man who chose to spend his life living in the woods, in almost complete isolation; the man who treated going into town for groceries like most would greet an afternoon of creative torture, simply because there would be *people* around. Not a chance.

Maybe the wendigo poison was messing with his brain.

Eli chuckled soundlessly, clearly amused by my own amusement. "Dead serious. Not surprised he didn't mention it, though. It's not the sort of thing an already private person would likely openly share. I only know because of my father. And it's one of those topics he'd only occasionally bring up because he was drinking and his guard was down—that's the only time he reminisces about the good old days."

I could feel my jaw dropping as I turned towards Eli, every atom of my body focused on pulling the story out of him. "You have to spill, Eli Bentley. It's basically mandatory."

I tucked my legs under my ass and settled in for his tale, like I was a giddy schoolgirl.

He scrunched up his nose, considering, before finally turning back towards me. "There's not a whole lot to tell. Sorry to disappoint. I don't know much. Just that he was in love with Alleva—"

"What?" I yelled, far too loudly for someone hiding out in an old warehouse, trying not to pull in unwanted attention from wandering neighborhood demons. "You can't seriously mean to tell me that he and Alleva were into each other...like that?" I added with a whisper, as if that might negate my earlier exclamation.

His eyes danced with amusement as he studied me, and I could tell that he was pleased that his big reveal didn't disappoint. "The one and only. They were in love and on the same field team way back when. There were supposedly big plans for them to bond, but at the last minute Alleva pulled out and bonded to two other people. I think it had something to do with her father. Cy was, believe it or not, a bit of a rebel back in the day, and while he was top of his class, a lot of people were wary about being tethered to him. But I'm not really certain of the details."

I toyed with some of the cloth we were lying back on, trying to picture a world in which Cyrus could be in love with someone. He'd barely so much as even looked at any of the women in town and never once mentioned a previous relationship. Was this why he'd kept us from this world for so long? Why he'd chosen to hide out on the side of the mountain, adopting two abandoned kids as his duty to his heritage? Heartbreak?

My chest squeezed at the thought of him going through that sort of pain, at the possibility that he'd changed the entire course of his life because of it.

And then I thought about Reza—and how close he could have come to being her father instead of mine. Or, well, not her father exactly, since she wouldn't be the same person if she had his DNA, but the father of someone like her all the same.

"What happened?" I asked, leaning towards Eli, hanging on every single syllable of what he had to say. He might not be able to give me much on my own history, but I'd eat up every bit of Cy's that he offered.

He shrugged and scratched the back of his neck, thinking. "Our dads are stubborn men. And I know that mine took heartbreak very hard. Cyrus is even more intense, so it makes sense that he couldn't handle being around Alleva after that. He did save her though, before leaving."

I'd heard part of this story, but I didn't know the details. That Cyrus had taken on two vampires solo, walking away with nothing but a few bruises, cuts, and some permanent damage to his leg.

"Do you know the details of that night?" I asked, almost ashamed that I didn't know them myself. Cyrus was, after all, the person I'd known the longest in my life. If anyone should have known about his past, it was me. But he'd kept everything from me, which left an uncomfortable ache in my belly every time I lingered on that fact.

Eli's dark eyes filled with what looked alarmingly like pity again. A realization that sent a jolt of discomfort and further embarrassment through my chest. I didn't want pity. It was the one thing that could make learning all of this secondhand even worse.

As if recognizing this just as I felt it, Eli gripped my hand softly in his and shook his head. "No one really knows the details of that night, not even my father. And if Alleva does, she's never spilled to anyone as far as I can tell. All I know is that as soon as Cyrus was well enough to walk on his own, he took off in the middle of the night." He shrugged, his brows tilted in focus. "My father doesn't talk about that time in his life too much. It was hard on him—having his best friend leave like that. He looked up to Cy, admired him intensely." He paused and glanced over at me, a wistful smile on his face. "They were on the same field team too, and were probably just as widely-respected and feared amongst their age group as Atlas is now. They were supposed to be the next big thing. I think losing that—losing his best friend and brother—sort of took something from him. Something he never quite got back."

I sat with that for a moment, thinking about how I would feel if Ro just up and left me one day to navigate this life on my own. The thought alone had my stomach tightening with anxiety. As soon as I got back to Guild Headquarters, I was going to make that dude sign a contract—in blood—promising never to ditch me.

And there had to be so much more to the story than Eli knew. Curiosity filled me as I sifted through the threads, trying to make the puzzle pieces fit together in my mind. I desperately wanted to know what happened between Alleva and Cy the night of the attack. Alleva was one of the most powerful protectors we had at Headquarters—what kind of situation had she gotten into that left Cy fighting off two vampires without her help? And with the rigorous details The Guild kept on missions, how was it that no one seemed to know the full story of this one?

And then I traced my version of Cy against what I'd just learned—the subtle anger and pain that he seemed to always carry, no matter what; the way he frequently used alcohol or excessive training to try and block out his ghosts, like he was constantly running away from them, lest they catch up. Had it all been because he was heartbroken? Or was there more to the story? And why had he chosen that night to abandon The Guild entirely, when he could have just as easily gone with his brother and joined another team at any of the other Guild satellites or headquarters around the world? If he was the top of his class, it wasn't like he wouldn't have had options.

There were so many dead ends, so many stray pieces that didn't fully make sense. After learning these few details, all that I was left with was the aching realization that I didn't know Cyrus very well at all. Only the parts of himself that he allowed me to see, which wasn't very much in the grand scheme of things. Hell, even complete strangers seemed to know more about his past and his life before our cabin than I did.

I felt a gentle pressure squeezing my hand and I glanced down, studying the way that Eli's fingers wrapped around mine. Seeing our skin touching, feeling his against mine, sent my mind flooding with visuals of my dream and I momentarily welcomed the shift in my focus. This was a sort of anxiety that was fun to linger in, an exciting sort of stomach plummeting. My mind filled with visuals of the way he'd pushed me up against the wall and kissed me like he was a drowning man and I was the only source of water for miles, the mind boggling sensation of his head tucked between my legs while Wade watched with a greedy expression in his eyes. As much as I didn't understand it, I wanted back in that moment, I wanted to bury myself in those sensations and forget all of the drama and violence of the real world. No more hell, no more family drama, no more Guild politics. Just feeling.

Heat flooded my body and I slowly lifted my eyes, heavy with lust, from our hands to meet his face. He was a terrifyingly beautiful creature. His dark hair was still mussed from our fight with the wendigo, and the lower half of his face was coated in a dark shadow from going days without shaving. That typical cocky smirk tilted his lips, as if he knew where my thoughts had suddenly turned, as if he was navigating them there himself, just through willpower. He leaned forward slightly, like he wanted to close the distance between us as much as I did.

My lips felt like magnets, like they had no purpose in the entire world, other than to latch against his—and the longer we waited, the more desperate it felt.

I could feel my heart beating like a rabid animal against my ribcage as I watched him inch closer and closer to me. But at the last second, panic took over and I pulled back.

"I'm sorry about the dream," I blurted out, pulling my hand from his. My eyes dropped instantly from his tempting-as-fuck grin, to stare instead at my lap. I needed to not feel this way about Eli. He'd made it very clear that he wasn't exactly the relationship type, and while losing myself in him for a little while would be fun, I wasn't certain I'd be able to resurface. Not now, not anymore. I knew him now—he was so much more than just a hot guy I saw at school. Our lives were permanently woven together through Cy and Seamus. There wasn't an option to kiss and forget, to go back to pretending like nothing had happened.

Firm fingers tilted my chin up so that I was staring into his warm brown eyes, any sign of his usual taunting smirk nowhere in sight. There was an almost angry edge to his face as his eyes studied me. "Why the hell would you be sorry for that? It was, by far, the best fucking dream I've ever had in my entire life. Without a doubt. And I have a pretty good imagination, so that's saying something."

I sucked in a deep breath, trying to force my racing pulse to calm down. "I mean, the thing with Wade's powers is that it heightens any kind of—urges. And that was your first time being in a dream with an incubus and you were already in a weakened state. I should have known better and stopped before things got so car—"

My words cut off as Eli's lips pressed into mine, somehow the perfect combination of hard and soft. Memories of the last time he'd kissed me came flooding back, memories not of a dream, but sitting quietly at a pond—our pond. He was so different there, so open. As if it was muscle memory, my body seemed to sing when his was pressed up against it, just as it did then.

There was a sort of rightness about being pressed against Eli, an all-encompassing feeling of home.

But then I remembered the rejection. The way it felt when he'd pulled away that day, the shame that had consumed me.

I pushed away from him before things could deepen and shook my head, desperately trying to find the words I needed.

His face looked so dejected as he stared at me with a mixture of hunger and something I didn't quite know how to place. The usual arched brow and lip-tilting smirk were completely erased, making him seem so much more serious, more vulnerable than he usually did.

"I-I'm sorry," he said, leaning back and rubbing his hand over his face. He let out a frustrated sigh. "I didn't mean to take advantage. I thought—"

Confusion flooded me at his apology. "I just—last time, it didn't seem like you wanted this. Like you wanted me."

His face flushed as his eyes found mine, the hunger in their depths amplified. "Max, you didn't take advantage of me in that dream. I knew what I was doing, and whatever I was feeling there had nothing to do with Wade. Once I saw you, he all but disappeared from focus for me. And before—" he shook his head, his tongue peeking out to wet his lips as he considered me, searching for the words. I followed the movement with a hollow hunger, my eyes fixated on his plush upper lip. "It was compli-cated, and my head wasn't straight—it was just, I needed—look, I shouldn't have just left you like that and then pretended like it didn't happen." He let out a humorless, deep chuckle that did strange twisty things to my stomach. "Sometimes I can be an absolute ass. But trust me when I tell you that it's all I've thought about since it happened. The way you felt against me, the way you tasted—" He blew out a frustrated breath and ran his hands through his hair, "I know on some level that this is a bad idea. Like a colossally bad fucking idea. I just—I don't think I care anymore. That's not a good enough reason."

His voice was low, gravelly almost, and I could feel myself practically panting, lingering on every word.

Warmth spread through my limbs as he studied me, my entire body filled with a tingling energy. It was a heady thing, having Eli Bentley focus all of his attention on you. His eyes left no question as to what he wanted to do, what he wanted from me. The way he stared at me now, I might as well have been naked already. And maybe I could survive just one encounter—just one desperate attempt to erase the heated desire from my system. Maybe then we could focus on other things, if we just took care of this tension now.

"I just, I understand if you wanted it to be a one off sort of thing. I know that you have a rep—"

He swallowed the rest of my words and this time when his lips pressed against mine, there was no gentleness, no question of what it was that he wanted.

"Do you want this, Max?" he asked, the question forming against my lips as he kissed the seam of my mouth, before trailing down to my neck, the pressure feather light and intoxicating. "That is all I need to know."

I nodded, my tongue tied up in knots from the sensation of his tongue pressing against my skin.

I could feel his grin against my skin just before his teeth nipped my pulse point with a playful bite. "I'm going to need you to say it," he said, his tone cocky and voice deep. He knew exactly the kind of effect he had on a girl. And while I would have thought the reminder that he was so experienced would have turned me off, it only heightened my excitement. I wanted nothing more than for this to continue for as long as he was willing. I wanted the distraction, to get lost in something fun and frivolous, if only for a few moments. I wanted the full Eli experience—wanted to know exactly what it was I'd been missing out on.

He drew his fingers down my arm, light as a feather and pulled my wrist to his mouth. With eyes focused on mine, he kissed my wrist, the sensation sending a shocked jolt up my arm. Who knew that a wrist could feel like that? Then he drew my arm towards him and nipped and licked the inside of my elbow.

I clenched my thighs with need as he brought his face up to my neck, his lips tracing a design into my clavicle.

"What do you want, Max?" he asked, his voice a whisper that sent chills along my skin.

"Right now, I want this," I said, my words coming out as a pant as he slowly threaded his hand up my shirt before gently pulling it off in one graceful move. Even the sensation of the fabric grazing against my skin felt like playing with a delicious fire. That he could make my body feel like it wanted to explode from such a simple gesture, sent heat through my core in anticipation.

He pulled back as the fabric fell away and studied me, eyes languid and reverent. The sight of him staring at me in nothing but a bra sent my pulse into overdrive. His eyes narrowed as his gaze met mine, his lips pulled up in that half-amused grin he wore so often.

"And what exactly do you mean by this?" he asked, his hand wrapping around my back to unclasp my bra in a move so quick and deft that it fell away with far more ease than I could have managed myself. My breasts felt full, heavy under his perusal. "I want you to tell me exactly what it is that you want."

There was an authority in his words that licked at my insides like an impossibly dangerous fire. I glanced down at his lap and the realization that he was just as affected as I was filled me with a delicious power—and with a desire to let him take all of the control, at least in this instance.

"I want to escape for just a little while. I want you," I said simply, surprising myself with the honesty in my voice. Because while I knew that Eli was a fucking force to be reckoned with, and that we were in hell on a rescue mission that we quite possibly wouldn't survive—in this moment, I wanted all of that to slip away, to just be a girl with a boy and enjoy it. Every last second of it. No more protector bullshit, no complications, just sensations. "That's it. Just you."

His eyes flashed with heat as he studied me, his hands dancing excruciatingly slow up my stomach and then my chest as he lightly pushed me back until my head landed on the bed of clothes. "Then that's what you'll get. That, at least, I can deliver."

His deft fingers circled my nipple as his other hand held mine above my head with enough force to keep me still as my back arched towards him, like my body was possessed.

He laughed against my skin, which felt like electricity was rippling through me, before moving to my other nipple, each breath making my nerves light up.

He looked up at me, the sharp angles of his face and that look of confidence in his eyes enough to undo me right there. This time when his lips met mine, there was a sort of knowing in the gesture, a desire to draw the moment out as much as possible—no rush now that we knew exactly where this encounter was going. We'd done the work of ironing out the details, and now we could just enjoy watching them unfold.

My tongue met his with a flash of sensations that already had my toes curling. And I realized then that while it was intoxicating being with him in our dream, it paled in comparison to being with Eli in real life, to feeling his body pressed against mine.

Despite being in a grimy warehouse, in which we'd both almost been killed by a flesh-eating demon a few hours ago, all I could feel and smell and focus on was him. And for just this once, I was going to let myself do just that—no apologies.

I slid my leg between his, until I could feel him hard as a rock against my thigh, grinning as he exhaled from the friction.

He deepened our kiss, his tongue fighting against mine as he wound his hands to the base of my neck, his fingers tangling in my hair. I found myself happy to be lying back on the ground, because I knew with absolute certainty that my knees would buckle immediately if I was standing. It was like I was a puppet, my limbs made of jelly that he alone could support.

It was strange, but even after hiking for miles over hell's terrain and fighting a creepy demon, he still smelled great—the perfect mix of musk and spice.

Slowly he dragged one of his hands down, his fingers teasing the skin of my neck briefly until he reached my left nipple and pinched. I gasped into his mouth as the sensation sent a wave throughout my body.

He grinned against my mouth before playfully biting my bottom lip.

Not wanting to give him all of the control just yet, I wrapped my legs around his lower body and twisted my hips until our positions were reversed and he was underneath me.

His expression was filled with surprise as I wrapped my fingers around his wrists and pinned them against the floor. I might not have a ton of sexual experience, but I was excellent at sparring—and if the thick bulge pressing against my core was a sign of anything, the two methods of contact weren't all that far from each other.

Keeping him pinned, I brought my lips down to his, biting his bottom lip in an echo of his move, before kissing down his jawline and neck.

"I'm not used to giving up control in the bedroom." Even though I couldn't see it, I could hear him smiling. I bit softly down on his pulse point, smirking as the move caused him to throb with excitement. "But clearly it's worth considering every now and then," he whispered, his words sounding almost like a hiss.

I let my weight fall down on him and let out a gasp. He was hard as a rock and larger than I'd realized—and the feel of him against me sent a wave of uncontrollable desire through my body. My core tightened as I rubbed up and down against him. Letting go of one of his wrists I unbuttoned his jeans, my fingers a tangled mess from the anticipation and nerves.

Just as I finished unzipping him, I found myself on my ass, staring up at the ceiling. Eli's hands grabbed my hips and dragged me back toward him so that my knees were bent and his head was planted between my thighs. Memories flooded back to the last time he'd been in this position in my dream.

He cocked an eyebrow, not breaking eye contact as he bit my inner thigh. The mix of pleasure and pain made me feel dizzy with anticipation—every move he made as deliciously unpredictable as the last. "You're not the only one who knows how to blur the boundaries between fighting and fucking, love."

With far more composure and grace than I'd managed, he pulled my pants and underwear down, until I was completely bare before him. The cool air against my skin made my body erupt with goosebumps.

My body hummed with excitement as I waited for him to close the distance between his mouth and my clit. And once he did, I almost fell apart right there. Every sensation was amplified so that the dream felt like an echo of reality. How could I have even once thought that I had had him in that dream—it was nothing but a shadow.

His tongue moved with slow, teasing movements, his eyes taking me in with greedy excitement. "You're delicious," he murmured, his words a low growl that added to the already dizzying feeling of his tongue against me.

I heated at his words, but before I could get too self-conscious, he slid a finger inside of me and I bucked against him.

"Jesus," he said, his expression filled with awe as he watched me, his mouth and his finger working together in a perfect cadence. "So fucking wet."

My breathing picked up as he inserted a second finger. I could feel my walls tightening around him, like my body was trying to keep him inside of me, terrified that he would stop doing whatever magic he was doing.

His lips trailed along my thigh, alternating between long, languid kisses, and soft nips. When his mouth made its way back to my opening, I wound my fingers into his hair. He pulled his fingers out and replaced it with his tongue, drawing a loud moan from my lips as his fingers rubbed along the sides of my clit.

"I want you to come for me," he said, his eyes on mine and filled with challenge. He pinched my clit lightly between his lips and grinned. "Now."

As if my body was his to command, an orgasm went rippling through my body. I'd come before. It wasn't a new thing for me. But this? This was something else. I was half convinced that my body was growing addicted to Eli. That I'd never be able to do anything ever again other than fuck him on this floor.

His tongue drew lazy patterns as the convulsions ran their course. His expression was smug, that cocky grin I was growing frustratingly fond of plastered on his face.

With a smooth movement, I yanked on his hair until he got the hint and crawled up my body.

"Eli," I said, my voice hoarse with need, "I want you inside of me. Now."

Whatever he was expecting, that wasn't it, because the arrogance on his face melted away until all that was there was pure need, and maybe a little fear.

"You're sure?" he asked, his voice husky as his eyes bored into mine, his arrogance drying into something softer, more serious. "We don't have to."

"I'm sure."

He nodded, his hand sliding into his pocket. He pulled out a shiny wrapper and peeled it open. Leave it to Eli Bentley walk into hell prepared to fuck.

With quick, studied fingers, he pulled off his boxer-briefs, finishing the job I'd started in my frantic excitement, and slid on the condom.

He lifted my head slightly and brought my lips to his. He tasted sweet and a little like salt, and a wave of heat flooded me as I realized that what I was tasting was me. While I would have thought it would gross me out, tasting me on his lips just turned me on. I could feel my own wetness coating my thighs. His kiss was gentler than it had been, almost reverent, as he slid himself between my legs.

There was pressure, but it didn't hurt like I thought it might when he pushed into me. His movement was slow and steady as he waited for me to adjust to his size, until, with one small thrust he was buried all the way in.

He stilled, his body tensed as my walls closed around him.

"You okay?" he asked

I nodded and deepened our kiss until our tongues were just as entangled as our bodies were.

He groaned into my mouth and started to pull out until the tip of his dick was at my opening, and then he slammed back into me. The feel of his cock sinking into me made me feel dizzy with need.

He repeated the gesture, groaning into my mouth as I bit down on his lip.

I wrapped my legs around his waist, pulling him closer to me as he pumped in and out, my body climbing with each thrust towards another release.

"Jesus," he whispered, as I met his eyes. The brown depths were filled with a desire so hot, I was half convinced I'd melt into a puddle from it.

I used the momentum to push us towards the side until I was the one on top now. My hands pressed into his firm chest as I rode him, hovering a few inches above until his hands dug into my hips and impaled me. I could feel each finger leave a soft indentation against my hips as he lifted me up and down, over and over again, guiding me, building the pace up. I was jelly now, no longer able to even act under the illusion that I had control of the situation.

I bent down and kissed him, as he pulled me closer and closer to the edge. He held me against him and flipped us until my back was against the pile of clothes on the floor. With one final thrust, I exploded, my nails digging into his back as he swallowed my moan with his lips, following me over the edge himself.

For a long moment, we laid there, both of us throbbing from the aftershocks, until he finally regained the ability to move his limbs and lifted off of me. With a loud, satisfied exhale, he leaned back down and pulled me into his side, my head resting against his chest.

"I can see why you're so fond of that," I said, my words breathless and relaxed in a way that sparring never quite managed, though it often came close.

He stiffened below me, his arm tightening around my body like he was pinning it to him.

"Yeah," was all he said, though I could tell that there was more there, beneath the surface.

Instead of pulling it from him, I closed my eyes and fell slowly into a peaceful sleep, feeling somehow safe and sated, despite the fact that we were in hell, surrounded by the remnants of a wendigo nest.

☙ 15 ❧

ELI

"Umph, go away," I said, my body relaxed and fighting its way back to sleep from whatever the hell disturbed it in the first place.

I curled my head back down until it was met with that intoxicating vanilla scent again. I breathed in deeply, grinning as the scent tickled my nose. My body seemed to relax as it washed over me, like a peculiar sort of magic. My back hurt like bitch and there weren't enough blankets, but I couldn't remember ever being this comfortable, this relaxed.

The soft nudge in my side grew into something less gentle. I opened my eyes and found Max curled up against me, her head resting on my chest. I watched her form lift with each of her breaths as panic filled me.

I'd never actually slept with a girl before. I mean I'd slept with more girls than I could count, but we never actually did any sleeping. Usually after I fucked, I either went home or sent them packing back to theirs. There was something wildly intimate about sleeping next to someone—it was a sort of vulnerability I was never comfortable with. Ever. It was the sort of thing that was a breeding ground for...feelings. And I was not reckless enough to head down that path.

Or so I thought anyway.

As if in a rush, images of Max tangled up against me came rushing back. That was new too. I'd fucked a lot of girls, but I'd never once done that—never once came at the same time as one of them or been so fucking mesmerized by watching them fall into a million pieces beneath me. Hell, I'd almost come just from watching her body spasm while I was going down on her. My body reacted to hers like a finely-tuned instrument, and the second I was inside of her I'd almost lost it.

It was like I was a damned teenager all over again and I had to actively try not to come instantly.

My hand ran over her hair, soft enough that I wouldn't wake her. Lazily I dragged my fingers down her back, feeling the dips and wells of her curves, lingering against her impossibly-soft skin. I needed to find out what kind of lotion she used, because damn if I wasn't addicted to it already.

We'd been gentle this time, softer than I usually was, but just the thought of her on top of me, riding me until she found her release—or the image of me ramming into her from behind with her wrists tied to my headboard was enough to get me hard all over again. I was ready for round two. Which was a huge fucking problem, because I had no idea how the hell I was supposed to survive this place if all I could think about was getting lost between the sheets with her body tangled against mine.

"Get up you asshole," a voice whispered next to me, "Atlas is ready to murder you and, for once, I can't even blame him."

I jumped from the sound and instinctively covered my erection. My head snapped as I turned my attention from Max and saw Declan's black boot inches from my face. When my eyes drew up, I saw that hers were narrowed and glaring daggers at me—like bright green pricks of light that wanted to peel my skin back layer-by-layer.

Fuck.

I nodded, and slowly crawled out from underneath Max, lifting her head so that I could gently rest it down on some of our makeshift bedding. Declan had seen me naked often enough that I didn't sweat her stare too much as I fished around for my clothes. And right now, it was easier to let her stare at my ass rather than meet her judgy little eyes.

This was not supposed to happen. I was not supposed to fuck Max. And I was definitely not supposed to get caught if I did.

With one last glance down at Max, Dec spun from the room, her mouth set in that firm way of hers that let me know instantly that this was no joking matter—she was livid. Fan-fucking-tastic. If she was that pissed, I didn't even want to think about how Atlas would react.

My limbs were drained as I stuffed one leg and then the other into my pants. I could feel my pulse thumping like a jack-hammer and I simultaneously wanted to get as far away from Max as I could, all while bringing her with me in the process.

What the hell was that about?

I looked at her, at the way her dark hair fanned out around her head, a few strands covering her face as each of her exhales blew softly against them. I bent down and carefully swept them off of her cheek, my fingers lingering near her mouth. Her lips were impossibly soft and all I wanted to do in that moment was press them against my own, to taste every atom of her.

She shifted slightly so that her face pressed against my palm. The movement shifted the fabric scraps and I damn near lost it all over again when I saw her chest.

For months I'd been convinced that if I could just get her out of my system, that I would be able to move on. But now that I'd had her, I didn't think I could ever go back to fucking random girls again. Every single molecule of my body had been alive as I entered her, it was like she was made for me and I wanted all the time in the world to explore every inch of her. Again and again and again.

Jesus fucking christ. I was screwed.

It took every ounce of willpower to pull my hand back from

her, to take a few steps away and follow Declan out into the other room—not least of all because I knew what awaited me when I did.

I shut the heavy metal door softly behind me and the second it latched, I went flying into the wall and landed on my ass.

"What the fuck," I whisper-yelled as I stared up, expecting to find myself confronted with another demon. Instead, all I saw was Atlas. My back straightened as I studied him, trying to keep the shock from my face. He'd never attacked me like that before. And I'd had years of pissing him off, half the time just because I wanted to see how much I could push him before he broke. This—this was what broke him? "What the hell are you doing?"

I stood up, ignoring the sting in my shoulder from where I'd landed against it. As soon as I was on my two feet again, Atlas pressed his forearm to my throat, pinning me against the wall. I opened my mouth to call him out, but then I noticed his eyes— bright yellow without a brown speck in sight.

I raised my hands in surrender as I watched his ragged breathing convulse through his body. "Alright man, we're good. Calm down."

He growled in response. Fucking growled. It was easy to forget that Atlas was sharing his body with a monster these days, but moments like this made it alarmingly clear how out of our element we were when it came to his transition. We'd been tricking ourselves into thinking we were in control of the situation.

"Atlas," Declan whispered from a few feet away. "Breathe. It's Eli. You need to calm down. Get your wolf under control."

She was the best at calming him, but it didn't escape my notice that she was standing several feet away—like even she wasn't sure if she could talk him off this ledge this time.

"What happened out there?" I whispered out of the side of my mouth to her, as if Atlas couldn't hear every syllable with crystal-clear precision. "Why's he so riled up?"

"What the fuck do you think happened, you fucking dick-head?" she snapped.

I didn't want to look away from Atlas because I was pretty certain that if I did, he'd go for my jugular, but I glanced out of the side of my eyes and saw Dec pinning me with a glare, like I was the one attacking my teammate and not the other way around.

"What the hell were you thinking, Eli?" She took a few steps closer, but made sure to still stay out of range of Atlas' limbs, just in case he shifted his aggression on her. "You fucked his mate. And a mate he's using every ounce of willpower to reject—in that way. And then with a shrug you just go and fuck her your-self." She shook her head, letting out a humorless laugh as she ran both of her hands through her hair like she couldn't believe she had to deal with my tactlessness, here of all places. "I mean Jesus, we're gone for three hours. Three hours. And you were supposed to be healing. And yet you still decided that your fucking libido took precedence. We're in hell one day and you decide it's the perfect time to get your dick wet. The fuck is your problem?"

My stomach dropped at the mate comment. After everything we'd been through over the last week, I'd almost forgotten that Atlas's wolf seemed to be just as drawn to Max as the rest of us were. But he'd assured us he was resisting it, that it wasn't a true wolf bond and all of that garbage he liked to spew wherever she was concerned. The only thing Atlas ignored more than his interest in Max was his wolf.

"It's not like he's claimed her," I responded, my voice drip-ping with frustration as I stared at Atlas. I could see from the way his body was shaking that it was literally taking every ounce of control he had not to wolf out right now and tear me limb-from-limb. "I mean, you did say you weren't going to act on it. And she's a consenting adult. There's no rule—"

The pressure against my throat increased until my airways were cut off.

Fuck. Fuck. "Wrong thing to say. I can see that now," I choked out, my voice sounding like it got in a fight with a garbage disposal and lost as I tried to create some space between his forearm and my trachea.

"Atlas," Declan said, her voice as soothing as she was able to make it, but Declan wasn't exactly great at disguising her own anger. I watched as she extended a tentative hand to his shoulder —a thoughtless move to touch a rabid werewolf, but she tended to have her head in the sand where Atlas was concerned. "Calm down. He's an asshat, but it's Eli. You'll hate yourself if you accidentally kill him." She glared over at me, her green eyes filled with more rage than I'd seen in them in a long ass time. "While ending him doesn't sound like the worst idea right now, I don't think you'll come back from that. So calm down and wait for another creature to decapitate him. Not you. I can't deal with every single member of this team losing it all at once."

"She's mine," Atlas growled, though he released some of the pressure against my neck. He was so close to wolfing out that I was surprised he was able to get even two words past his lips while trying to fight it down.

Rage boiled in my eyes as I stared at him. Max was not his, and the thought of someone else claiming her had my chest tightening like I was being hugged by a metal robot. I kneed him in the dick—a break in bro code if ever there was one—and cranked my fist back as he bent over.

Before I could punch him, Declan elbowed me in the stomach, pulling a surprised groan from my mouth.

"What the fuck?" I choked out, doubling over like Atlas had just done.

I looked up at her and noticed her eyes were wide with shock —and maybe a little bit of disgust too.

"What the hell are you doing? Kicking a guy on the edge of a battle with his monster in the dick? You're going to get yourself killed, you fucking twat." She turned away from us both, her hands clutching her hair as we both turned to watch her.

"You'll get along with men, they said; join a team with guys you're friends with, they said; not all guys are fucking neanderthals, they said." She spun back around, leveling us both with a glare. "Well, they were wrong. You're both absolute wanks. Max is not a fucking possession. She doesn't belong to either of you no matter how much your raging hormones might seem to think otherwise. Jesus, I thought you both were fucking feminists?" She crossed her arms in front of her, nostrils flaring with rage as she studied us both. "Personally, I think she's fucking daft if she chooses—or even eyes—either of one of you. The fact that she let you inside of her absolutely blows my mind."

My jaw tightened at that, and I straightened my posture as the sting of her elbow started to dissipate. I glanced down at Atlas and while he was still raging hard, and while most of that rage was directed at me, I could see that some of the brown was bleeding back into his eyes. I nodded at him in acknowledgement.

"Sorry man," I muttered, even though it was only partially true. Declan was right. I wasn't one to claim a girl or even fight over one. But it was like something in me was shifting, and the thought of her belonging to Atlas—or maybe belonging only to Atlas—made me snap. "You're right, Dec. We're being dicks. Sorry." I cleared my throat and glanced briefly at her. "And I am a feminist. A raging feminist, in fact. Put that on my gravestone when Atlas decapitates me, please."

I shot her a cheeky grin as she continued glaring at me—a grin that only widened as I watched some of her anger dissolve into reluctant amusement.

"What the hell were you thinking, Eli?" she asked, exasperation filling her voice as fury drained from it. "How could you possibly think that right now was a good time to hook up with Max. I mean—"

"Holy shit," I said, cutting her off, not even bothering to hide the grin I could feel splitting my face. "You're into her too, aren't you? That's where so much of this anger is coming from. It's not just anger. It's jealousy."

I watched, amusement only growing, as her cheeks shaded with red and she dropped eye contact altogether—something she almost never did because it signaled weakness to the enemy.

"No," she said, her voice higher than usual. "No, I'm not, I just—"

"Enough," Atlas snapped. When I glanced his way, I could see that while the wolf was still fighting for attention, it was no longer running the show. Uptight Atlas was back. "We have more important things to discuss right now. And Max stays off limits. We don't have time for this shit. And we can't afford to turn on each other."

I opened my mouth to argue, but he shot me one of those looks of his that was almost as good at shutting me up as his wolf was.

"I mean it Eli." He took a few steps back, his chest expanding with each ragged breath as he tried to compose himself. "We know nothing about her. And if the last few days have made anything clear, it's that whatever she is, she's not one of us."

"What do you mean?" I asked as I slid against the wall until I was sitting on the grimy floor. "Just because we're all drawn to her doesn't mean she's evil. I'm sick of us dancing around this conversation just because you're not used to actually wanting somebody. Or because you're afraid she won't want you back."

It was a low blow, and I regretted the words as soon as they left my mouth, which in all fairness was a pretty rare occurrence for me.

"You're thinking with the small brain again," Declan muttered, but she walked closer and leaned her shoulder against the wall just above me. "You can't honestly have gone through the last few days and still think she's just a typical protector. Even you aren't that thick."

I narrowed my eyes at her, but mostly because I wanted to be that thick. Now that I'd had sex with Max, I couldn't stop thinking about the fact that I'd been betraying her. That I'd lied to her. Multiple times. I let out a sigh and ran my hand roughly over my face like that would help wake me up from whatever the hell my libido was doing to my brain.

"My dad doesn't think she is either." I looked up at both of them and cringed at the look of shock cannibalizing their expressions. We didn't keep shit from each other. They'd had my back for most of my life. And I'd been lying to them. "He had me steal some of Max's DNA a while back."

Declan's brows met as she stared at me. "How the hell did you steal her hair? Creep around in her room like a stalker?"

Shame filled me and I couldn't keep eye contact as I answered her. Taking it from her hairbrush would have been a smarter move. "I kissed her out at the pond," I exhaled sharply from the memory, "and when I held her head, I swiped a strand of hair."

When I glanced up at Atlas, I could see his mind running through loops as his jaw pumped with a fury that had me cringing.

"You're an animal," Declan spat, her face scrunched up in disgust. "Doubt your sleeping beauty will want much to do with you once she finds out that piece of history."

Fear like I wasn't prepared for licked at my stomach and I dropped my head into my hands. How the hell was I even going to broach that conversation with Max. I didn't know her all that well, but something told me she wasn't going to be stoked by the fact that I swiped her DNA in more ways than one while sucking her face. Dec was right. I was a raging dickhead.

"Why did Seamus want her DNA?" Atlas was pacing now and I had the feeling that he was once again trying to keep the lid on his wolf. "What did he suspect? And what did he find?"

I shrugged as I heaved myself off the floor, to start my own bout of pacing. Nervous energy was starting to make my hands shake. "If he did find something, he hasn't told me. But he thought Cyrus was keeping something from him—he's too protective of her. He said he knew some of the details of how she came to live with him. But that something was off. That Cy was deliberately hiding an important piece of the story. He wanted to know what that piece was." I glanced at them both and shrugged. "You know how my dad is. He doesn't like not being in the know."

Atlas nodded. He paused like he was debating something, but then let out a heavy exhale. "I overheard them talking about her a while back. Before things went down with Wade. They seemed to think she was in danger, like something was coming for her. Like there was a reason why she kept getting attacked. And probably the same reason Cyrus adopted her in the first place. We just don't know what it is."

Declan rolled her eyes. "Yeah, that's because neither of them realized that the werewolf who attacked her was you."

He narrowed his eyes, every muscle in his body tensed. "I didn't attack her."

"Right," I added, remembering some of the details of this story from Dec. "You attacked her human boyfriend. Like that's so much better."

"He wasn't her—" Atlas shook his head, crossing his arms over his chest. His face got that stern expression he got whenever he was deciding something. "Seamus suspected something. And clearly his instincts are still on target. She fucking conjured up fire and literally burned a mountain of vampires attacking you to flames. That's not normal. She's not a protector. At least not *just* a protector."

Right. I deflated slightly at the memory of her standing there like an avenging angel straight out of hell.

We hadn't discussed it since it happened, not openly anyway. Probably because she was always around and we were afraid of the fang twins overhearing anything.

"And then she helped heal you," Declan added, her tone monotonous and unreadable, like she was reading from a history book—detached. It was something she did well, when she was afraid of getting hurt—turn off, like her emotions were attached to a switch. "With that girl from the vamp's house. What if she's like her?"

"Like Khali?" I asked, trying to impose the image I had of the mysterious girl at Claude's against Max—who was also mysterious, sure, but in a different way. "I don't think they're the same breed of demon."

"Demon?" Declan asked, surprise momentarily breaking through her steel wall. "You don't really think Max—" she cut off, her eyes filled with a distant expression. "Have either of you heard of someone being part demon? Maybe she's some sort of hybrid. Do you think she's actually unaware of her powers or is it just some weird innocent act?"

"I mean, Wade is part demon," I said, before nodding towards Atlas. "And so's he. Maybe Max is too. The rules are all changing on us. It's new territory."

Atlas shook his head. His hands were fidgeting as they always did when he was feeling useless. For once, I got it. I didn't know how the hell to feel about Max. And if she was actually a demon —did I really give a fuck?

"I don't think she knows," I added, feeling the truth as the words settled over the room. "She's been pretty clueless about our world the whole time—to an extent that it would have been senseless if it was all an act and she was trying to blend in. I think Cy kept everything from her. And maybe he doesn't even know everything. I doubt he'd bring her to Headquarters at all if there was any concern she'd light up like a torch when attacked by demons."

"And Rowan?" Dec asked as she scratched at some of the paint chips flaking off the windowsill. She was deliberately avoiding looking at either of us. "You think he's—whatever she is too? Hard to believe Cyrus Bentley is the type to harbor demon fugitives. I don't understand where he found her or why he kept her alive. She's clearly dangerous."

"More dangerous than our entire team combined, and right now that includes a werewolf and an incubus, so that's saying something," I added with a smile, though the situation was anything but funny.

"So what now?" Dec asked, but her focus was on Atlas. He was the one she would listen to, the one she depended on for answers. Not me. As always.

"What do you think we do now, Dec? It's our job to kill monsters. There's our answer," I added with a healthy layer of sarcasm and a humorless laugh, though the words felt hollow to my ears. I hated even joking about something happening to Max. Fear did weird things to my brain. "It seems our team of protectors is just going to continue expanding until we have every shade of hellbeast under the sun. After we rescue Wade, it's probably best if we just cut ties with The Guild altogether, before we all wind up locked in the research lab, getting our brains fucked with just like our newest vampire bestie."

16

DARIUS

"What do you think? It's our job to kill monsters. There's our answer," Eli said, his voice dripping with a cruel edge that didn't particularly suit him. He was supposed to be the fun one of the group, the one who kept everything light and reasonably entertaining. It was part of the reason I saved him in the first place. That level of sardonic nihilism was better suited to his slightly older peers.

"Are we eavesdropping now, little protector," I whispered against the shell of her ear, grinning when she jumped in response, her skin pebbling from the sensation. For someone who could basically self-combust and destroy a pile of my kind, she was unusually jumpy. "I have to say, I'm quite shocked. You don't seem the type to listen in on private conversations."

She spun around towards me, her pulse beating frantically against her skin, her eyes wide and glazed over with a liquid that made my stomach sink.

My grin slid away. I didn't do tears. And something about her being sad rubbed at my chest in a way that made me want to tear into something. Or someone. What the fuck was that about?

"Is it true?" she whispered, her voice a low whisper that didn't quite cloak the fear lacing it—there was hope there too, and I realized that she wanted me to tell her that everything she'd overheard was false. That she was just the average, run-of-the-mill, neighborhood protector.

I cocked my brow when I glanced down at her, noticing that she was wearing nothing more than a much-too-big shirt that was down to her knees. My lip curled in disgust when I scented the obnoxious protector all over her. So much for him being entertaining—now I almost wished I'd just let him die. Seemed she had gotten up to some fun while I was away. Explained why the room smelled like sex, but I couldn't figure out why the thought of her tangled up with one of the dimwits in the other room had my blood boiling.

"Let's go for a walk," I said in answer, and while it stung that my words couldn't bring her the comfort that she was so clearly craving, she exhaled softly and nodded in response.

"Let me just," she glanced down at the cloth covering her and let out a ragged breath, her posture dejected and insecure. "I'm just going to put some clothes on."

I nodded and waited at the doorway for her to finish, keeping my back to her to help prevent any further embarrassment. Now that she'd agreed to come for a walk with me, I no longer needed to listen in on the others. It was clear that whatever she'd overheard, she was not pleased with—and I was self-aware enough to admit that her disapproval pleased me. Meant I'd have less trouble getting her to agree to keep her side of the bargain. Not that I fully understood why I even made that bargain in the first place. I wasn't the type of person who wanted to keep someone around for any extended period of time—not unless their presence could benefit me somehow.

Something about her just had me...intrigued. And since I didn't exactly have a ton of people excited about my miraculous escape from The Guild's creepy ass dungeon, she was the best thing to keep me occupied for now. And the only person who didn't look at me with the desire to skin me alive drawn across her features.

"I'm ready," she whispered, and I could hear the heavy sadness swallowing her up. Could practically smell it, like it was caking against my body, like it was my own sadness.

I looked down at my fist and noticed that it was clenched, hard enough that my joints cracked from the pressure. Clearly I didn't like it when she was sad. Interesting.

But a worry for another day. We had more important things to focus on. Like finding a way to survive this place. We'd been here for only a few hours and already had two close calls. That didn't bode well, especially considering how preternaturally quiet this place felt now. Such a radical difference from the last time I was in town.

I glanced down at her and saw she was wearing what I was fast-considering her own little uniform—black leggings and a black tank top that revealed just enough to keep things interesting.

Without another word, I grabbed her hand in mine and pulled her to the door. I tried not to focus on the feel of her soft skin against mine—used every ounce of willpower I had to pretend I didn't smell the lingering scent of that boy wafting off of her.

"It's dark," she said, her curiosity eclipsing some of the sadness from before. "I didn't know if it actually got dark here. I didn't really notice a sun."

"Hell isn't all that different from the human realm," I said in answer, pulling her along at my side, away from the warehouse. Part of me was giddy with the idea of leaving the other protector assholes behind. They'd be furious, of course. But this had been what I'd wanted all along.

Still, the fact that it happened at the girl's expense stole some of the victorious feeling away. Which was its own brand of annoying. Another thing to hate protectors for.

"Is it true?" she asked again, her voice still soft, like the three goons could overhear her even out here. She really knew next to nothing about this world and her people. Protectors were just glorified humans. Though the wolf had some added strengths, of course.

"Yes," I answered, tone matter-of-fact. "You fried a bunch of vampires and they decided to keep it from you." I glanced around, checking the perimeter to make sure that nothing was nearby. "Not sure why they're making such a big deal. It's not like you fried any of them. If anyone should be concerned, it's me."

My arm grew taut and when I turned back, I realized that she'd stopped walking, her jaw tense and brown eyes wide as a doe's.

"What kind of creature can create fire? Out of fucking nowhere?"

Good question. I'd been trying to come up with an answer since the second I witnessed the event, but I was drawing a blank.

"I'm not sure," I answered, figuring I'd go with the approach no one else had taken with her before—the truth. "I've been trying to figure it out, but hell is a diverse place. I'm not familiar with every sort of creature that lives here. And the most dangerous ones are notoriously few and far between."

Especially since it had been years since I'd been around my own kind—and even more since I'd been to hell.

"And the only creatures I can think of off the top of my head aren't humanoid, don't reproduce, or haven't been seen in ages." I added, winking at her. "And you're definitely humanoid."

"So you think it's true then—that I'm a demon?"

There was that hope again. And I knew what she wanted from me in that moment. For me to look at her and say 'no,' that there was probably some perfectly reasonable explanation for why she could heal creatures on the verge of death or turn others into a raging inferno. That she was just a protector with a few wires crossed or something.

"Probably," I said instead.

Part of me expected her to start crying at that. To drop to the ground and ball up—hiding from the reality of her situation until she couldn't avoid it anymore. And I wouldn't even blame her. It was a wild thing, having your entire universe turned upside down.

But, once again, the little protector surprised me. She seemed to do that a lot. Which was equal parts refreshing and frustrating.

I watched as her posture straightened, her face regaining that angled, intelligent expression I was growing so fond of.

"Thank you," she said.

"Of course." I turned back, ready to continue on our journey, but stopped mid stride. "But what are you thanking me for again, just so I'm clear?"

"For telling me the truth. It seems rare for people in my world to be straight with me. I'm getting really sick of it, to be honest."

I nodded, narrowing my eyes at her. "You really have no idea where you come from, do you?"

She shook her head, her eyes tight with emotion, though I wasn't sure which. "What about Khalida? She said that I could heal like her—that I helped heal Eli. Am I like her?"

"Khali is very powerful," I said slowly, "but she can't create fire from nothing." I paused a beat, and grinned. I'd forgotten how much fun Khali was to be around. I'd missed her. I missed so much. "She'd probably kill for that sort of power though. Girl loves fire. And most things that are dangerous and deadly, if I'm being honest. Bit of a wild bag, that girl."

"What is she?" she asked, glancing down at our hands that were still intertwined for some reason that I couldn't actually provide.

I wasn't going to pull away though. It felt nice having her close by where I could keep an eye on her. The girl was a ticking time bomb and the closer she was, the less of a chance of her getting dead. My eyes moved from our hands to her neck and I swallowed, forcing my gaze to her eyes. I needed to feed. Ideally soon. Or wendigos wouldn't be the only thing I needed to protect her from.

"Khali is unique," I said, grinning when I saw Max's responding glare. "Can't divulge all of our secrets all at once, little protector. Have to give you a reason to keep coming back for more. I've been starved for good conversation far too long to use it all up in one go."

She snorted but moved on. "Where are we going then? Did you find your friend earlier?"

My stomach dropped at the reminder. After hours of hunting for her all that I came up with was a series of disappointments and one very close call with a couple of vampires who didn't take kindly to unfamiliar faces. I shook my head. "No, I didn't. But I'm going to hit one more old spot to try and find answers. I just was really hoping to avoid this particular part of my past. Having company will help."

Max studied me as we continued walking. I could feel her eyes practically drilling into my skull. After a long moment, she pulled on my hand until I stopped and spun towards her.

"You're worried," she said. It wasn't a question, and my breath stuttered at the intelligent focus on her face. She was naive, that was for damn sure, but she wasn't dense.

I stared at her, trying to figure out how she could read that expression. I was notorious for being a closed book when I wanted to be. But maybe that was it. Maybe something about this protector—or whatever the hell she was—made me not want to hide every little thought or feeling that went flitting through my mind. Made me almost want to open up and let her look around at all the mess that lurked beneath the surface.

"It's okay to be worried for your friend, Darius," she lifted her lips in a coy grin that I had the strangest urge to lick. I needed food. And I needed to get laid. And both needed to happen soon. "I promise not to tell anyone that you actually care about someone other than yourself. We don't want to ruin your reputation all in one fell swoop."

I pulled my hand away from hers in response, and missed the feeling of holding it as soon as I wasn't. Maybe she did have some succubus buried somewhere in her genes. I'd seen weirder things.

But I'd been with a succubus before, and I knew that wasn't the sort of draw I was feeling. It was like there was some strange force inside of me, desperately reaching for something in her.

"How far away is this friend we are looking for?" She took in every sight with such curiosity and fascination. It had to be strange—spending a lifetime hating hell and all the creatures who lived in it, only to find that she might damn well belong here herself.

Part of me wanted to see this world through her eyes. A lot had changed since I was last an inhabitant. The magic here felt off, chaotic even, in a way that had the hair on my arms standing up with each new turn. There were fewer creatures too than I'd remembered. More rundown buildings, the scent of desolation and desperation almost pungent. And something about the silence—the lack—had me more concerned than I wanted to admit.

An involuntary shiver ran through my bones. I didn't miss this place. Not at all. And after spending so much of my life trying to leave, it was strange to take the plunge back into this realm by choice. Claude was right in his anger and confusion. My decision to join them on their quest made no sense, especially given the fact that the wolf offered me the opportunity to walk away.

"For a protector? She'd be a good night or two of walking," I said, lifting my brow as I studied her. "For us, we can make it happen in a few short hours if we run."

Her face scrunched up as she looked at me. "I'm no faster than a protector, Darius. I might be something different, some-thing...more maybe, but I don't have a vampire's speed."

So she hadn't noticed how fast we'd been going when we were

hunting down Eli and the monster tormenting him. I'd thought as much, but this confirmed it.

"You're as fast as I am, little protector." I'd need a new nickname, once I had the time to come up with something that fit better. This one certainly no longer did. "When we went after the useless one, you were able to keep up without a problem."

I grabbed her hand in mind again, determined to hold onto her so that we weren't parted during our travels. At least that's what I told myself. Her pulse on the inside of her wrist was jackhammering against mine and I ran a tongue against my canines. They were descending. I needed to find something to eat. And the sooner the better. I was generally pretty good at holding off my appetites, but captivity had done strange things to my body. As had the physical exertion of fighting my brother and a couple of wendigos.

And the girl was far too tempting on days I'd had my fill, let alone on those I hadn't.

Confusion and fear marred her features, and I tried not to grin when I felt her hand squeeze mine. If I didn't know any better, I would think she wanted me near, to help her navigate her own anxieties about her identity.

Not giving her time to overthink things too much, I took off at a swift pace, a wild smile stretching across my face as I felt her keep up stride-for-stride. For a long moment, if I closed my eyes, I could almost forget that the last decade of my life happened, could almost let myself feel something that was peculiarly close to...joy?

We ran for hours, making sure to take the necessary routes to avoid any creatures that I heard off in the distance. I didn't have the best hearing compared to some of the creatures in this realm, but it was pretty damn close. And for now, everyone we came across would be considered an enemy. With only two of us, and with so little information about the social hierarchies these days, it was best to stay clear of everything and everyone altogether.

I took her near one of my favorite spots, a large river that connected two territories, spending just as much of my focus on watching her take the scene in as watching the soothing whirls myself. The Styx was the feature that most closely aligned with my memory of it—the water a clear steely gray that swirled in places so dark that it almost looked iridescent, like I was looking into space instead of the sea. It was a somber place, but it had always been a favorite of mine growing up, a place to get away for a few hours and dream of better lives for me and my family.

"It's beautiful," I heard her whisper as the wind carried her voice behind us, her quiet laughter soliciting some of my own. I swallowed that shit back though, because giggling next to The Styx alongside a pretty girl was not really my vibe.

"It is," I agreed as I studied her dark brown eyes, watching as they reflected the world around us back to me. Somehow, it was almost more appealing through that lens, even if a little less complete, like a strangely enticing mirror that held a healthy dose of mystery.

We lost track of time and, for a moment, I was convinced that even if Nika wasn't to be found, I could convince Max to abandon her silly quest and spend time trying to nurture and understand her powers, where they came from and what she was. Now that she'd turned against the others, a small buoy seemed to be lifting me, my spirits higher than I'd remembered them being in ages. So long as the prick back there didn't go and get himself almost killed again, it didn't matter what they did with their time in hell.

My stomach dropped slightly, as I thought about my eternal connection to the ass. What had I been thinking, tying my life to one of them? I didn't blame Claude for attacking me for it— I'd have done the same to him if the situation was reversed.

When we slowed outside of the familiar town, I watched the joy melt from her expression and make way for fear. "They'll be worried. If we spend much longer away."

I dropped her hand from mine, trying to control the grip

around my chest. "You want to go back? To them? Even after they've kept so much from you, betrayed you? Even knowing what they might do to you once you're back in the human realm?"

If we ever made it back to the human realm, that was.

I didn't take her for being irrational, but maybe I was just as naive as she was.

Her face was drawn, a sad reluctance visible across every feature. She wasn't good at keeping her emotions discreet, and I wasn't sure whether her openness was pleasing or disturbing to me.

"We need to find Wade. That's still the goal, regardless of what happens after." She rolled her bottom lip against her teeth as I paused behind an old building, familiar and worn. "Besides, I don't really blame them. I don't know how I would respond to traveling around with someone who had unwieldy powers that only demons possessed. We're trained from a very young age to hate everything that is associated with the hell realm. It's literally encoded in our DNA to want to kill and protect in equal measures."

I bit my tongue, not wanting to argue. That was a discussion for another day. Her world wasn't what she thought it was, but I knew it would take more than my telling her so to convince her. Protectors were a stubborn fucking bunch, and even if she wasn't one of them, she was raised by them. "For a team that currently consists of a werewolf and an incubus, you all have a rather inconsistent view of the world."

So maybe I wouldn't keep totally silent on the issue. But I wasn't exactly known for keeping my thoughts to myself. Years of captivity had seriously loosened my already loose tongue.

She opened her mouth to say something else, but I placed my fingers against it before any sound could escape. Someone was coming, but I couldn't quite triangulate the sound and figure out exactly which direction it was coming from.

I knew Nika's movements like I knew my own. This wasn't her. Which meant that—

My back slammed against the stone building, my fingers digging into the moss and vines growing in the crevices. This part of the world seemed relatively abandoned, like it had been left for the environment to reclaim it. The musty scent of the vegetation coated my nostrils with every breath I took, like it was the environment's cloying attempt to take back the world we'd all destroyed.

"You have a lot of nerve showing yourself here," a deep voice filled with anger reached my ears a second before I registered the face.

"Nash," I said, an echo of fear slinking down my spine. We hadn't exactly left off on a good note.

He looked just as I remembered—deep gray eyes with hair so dark it was almost reflective. The typical scowl was plastered to his face, only it was rare for his anger to be directed towards me.

"What are you doing back here?" He shoved his forearm against my throat, pinning my spine to the wall like I was nothing more than plaster.

"Good to see you too," I choked out. "It's been ages."

I glanced over at Max, tempted to tell her to get out of here while she had a chance. She could set shit on fire, so she might even survive without me there to protect her. Nash was an unpredictable motherfucker and I hadn't fully expected to encounter him while chasing down his sister.

"I'm looking for Nika," I added quickly, as his eyes narrowed and followed my gaze to Max. The last thing I wanted was for him to focus too much on her. He had even less impulse control than I did, and he wasn't known for taking kindly to strangers. Especially one as difficult to get a read on as she was.

His lip curled in disgust and he gripped my shirt, pulling my head away from the wall just far enough that it made a heavy impact when he threw me back against it. Fucking obnoxious ass.

"Nika's gone."

I knew him well enough to hear the sorrow lacing his anger. Every muscle in his face was tense, like he was trying desperately to keep from revealing any cracks in his composure. Which would be effective for most people, but not for me. Nash and I grew up with each other. I could read him as well as I could read my brother. Maybe even better.

"Gone where?" I asked, though I wasn't certain that I actually wanted to know the answer. Gone in this place was never a good thing—and always spoke discreetly of an excruciatingly painful going process.

"Do you care?" he exhaled a humorless chuckle before letting me go like touching me disgusted him. "You left her. She needed your protection and you left her to the wolves, like the selfish animal you are. She's been gone for years."

My stomach squeezed as I absorbed his words. He wasn't wrong. I had left her when I found a way out of this hellhole, and I'd left her knowing that when I did she'd lost a valuable source of protection. But I knew Nash well enough to know that some of that disgust on his face was directed at himself as well.

"What happened?" I asked, trying desperately to ignore the annoying tightness wrapping itself around my chest. Nika wasn't my responsibility—not my only responsibility anyway. And while I wasn't a good friend to her when I left, she knew exactly the kind of person that I was. It wouldn't have come as a surprise that I left this place at the first opportunity. I had other priorities.

"What the fuck do you think happened?" Nash shoved away from the wall, both of his hands combing through his hair in the universal sign of a guy at his wits end. "Have you actually managed the impossible in your travels to the human world and back? Have you somehow found a way to become even more thoughtless?" His voice was soft now, like he was talking more to himself and we were just given the privilege of listening in on the conversation. "What the fuck did Nika ever see in you? Maybe she was fucking dense too."

"Erm," Max cleared her throat, her dark eyes bouncing between the two of us like she was watching a slightly terrifying match of tennis, one in which the ball might morph into a rabid bear and attack the audience with relish. "I'm Max."

I resisted the urge to drop my face into my hands at that comment. The girl clearly had no idea how to read a room.

Nash stopped his pacing, every muscle in his body filled with a predatory stillness as his eyes landed on her. I knew him well enough to have a guess at what was going through his mind. Here I was, carting around a girl of mythical originals, who looked like she could do little more than fight off a stray dog, let alone any of the creatures traversing the hellscape. And while he wouldn't immediately be able to pick up on the strangeness that was Max Bentley, her innocence was practically plastered across every molecule of her body.

Good. Let him underestimate her. It would be fun to watch her kick his ass if it came down to it.

His head swung back to me, like I could somehow explain Max's desire to insert herself into a conversation between two very volatile vampires.

"Do you have any food?" I asked, shrugging one of my shoulders lazily. Maybe it was best to just embrace the absurd—it had served her well enough over the last few weeks. Maybe her luck would rub off on me.

Nash bared his teeth and he flashed from standing in front of me to standing next to Max, his hand wrapped around her throat as his canines descended. "Looks like you brought your own blood bag. The only good thing you've ever been good for. At least that hasn't changed."

His dark eyes that always knew far too much studied me with a cool curiosity, like he was baiting me and waiting for me to explode. I was notorious for hating when other people touched my things.

I swallowed the growl building up in my lungs and froze in place, eyes wide as I sent a silent plea for him not to do anything rash. If I said something outright, he'd probably snap her neck just to spite me. And while I knew that Max had survived at least one bite with shockingly little effect, I wasn't confident enough that she could do it again—not while her developing powers were all wonky. And who knew if a blood-bond could save her like it had the useless one.

She rolled her eyes. Rolled. Her. Eyes.

And then did the unthinkable: elbowed him in the dick.

As he doubled over, rage and pain swallowing his expression, she grabbed the dagger she kept pinned to her thigh and brought the blade to his neck.

"Max," I said, my voice a hoarse whisper, as I tried to dial the deadly energy back to something slightly more pragmatic. "Let's not infuriate the blood-thirsty vampire any more than you've already done, okay? I'm sure it's all good fun, but I'd rather not have to murder my best friend's brother if that's alright with you."

"I don't like being threatened," she said, her eyes flashing black as she studied Nash with a mixture of intrigue and anger. I wasn't sure if it was her power—whatever the hell that power was—coming out or what, but I needed to dampen it. She didn't seem to have much of any control at all.

"Nash," I said, stretching my arms out wide. "It's been great fun catching up with you. We'll have to do it again sometime. But since you can't help us, we should get going before this devolves into bloodshed. We only brought one spare change of clothes, so it's best to keep this set clean." I glanced at Max, her top and pants covered in dust and ripped to tatters from the wendigo. "As you can see, we're already sartorially fucked, as they say."

"No one says that," Nash ground out, his jaw tensed as he stared Max down with a mixture of white-hot anger and what looked terrifyingly like intrigue.

"Wait," Max said, her grip on the blade still poised, but her eyes returning to their more conventional shade of chocolate brown. "Maybe he can still help us." She looked back towards Nash and tipped her blade forward so that it touched the skin of his neck just slightly. He bared his teeth and she pulled back, hands up in the sign of surrender. "Sorry. It's just that our friend was taken by someone who can teleport, which seems to be a pretty rare ability. And he's being kept in this creepy ass crypt or dungeon. Sound familiar or ring any bells?"

It took every ounce of self-control not to drop my face into my palms and leave her to Nash's whims. This girl had a death wish. And the tact of a goldfish.

Nash narrowed his charcoal eyes and I knew in my gut that he had an idea where the incubus was being kept, but I also knew with just as much certainty that he would never tell us where that was. Not because Max had threatened to decapitate him, but because of the fact she was with me.

"Leave. Now." He glanced up at me, his jaw clenched. "And if I see you in my territory again, I will remove your skull from your spine. I don't care who you are or what history you think we have. Is that clear?"

I nodded, before taking a step forward to grab Max's hand, pulling the dagger from her fingers and sliding it back through the sheath on her thigh. I felt her body relax slightly when I touched her, and tried not to read into it too much. That line of thinking would get too muddy and dangerous, much too quickly. "Aye aye, captain. As always, it's been a real pleasure."

Without another word, I started to run, dragging Max with me like a dog on a leash and trying not to audibly chuckle at the way her "erm, bye" was swallowed up by the wind.

After a few long minutes that each seemed to last a lifetime, I paused, ears poised at the sound of ruffling in the foliage.

"Your friends all seem to hate you," she said, her eyebrow arched as she set her hands on her hip in a power posture she'd likely picked up from a ridiculous sitcom or one-too-many episodes of Wonder Woman. "Care to elaborate on why?"

"Khali doesn't hate me, or did you not notice that?" I asked, pressing a finger to her lips to stop the endless flood of words that seemed to leak out whenever she was nervous. "Food."

She opened her mouth to argue further, but I was spared the disturbance by the loud growl emanating from her stomach. Her lips tightened into a thin line in response and she nodded, fully aware she didn't have a leg to stand on if she wanted to argue with me.

Hunting in the hell realm wasn't always the easiest thing. Food was around, but it was much more sparse than it was in the human world.

This was a realm occupied to the brim with predators, so competition was fierce. And if I was alone, I'd settle for something much larger and tastier than a deer, but I had a feeling that I could only push Max so far in one night.

I flashed away from her at a speed no deer could outrun and grabbed the creature around the neck, twisting in one quick motion so that it was dead long before it had a chance to realize it was even in trouble. I turned back to the little protector with a smug look on my face, expecting her to praise me for being so thoughtful—both for ending the creature's life so quickly and for providing a meal for her.

I wasn't expecting her eyes to be wide and glazed over with moisture. Fucking tears. I hated when women cried, it should be illegal. "What? What's wrong? Are you hurt?"

"That was just unexpected," she said, and I could tell she was swallowing back some emotion, frustrated with herself for showing any at all.

I dropped the beast with a loud thump and shrugged. "We don't exactly have the luxury of a grocery store right now. Those establishments exist—well, sort of—but they're sparse. And we're trying not to draw too much attention. If you wanted all the glamor that comes with being a human, you should have stayed in your realm."

Her eyes hardened as they locked onto mine, but she nodded. "You're right."

I almost fell back from the shock of hearing those words leave her lips. It was so rare that anyone actually agreed with me. On anything.

"I'll get a fire started and then help you skin it." She walked around me, glancing briefly at the creature with resolve in her eyes. She picked up some dry sticks and brush from the forest floor and looked back at me. "I draw the line at raw meat. Have your fill of the blood while I get the flames up and going," and then, under her breath, she added, "slurping up a deer like he's a Cullen now. Hell is weird."

She paused, every muscle still as she turned back to me. A shadow seemed to ghost across her features and I knew instantly that she was thinking the same thing that I was. That if anyone could start a fire quickly, it was her. But neither of us knew how exactly to get her powers going. I made a mental note to devote some time to it once we had our bellies filled. I had a feeling if we didn't figure out whatever the fuck she was soon, we'd be in trouble. And while I was always down for some good trouble, something told me that her powers were beyond what I was capable of handling alone.

A worry for another day.

I leaned back, partially sated, and watched her. For someone who'd initially had reservations about her meal, she dove into the deer like it was the first time she'd eaten in months.

"This is great," she said, her mouth half full. "I feel like I could eat three of these beasts myself. They're a bit leaner than the deer that exist back home though." She swallowed, her eyebrows meeting in the middle as she stared at me. "Are there a lot of similar creatures here? To the human world, I mean? And other forms of retail besides grocery stores?"

I nodded, feeling significantly better with some blood in my system, but I was still studying the pulse throbbing softly in her neck as she chewed. Part of me just wanted to know what she'd taste like. And that part was slowly growing into an obsession. The only thing stronger was the strange desire to keep her alive and safe.

"A lot of this world is similar to the human one. Many of the beasts that live here need food just as you do. And the few who've left this realm and returned have shared some of the technology you all have—the way you do things, the way you survive. We've made use of what serves us and mock the rest." I grinned at her, watching with joy as her cheeks reddened slightly, like she couldn't tell whether or not to defend humanity.

"How long have you been in The Guild lab?" she asked, her voice was calm and collected, but I could tell that the question had been dying to burst from her lips for a while now.

"About four years."

"How old are you?" she pressed.

"My body is about twenty-five. But I've been alive longer than that."

As I expected, her face scrunched up in confusion in that way I was begrudgingly finding endearing. "What do you mean?"

"When we mature in the hell realm, we are often suspended in that state. It's part of the magic of this place. And we live for a very long time."

"Interesting." She took another bite of her meat, chewing as she processed. "How many years have you lived then?"

"Not as long as most. I'd be about forty in human years. After my family and I were able to escape this place, we lived in Seattle for a couple of years. So it's been about six or so since I was last here." I glanced around our makeshift rest spot, thinking back to everything I'd encountered here. "A lot has changed in that time, more than I thought possible. Time was difficult to measure while imprisoned, so it's hard to say for sure. I'd have to ask my brother. I'm sure he savored every second that I was out of his hair." I cleared my throat and stood, dusting invisible debris from my pants. Talking about my past was not something I wanted to do. Ever. "We should go."

Not missing a beat, Max stood too, unsheathing her blade like she was afraid something would sneak up on us. "Did you hear something?" When I shook my head, she relaxed a bit. "Then where are we going?"

"Nash wasn't being honest. Not fully." I grabbed her hand, half out of habit now, but also because I liked the feel of it, and started walking slowly through the forest. "He knows more than he's letting on, and I expect that if we stalk him long enough, we might find out what it is." I looked down at her and could feel the smirk crawling over my face. All of her focus was on me, her expression similar to one I often saw when she looked at the others. Like I was an equal. "We'll need to be stealthy though. Nash isn't as strong as I am, but he's pretty damn close. And he's far more familiar with this world now than I am. He's always had a knack for survival."

"You're quite arrogant," she said, cocking an eyebrow. Thankfully she didn't pull her hand from mine as she followed me through the woods, just on the outskirts of the smattering of buildings I'd lost familiarity with over the years. "Are you ever going to tell me why you and your brother are so strong? Or why you hate each other so intensely?"

I stiffened at that question and shot her a quick glare. My fangs flashed briefly, out of habit more than threat. Though as the canines descended, I couldn't stop my eyes from landing once more on the pulse point in her neck. The deer was not enough. Not when I'd been starved for years and beaten down by my asshat of a twin. "Who says we're stronger? And no."

She rolled her eyes but, despite her conjectures, she didn't appear like she was afraid of me. I wasn't sure whether that made me happy or angry, so I ignored it for now—something to deal with later.

"Weird thing to play coy about, but whatever." We walked in silence for several moments, so I thought she was ready to drop it. But clearly I was wrong. She was even more stubborn than I was. Maybe even more stubborn than Nash. "I mean really, it's a bit ridiculous. Are all vampires this insufferable?"

The question was more of a mumble and I had a feeling that she didn't really care if I'd heard it or not, so I left it lingering in the air as some unrecognizable emotion gripped my chest. I was getting tired of these unrecognizable feelings that kept cropping up more and more often these days. I blamed her for most of them.

"What's the story with you and Nash then? And his sister, Nika—what's that all about?" She said, clearly in a chatty mood now that we were tromping around after a vampire. The girl had a death wish, if ever I'd seen one. You'd think that for someone who'd had more brushes with death in the last few months than most, that something would have instilled a sense of fear and self-preservation. Obviously not.

"Did you miss the part where I mentioned that Nash had pretty good senses? And that we're supposed to be spying on him?" I swallowed back my smile, aggravated with myself that it was starting to form against my will. "You talking sort of ruins any semblance of stealth we have going for us. They don't teach you much in that school, do they? No wonder your lot dies so young."

Her mouth narrowed into a straight line, but there was humor in her dark eyes as she studied me. She mimed shutting up by doing that ridiculous zip-lipped gesture that human children often did. She even tossed away the key. Like, why the need for the performance? Just don't talk. Simple.

Still. When she did it, it was almost...endearing. Which was its own brand of infuriating.

"We grew up together," I said after a few moments of silence that were making me itch with discomfort. "Nika was my closest friend. I can't—I refuse to believe that she's gone. Nash is keeping something from me. And I want to find out exactly what it is."

Her hand squeezed mine gently, like she was encouraging me to continue, but I didn't want to. Not least of all because if Nika really was dead, it would be because I wasn't here to protect her. She was always getting into trouble, largely because I encouraged it. The thought that I could be responsible—

"Something tells me that he might know more about where your friend is being kept as well," I added, forcing the other line of thought to evaporate before I suffocated on it. "Nash is sort of top-of-the-food-chain material if you catch my drift. If anyone knows details about what's been happening in this realm during my absence, it would be him."

I was blessed with a few more moments of silence, and tried not to get too annoyed by the fact that a reminder of her incubus was enough to get her back on mission. I hadn't met the kid, but he sounded like a bit of a bore—especially if his older brother was anything to measure him against. Not to mention he was literally draining her each time they met. Which bumped me up on the good guy list, as far as I was concerned. Not a drop of her blood had so much as touched my lips, despite the heavy temptation. I was the good monster of the group.

I scented Nash inside of an old building, the cement siding was run down and looked like it was being reclaimed by the nature surrounding it. These buildings had all been occupied by his people when I'd left—there had to be at least twenty or thirty vampires living in these parts back then. And now, judging from the silence and general apocalyptic feel of the place, it seemed that Nash was the only one left. While I wasn't one who liked to embrace curiosity when it put my life at risk, this particular scenario had my interest peaked.

Dragging the girl, I climbed to the top of a building across the street, figuring it would give us a good view of the area all at once, see if anyone else was wandering about. I settled over the edge, tempted to dangle my legs as I used to as a child. But that didn't exactly align with my goal of keeping to the shadows and not standing out.

Max curled up next to me. I could feel her eyes boring into the side of my head and I pushed away the annoying tingling sensation creeping along my skin. That had been happening more and more recently. It was like every molecule of my body wanted to merge with hers through some weird sort of magical osmosis.

Honestly, maybe I should just kill the girl. That might stop all the weird swirly shit going through my body. Maybe her death would bring me some peace. Or at the very least, a momentary reprieve. It was a disturbing feeling—not wanting to disappoint someone. And I wasn't sure why this girl inspired it in me all of a sudden.

"What?" I bit out, no longer able to stomach the silence. That was strange too. Why did I seem to encourage her obnoxious commentary?

"You're not afraid of me," she said, her words soft enough that they didn't carry beyond our small little bubble.

I glanced down at her, and felt my face scrunch up in confusion. "Why on earth would I be afraid of you? You're pint-sized. You're the one who should be afraid. I could break your neck and drain your veins in the time it would take you to say Taylor Swift."

"You're very strange, you know." She crossed her legs and leaned back on her palms, studying me with a shrewd focus. For all of her innocence, she could hold her own—I could see it in the way her eyes clocked everything, every movement. Hell, she'd even threatened Nash. Something I hadn't seen anyone do and survive since we were children. "I literally conjured fire and barbecued a pile of vamps. And I have no idea how I did it. Aren't you afraid I might do the same to you, even if by accident?"

Huh. When she put it that way...

I shrugged. "You wouldn't kill me, accident or not."

Her lips turned up in a smirk, but she tried to disguise it by looking away. "What makes you so sure? You're pretty insuffer-

able and your arrogance just might be the end of you. My unconscious self, or whatever the hell is lingering inside me, might
eventually get fed up with it, you know?"

Was it weird that I was getting turned on by a death threat?
Probably better not to analyze it.

"I'm not as easy to kill as the leeches back at the hotel." I
grinned at her. "But I would welcome you to try. Though it
might be better suited for a bedroom."

As I'd hoped, her cheeks turned a burnished pink, bright
enough that it was visible through her golden skin. I watched as
her throat bobbed with an exaggerated swallow. I breathed in
deeply, catching her scent as she turned away. She was...aroused.
How interesting.

"Thought you said you weren't more powerful than other
vampires?" she mumbled, but paused for a long beat. "Darius,"
she started again, her voice uncertain. Was she going to push the
flirtation further? "Are you sure that you don't know what I am?
Do you promise?"

I tried to disguise my disappointment at the turn in conversation, but reached for her hand nonetheless. For some reason, I
wanted to comfort her, to erase that fear from her eyes. Fear had
a place, and I would welcome the chance to explore her fear in a
different, more enticing context. But not like this.

"You have my word, little protector. I may not tell full truths
as readily as many, but I do not lie. I have no idea what sort of
monster you are."

Her face dropped slightly at the word, and I tried not to take
it personally. Protectors were always so goddamn sanctimonious,
even the ones who weren't really protectors—or not only protectors anyway. The wolf and the girl were proof enough that all you
had to do was grow up amongst them to adopt that particularly
insufferable trait.

"But I can't wait to find out," I added, my tone laced with
insinuation. I was growing strangely addicted to her blushes and
when one answered my comment, I shot her a coy smirk before

turning back towards the building Nash had entered. I had a feeling that he was in for the night. After all, it was close to dawn at this point. I just didn't understand why the hell he was spending time in abandoned buildings alone. Where were his people?

"It wouldn't be your fault, you know," she said, any sign of embarrassment wiped away from her face. When I narrowed my eyes in confusion, she continued, her eyes meeting mine fearlessly. "If something happened to your friend. While you were gone. You can blame yourself for many past grievances, Darius. I'm sure you've killed more creatures than you can count. But that shouldn't be one of them. If she died or was taken or whatever happened—that isn't a guilt that should resonate inside of you. You left trying to make a better life for yourself. I've seen enough of this place to know that life here was probably filled with many hardships."

My stomach tightened at her words and I turned away quickly, trying to get my breathing under control. What the hell was wrong with me? What the hell was wrong with her? What right did she have to have this effect on me? And why the fuck couldn't I seem to control it? Maybe I should just end things here and now. Leave her on this roof to her own fate, navigate hell on her own.

Or better yet, maybe I should just kill her. Have a good meal. Her scent alone promised that I wouldn't be disappointed.

Her small hand slid under my jaw and gripped the side of my face, pulling gently until I faced her again.

Steady eyes. Filled with a piercing strength and a kindness that made my stomach dip.

She was so determined, so sure in that moment. How could she be some small, innocent creature one moment, and this fucking force the next?

"I mean it," she said, her words carrying a heavy weight, a demand. "You can—"

I pressed my lips to hers, half to swallow whatever nonsense she was going to push into the air between us, and half because I simply couldn't not.

Her lips parted on a shocked gasp, and I took the opportunity to deepen the kiss, to taste her in a way that wouldn't end with her as nothing more than a shriveled up corpse. I knew right then that all of my joking aside, I couldn't kill her, no matter how infuriating she was. The thought of her no longer breathing, no longer around to entertain me, caused a sharp ache so deep that I couldn't find its source no matter how hard I tried digging for it.

I groaned in surprise as her tongue danced along mine. She tasted like the perfect mix of spice and something sweet, but not cloying. The blood of our feast lingered just slightly, and the monster beneath my skin slowly rose to the surface, intrigued. I pushed it back, subtly, gently, knowing that my balance and control over it was tenuous and delicate.

I pulled her closer to my body, my fangs descending, begging for a taste, even a single drop. She moaned softly and it was enough for my dick to throb—the monster and I both desperate to make her make that sound again. Over and over.

This—whatever this was—was new. My heart was racing against my chest and my breath was oscillating between stopping altogether and coming out in desperate, greedy pants.

I gripped her hips, needing her on my lap five minutes ago. But in an instant that I couldn't fully process in my lust-filled brain, her lips were ripped from mine.

❦ 17 ❧

MAX

Kissing a vampire. I was kissing a fucking vampire. Willingly.

Somehow, that realization hit me harder than the wrecking ball of a body that ripped me away from said vampire in the first place.

My mind was still in a daze, still not computing what had just happened. What had I been thinking?

I pushed the mindfuck from my thoughts, trying to refocus. The force from whatever—or whoever—had shoved me towards the edge of the building. I gripped my fingers along the edge of the rooftop, just as my legs swung over the side. It was a tenuous hold, and I could feel my fingers slipping digit by digit, like I was in some low-budget action movie. I dug my feet into the side of the building and pushed, trying to get some momentum so that I could scale back up. With a large shove, I heaved my body into the air, but away from the wall and safety. At the last possible moment, I used the momentum to lift myself into better positioning, so that I could slowly peel my body back onto the roof. I sent a silent 'thank you' to Cyrus for forcing me to do daily push-ups since I was five. He would never hear a complaint from me again. Assuming I survived whatever this was.

As soon as I caught my bearings, I almost wished that I hadn't. There were werewolves.

So many fucking werewolves.

Darius was taking on four or five at once, each of them working in tandem, like they knew where their pack member was going even before they made their own move. If we weren't currently royally fucked, I'd be deeply impressed by their teamwork.

I stood, my legs shaky already from the rush of adrenaline and watched as five more approached me, their walk slow and predatory, shoulders pressed together as they closed in. I grabbed my dagger from the holster and unsheathed it just as the first one dove for me.

Dark black fur completely obliterated my sight, but I managed to step to the side just in time, so that the creature's claws only barely skimmed my skin. Centering myself, I dove onto the creature, tackling it to the ground and slicing into its abdomen with my blade, all in one seamless motion.

Warm blood spilled down my wrist, coating my forearm entirely, as the beast let out an anguished howl.

I thought of Atlas and my stomach clenched, like it was bracing for impact, for grief. Though I knew this wasn't him, everything I thought about these creatures had changed. I was no longer certain who the enemy was, or if an entire species could ever truly be considered evil. The beast angled its teeth and dove for my neck, almost gaining purchase while I was too busy dealing with empathy.

I pulled my blade back and shoved it back into the wolf's diaphragm, beneath its ribs, with all of my strength. In one smooth maneuver up, I pierced the heart and with a heartbreakingly small whimper, the body went still. Two down, and a seemingly infinitely replenishing supply to go.

I caught my breath as I saw two of its pack members leap towards me.

With one hand on either side of the dead beast's body, I dug my toes into the ground and flipped us both, so that when they landed, their claws dug into their friend, instead of into me. Their deep growls seemed to reverberate around me, and through me, until they were all that I could hear. The wolves dug deeper and deeper into their friend, until I was certain that they were determined to go through him entirely if it meant they could get to me.

I couldn't let that happen. Beneath two raging wolves and a dead one was probably the worst battle position of all time, and I refused to go down hiding under a carcass.

I pulled my dagger from the wolf's chest, disgust filling me as its blood drenched my own abdomen, like we had mirrored wounds.

Eli, Declan, and Atlas—hell, even Darius—all seemed to think that I could fucking turn into The Human Torch. And Darius was right, I was faster and stronger than I had ever been before, as if turning nineteen and dropping into hell was all a girl had to do to gain some extra juice. But how the fuck did I make the fire thing happen? Because if there was ever a time to self-combust, now was it.

I gripped the blade, prepared my body, and closed my eyes. I envisioned myself lighting up like a firefighter's worst nightmare, torching the wolves trying to tear me to bits.

Nothing.

I let out a desperately frustrated breath of air.

What the fuck was the point of a conveniently powerful superpower if I wasn't able to find the fucking on button?

A claw grazed my shoulder and I knew I was out of time, that my organic shield was breached and it was now or never.

Still no fire.

I remembered what Khali had said, that Ralph could probably come to me if he sensed that I truly needed him. And a burning fear rose in me at the thought. I didn't want him to come to me. Didn't want him to get stuck in hell, fighting and possibly dying, because of me.

With a determined, but annoyed grunt, I used all of my weight to shove the body to the side, desperate to crawl out from beneath it. My blade latched against the carcass, snagging until it dropped from my hands.

I was free, but my weapon wasn't.

The wolves wasted no time as soon as they realized I was out in the open. Both of them pounced at once. In a split-second, probably reckless, decision, I dove for one and tackled it to the ground, determined to take the beast on with just my hands. Bad idea.

We went down in a pile of limbs, and I punched, clawed, and kicked like a woman possessed. I felt just as much like a wild animal as the being I fought. A heavy shove knocked the breath from my lungs, and I realized that the other wolf had jumped into the fray. I didn't care. There was so much adrenaline that I couldn't feel any bites or claws, if they were indeed breaking through my skin at all.

I elbowed the creature at my back in the face, and used the returning momentum to punch the creature in front of me, like my arm was a bowling ball and they were the gutters. But I knew I couldn't last for long like this. I needed to get to my blade or I wouldn't stand a chance in the long run. No protector had ever survived a wolf attack weaponless. And while I wasn't exactly just a protector anymore, I didn't think I could survive without something sharp and pointy either.

Wrapping one hand on each side of one wolf's face, I tugged. The loud snap of the beast's neck rang through my ears and I felt the smile grow across my face. A neck break wouldn't kill the wolf, but it would knock him out long enough for me to get my weapon. Thank you Claude, for teaching me the utility of that fun trick. And thank you increased strength for making it a feasible maneuver for me.

Without a second thought, I decided to test my newfound

speed and hurry back to where my blade lay buried beneath the first wolf. I dug my hand under the creature, swallowing my disgust as its entrails spilled around me. Just as my fingertips found the familiar metal, I felt a jagged set of knives rake down my spine, ripping up my skin and probably a fair bit of muscle. I didn't have time to linger in the pain, or focus on the fact that a wolf's teeth were buried into my shoulder. The odds of me turning into one of them from the bite were much lower than the odds of me dying in this very battle.

I swung my arm around, swiping aimlessly. The muscles in my arm weren't moving with the usual agility and precision that I was known for. One of the wolves must've damaged it pretty badly, but the adrenaline was too high for me to notice.

I stabbed the creature in its side, again and again and again. I was vaguely aware of a low battle cry and I swung my head around looking for the sound, only to realize that it was coming from me. The momentary glance revealed three more wolves prowling towards me and Darius under a horde of what had to be at least ten now. There was no getting out of this.

Where the hell were they all coming from? It had been so silent just a few minutes ago—silent enough that neither of us noticed a single creature until it was too late.

This was what I got for making out with a fucking vampire.

My skin started to tingle, whether from the venom in the wolf's teeth or something else, I wasn't sure. I lashed out from all angles as the wolves surrounded me, like they were playing with a toy instead of going straight in for the kill now.

They knew they had me, and they wanted to take their time, savor it.

A chill ran up my spine and a sort of static electricity took hold of the air around us, raising the hair on my head and arms on end. I took a deep breath in, trying to dispel a sudden wave of dizziness that grew as the energy built, and when I exhaled, the energy around me seemed to short into nothing—no, into *something*, into a focal point.

My vision exploded with a flash of flames and I watched, stunned, as the wolves surrounding me were charred where they stood, a perfect circle of fire. A glance down at my hands revealed ground zero.

Swirls of red and orange that bled into deep blues and purples were coating my hands. I felt my pulse race against my chest, the pace so fast I was certain I was on the verge of a heart attack.

It was true. They hadn't been lying. I could create fucking fire from nothing, like a damn magician. On some level, even looking at the flames surrounding my body, watching as they ate away at the wolves, I still couldn't quite believe it, couldn't fully wrap my mind around it. The light scent of smoke, almost like a campfire, coated my nostrils as I turned towards Darius, prepared to focus some of this power towards the horde across the roof. Half were still fully trying to take him down, the other half were instead staring at their barbecued packmates.

How could I be sure that in trying to take them out that I wouldn't take Darius out too? I didn't know how to find the on/off switch, let alone focus the energy with any sort of specificity.

I hadn't killed Eli. I'd saved him. I had to believe that in this mirrored battle, I'd do the same for Darius.

Just as I took a breath in, trying desperately to gain control of the energy licking against my skin, an excruciating pain buckled my knees. I felt, rather than heard, myself screaming as my fire-coated arms circled my waist, desperate to contain the agony. There was no blood, no werewolf attack near me, no wound.

What the hell was happening to me? Leaning all of my weight on one knee, I planted my opposite foot on the ground, and tried to stand. Before I could move so much as an inch, the pain doubled. And then tripled. My vision blurred until all that I saw was the swirl of colors from the flame, and then, nothing but a deep, penetrating black.

"Darius," I yelled, though no sound escaped my lips. Or, if it did, it didn't make its way to my ears. My limbs felt like they were being burned and torn from my body, like now that the fire was done saving my life, it could move on to taking it.

My eyelids pressed together tight as I tried to use every ounce of willpower to stand, only no matter how I tried to move, the muscles in my body were spent, drained entirely. And no matter how much I focused, I couldn't move so much as an inch.

With a heavy inhale, my body wracked with a coughing fit, like my lungs were filled with water and I was drowning a slow, terrifying death in my coffin of a body. A heavy wind scraped past my ears, and I thought for a moment that I heard my name on Darius's lips, but just as soon as the sound formed, it was gone.

When I opened my eyes, my vision returned, but it didn't make any sense. There was no gravelly rooftop, no pack of were-wolves or uncontrollable fire. No Darius. Just thick, stone walls and a damp, suffocating sort of darkness that went far beyond a lack of lighting.

Exhaustion took hold, so I closed my eyes and focused on breathing slowly as a headache unlike any I'd ever experienced hammered against my skull. I gripped the digits of my fingers into the hard, cold floor, and with a slow, heavy ache, pressed my face against it. The gentle balm of the frigid stone against my skin felt like a glass of fresh water after a month-long hike in the desert. I swallowed back a whimper as fear and confusion made way for relief.

Slowly this time, I opened one eyelid, and then the other, giving myself time to adjust as dots of light blurred my vision. Something about the interlocking patterns of the graying stones was familiar.

The ringing in my ears started to disappear, the sudden lack of sound the only thing that made me aware it was there in the first place.

I tried to lift my head from the slab of concrete or stone or whatever the hell I was lying on, but I couldn't quite manage the weight of it on my neck.

"Ah, so it seems I guessed correctly," a deep, emotionless voice rang around the walls.

My eyes chased it hungrily, even as the edgy tone sent chills along my arms. Eventually, they caught a large figure in the corner of the room—no, two figures. Both creatures were shrouded in darkness, but one seemed to be shaking with a fragile sort of pain, barely able to hold its body any more than I could mine.

The other figure stepped forward until it was a mere few inches from me.

I inhaled sharply as recognition chased after an almost-forgotten image in my mind.

The shrouded man from Wade's dream. Was I sleeping then? I glanced around the room again, but I realized instantly that while it resembled Wade's dungeon, there were distinct differences. This one looked to be a bit larger, and there was a single slither of window where the high ceiling met the wall. A ghost of light filtered in, but it wasn't much.

Panic gripped around my chest as I stared at the figure in front of me, a form draped in cloth and a power so strong it made my blood sing.

"Where's Wade?" I bit out, the words a struggle to push past my lips.

A deep, humorless chuckle emanated from the figure in front of me. Without answering, he stepped back to the second figure and dragged it forward. With a final shove, he threw a body to the floor in front of me.

"No," I whimpered as I tried desperately to close the distance between us.

Wade's skin, which typically radiated with a soft, fresh glow, was caked in blood. His blue eyes were almost completely swollen shut.

And his stomach—a dark handle was protruding from his

abdomen, the material coated in a soft blue light. This wasn't a typical sort of dagger—there was something ephemeral, magical even, about it. And power. Power so immense that it made my teeth rattle as I stared at it.

"Wade? No," I said again, as I pushed myself forward, closing the distance between us successfully this time. I looked up at the shrouded figure, and though I couldn't see his eyes, I knew without a shadow of a doubt that they were piercing mine. "What the hell have you done to him?"

The figure seemed to shrug without moving, and then a large hand pushed through the folds of fabric and pulled the hood away, revealing a stunning, terrifying face. Smooth, olive skin, dark eyes, and a shadow of dark hair that lined a sharp jaw.

I choked on my breath as our eyes met, though I wasn't sure what exactly I was reacting too. Something about this man was so familiar.

"Are you the one who kidnapped Wade?"

He arched a dark brow and nodded, his lip curling in disgust as he glanced down at where my hand reached for the blade piercing Wade's stomach. "I wouldn't touch that if I were you. Not unless you want to kill the boy and die yourself."

"Can I even die in a dream?" I asked, regretting the obtuseness of the question as soon as I asked it. I blamed the cluster-fuck of exhaustion and rage coursing through my body. Would this man shove me from the dream again? I needed to stay. Needed to keep Wade alive.

"The boy isn't dying, so long as I want him to live, so do try to stop leaking so much fear and grief. It's a bit distracting. And you aren't dreaming. I had a hunch, and then I followed it. And, like usual, I was right. You're here in the flesh now, girl."

I choked on air as I closed my fingers around Wade's. Had he just read my fucking mind or was my desperation just that obvious?

The man smirked and crouched down until his dark eyes were level with mine. "Congratulations. You've completed your first successful shift. Most end up in a coma of sorts after their first attempt. It can be too much on the mind and the body."

"It?" I mouthed, my voice failing as a deep wave of exhaustion came over me. I felt my vision go blurry as I tried to hold the man's image in focus.

"Teleportation is a difficult skill to master."

ABYSS OF RUINS

Grab Book Five in The Protector Guild series:

Max and her team entered hell with the intention of bringing Wade back together. But they should have known that hell would have other plans...

Captured and alone in a place that looks like it was pulled straight out of a medieval novel, Max is desperate to get back to the members of Six. But not before getting what she came here for: Wade.

The members of Six, and the wily vampire who hitched a ride to hell with them, are learning quickly that while hell might not be all fire and brimstone like they had imagined it to be, sometimes reality is worse. Separated with no leads to follow, Declan, Eli, and Atlas navigate a realm of demons in hope of reuniting with Max and Wade. And while hell demons are certainly awful, the demons raging inside of them will prove just as haunting.

Hell is known for tormenting its inhabitants. The question remains: Will Max and her friends make it out alive?

ACKNOWLEDGMENTS

This book wouldn't be possible without the support of my family and friends. You know who you are, and I couldn't be more lucky to have you in my life. Thanks for always encouraging and pushing me to chase after my writing worlds.

Special thank you to my early readers, editor, Kath, and my cover designer, Michelle. This book is so much better because you've all contributed a piece to it. Thank you.

And to my very own 'Ralph,' thanks for keeping me company while I wrote this series for hours and months on end.

Printed in Great Britain
by Amazon